The Absent

Rosalind Palermo Stevenson

Rain Mountain Press
New York City

The Absent

Rosalind Palermo Stevenson

ISBN: 978-0-9968384-2-9

For all inquiries please contact info@rainmountainpress.com

Text set in Chaparall Pro
Designed by Sarah McElwain
First Edition

Printed in the United States of America

Library of Congress Cataloging-in-Publication Data

Names: Stevenson, Rosalind Palermo, author.
Title: The absent / Rosalind Palermo Stevenson.
Description: First edition. | New York City : Rain Mountain Press, [2016]
Identifiers: LCCN 2016045957 | ISBN 9780996838429 (trade paperback)
Classification: LCC PS3619.T4928 A64 2016 | DDC 813/.6--dc23 LC record available
athttps://lccn.loc.gov/2016045957

For my father and mother,
Harry and Rose

~

(loved)

So they all rejoiced... [not] because it was Falling Star,
but they realized the Star People would put a star up in the
heavens that is the biggest star of the universe.

Black Elk

Someone will remember us, I say, even in another time.

Sappho

Contents

1

Philadelphia, Pennsylvania, 1859

I had a dream last night of taxidermy. In some strange corner of my mother's house; that is, my mother's and my aunt's house—the two of them absent. But Lucie Beale was with me in the dream. We were on the floor sitting talking like Indians, as though we were children playing, the way as a child I used to play on the floor beneath the dining room table. There was a wolf with us on the floor, or was it a fox, if a fox a large one, although remembering the dream it looked more like a wolf. Sprawled on its side like a dog sleeping, but it was a wolf that had been skinned and stuffed. I began petting it in the dream, though Lucie Beale refused to pet it, and as I was petting it,

it came back to life and leapt up and ran away.

...what silence speaks of...there is that apt gesture of silence, the hand closed in a gentle fist, the index finger raised and placed over the lips. It's silly to stand there, the voice says, when you can lie down and rest. Yes, rest. Enough time has passed—too many days. How many? Do you remember? You look worn. You look tired. It's time. You agree that it's time, don't you? I see the figure of a woman with her belly bulging; she is still a young woman, but emaciated by disease so that her abdomen is distended and her breasts, though small, are sagging. She is not my wife, but she evokes my wife. I've come back to the last time I was in this bed—the last time I was in this bed my wife was with me. Her breasts were small; did I detect a change in them that night? I believe I did, I remember a greater roundness, fullness, something approaching a state of ripeness, the thing that happens to wives, to women...

Reminiscence. A shadow appears in the upper right corner of the photograph—at first taken to be a defect. Upon closer examination it can be seen to be a leaf that belongs to the floral pattern on the fabric of the backdrop—the leaf lifting upward. The figures posed, the necessity of their remaining absolutely still, the figures frozen on the print, for all time a reminiscence, a mother with her child at her side, and in her arms an infant, the infant sleeping, the unadorned gray of the woman's dress with its high-standing collar. The woman stares into the lens of the camera the way she has been instructed; the child clings to her dress; the closed eyes give an odd countenance to the infant.

There, I hear Lucie say, as she hands the finished portrait to the woman—you are fixed, the sun has captured you. It's extraordinary. Don't you think it's extraordinary? Your image has been fixed on this print by the power of light.

As she speaks her eyes are dark like someone brooding, her expression is serious which deepens the look of brooding, dark against the whitish skin, her loose brown hair, a hint of curl, the unspoiled chin.

12 May. We are married almost two weeks. She states her desire to continue to work in the studio with me.

—the adjusting chair with head rest; the adjusting head rest, with the heavy iron foot for full-length portraits.

to make love in the night. the mysterious water. the random words that come at night.

It is a nervous sensitivity. What is the nervous sensitivity? It is not Lucie who suffers from this condition; it is myself. Lucie has a calm disposition, her temperament is even. The nervous sensitivity is my own. Sometimes the inability to breathe, the sensation of my chest constricting, the inability to take sufficient air into my lungs. Or the inability to sleep. I lie in bed with only the pretense of sleeping. As if by imitating sleep I might attain it.

This is what I remember: a twisting in my sleep, that is a twisting of my body, a restlessness that had settled into my limbs, my arms and legs would not stop moving. And in that same way my mind would not settle down with all its wild thoughts and images—phrases spoken in my mind that had no meaning. It went on that way throughout the night—this inability to settle down—my thrashing in the bed woke Lucie, What is wrong, William? she asked—is something wrong? It's nothing, I said, nothing is wrong. She wrapped her arms around me as though to protect me, or to soothe and calm me as though I was a child. Something must have disturbed you, she said. I don't remember, I said. Nothing remains of it. Nothing with a shape to it. Were you thinking of your father? she asked. I answered, I might have been thinking of my father.

...and then the sensation of my wife's body pressing against mine. our rooms are in the rear of the house, on the third floor ell, away from the others.

in the vicinity of

there is something to be said

in the vicinity of the white

there is something to be said for

in the vicinity of

the three in view now standing

in the vicinity of the gas lamps the light is dim, flickering

In the dream I'm split in two, as though being viewed through a camera with a two-section bellows. All else is normal: it's morning; the night has passed; I'm with Lucie; we have come to the table, newly married. The buffet has been set with all the breakfast foods one would expect: boiled eggs, fresh breads, a platter of ham... I don't regard it as odd in the dream that my wife is in her bridal undergarments, her chemise and drawers visibly torn from where I have ripped them. No, it's not odd at all; we are proceeding with our meal in a correct and proper way; the conversation is light; we are discussing the weather. My wife comments on the sunshine, which she describes as "dazzling." It is dazzling, she says. I take two eggs from the bowl and put them on my plate; a slice of ham alongside the eggs. And all the while I do this I see there are two of me, each one faithful to the actions of the other; we are identical selves; each one filling his plate, every movement synchronized: every cut of the knife; every lift of the fork; each of us at breakfast a contented man with his new wife, who is in every way refined, and yet is sitting in her torn bridal undergarments.

I'm wearing a blue nightshirt,

it seems almost indecent, this talk of dreams, nightshirts.

it's the quiet part of the morning, the light still dim, I'm in bed with my wife.

the neighbor's dog is barking. the sound carries into the room. the dog has a shrill bark that pierces at the upper registers.

I consider the role of the husband. the word husband. husband.

when we come downstairs my mother and aunt are already at the table.

I have the sense. The sense of what? Arms and legs. The entirety of the body. Beneath the skin, bone. When cut there is blood.

for blood—that's what the red flag means. the blood of battle. the blood of killing. the blood of the hunt, the wanton killing. the blood of the scalp-knife. the scalp loosed and torn. a trail of red, the trail of blood. the blood loosed by the bullet. the ball loosed by the gun. daily an excess of killing.

the memory of my father and the way he died. it was during the early years when he had moved us down to Arkansas. my father had taken me on a hunting trip along the lower Red River; he was giving me instruction: ...*finish the animal to help it die.* he was a fair-minded hunter, perhaps because he was a judge. he was against the Indian way which was to wait until the animal bled to death. beast at the hands of a man. man at the claws of a beast. beast to beast. man to man. man to beast.

...and then to lie in the earth while the body disappears; first the flesh, eventually the bone; what is left of consciousness wakes to find itself removed, far from everything and everyone it used to know. no one to answer when it calls, only the faint response of the nearby newly dead.

Arrièrre pensée: a mental reservation; a hidden motive.
The Aru Islands.
The meaningless words that come at night.

To forsake. To renounce. To relinquish. To turn one's back on.

But why these thoughts when I have a wife? The marriage promise: the contentment that's due a man with a wife.

The morning is fair, already hot, tonight the heat will melt us in our rooms. I believe it was her grandmother with her, my mother is saying to my aunt. They are talking about a woman seen yesterday walking out by the tracks— alongside the stretch of trees in the wooded area that runs parallel to the railroad. She walked with her head down, very fast and determinedly... odd she should have been there, my mother says...

Lucie makes the remark that weeks have passed since the wedding and yet it still feels out of the usual to be here at breakfast.

To the women of the household: I'm making a record of things, Ladies. It will be something to survive me. The weather is hot, the air is heavy, it seems that the summers are getting hotter. Something purchased for a song. It's something my aunt is saying at the table. It means purchased for very little. Purchased for a song, or for less than a song. A story printed in *The Dollar*. And then the remark: They have turned quite profitable these stories. There is no attempt on my aunt's part to hide her enthusiasm for the plot. A man with a performing goat. A record of things created. Telling something about what they were. Like a skeleton stretched across the room, or the remaining skin and bone of birds, husks, all stopped in motion, the sun catching them at times, the sun illuminating them at times, carried by the air, or by the water, carried by the river.

In the afternoon we attend the Sunday ballet performance at the Walnut Street Theater. The story of a girl raised by gypsies. The troupe performs in the Russian tradition with Mademoiselle Mathias in the title role. The story from top to bottom convoluted, but unimportant as the story is only an excuse for the dance.

...after the ballet, a stop at Barnum's to have a look for ourselves at The Great Living Black Sea Lion. It's a bull and black as night and thirteen feet in length. It weighs 1200 pounds. The animal eats a hundredweight of fish every twenty-four hours and requires sixteen barrels of sea water every day. The eyes have great expression, Lucie says. It's obedient to its keeper—it strives to please him by moving in and out of the tank of water when he commands. We watch as the zoo keeper gives various commands, which the sea creature follows. Then we feed the animal with a one-cent stream of fish. The fish sell in one-cent, two-cent, and five-cent streams to feed the sea lion.

...at night a three-quarter moon. There's a name for it: gibbous moon.

This is my edge, the place I fall off, where I begin and end, where I'm on the verge, or on the brink, or at the outer margins. Reference was made to the Bosporus Straight today in an article in the Philadelphia Ledger—the article talked about a Russian cargo ship carrying wood for the telegraph. All the place names exotic: the Sea of Marmara, the Black Sea, the Dardanelles. But America too has its exotic portion... stretches of desert where crossing is to sleep beneath desert stars. Never a late spring like this one, the heat of a desert. Earlier in the evening in the garden with Lucie—where we sat talking about the darkling beetle, which lives on the ground and feeds on plants at night.

...the silence broken by a sound, and then the sound is heard again, there seems no air in the room, my skin is damp in the humid night, something comes back to me from sleep, a landscape stripped of living beings, in the distance natural forms made by wind and rain. I'm awake, my wife is sleeping beside me.

A glint of light on the dresser—from the fine-worked silver case.

The penetrating intimacy of another's presence: someone who seeks to penetrate another's soul. The rest of the night I sleep dreamless. Or if not dreamless, without images. All visual impact has disappeared. There are only sensations—at times pleasant—resting just below the surface of my mind. In the night a reference made to fire. *Was I on fire?*—the temptations and hallucinations that abuse the saint. When the flames rush into the mouth there is no retreat from the fire. Images from paintings, the Sistine Madonna, the amorous supplication of the female saint.

The marriage new and unaccustomed, the words strung together in my mind, wife and husband, dark room, dark night.

I close my eyes once again before the daylight.

In the morning the Old World view. I walk across Chestnut as far as 9th, stopping for a while at the ruins of the museum. A somber site to see the remains, the walls still standing on only the three sides where it is stone; all the wooden parts of the structure have been burned out, but not reduced to ash. The look of ancientness about it—our own small rendering in

Philadelphia of Rome...

...and then the length of the docks along the Delaware.

...the flocks of water birds have all come back in the midst of their migrations. the goldenrod not yet in bloom, growing along the stagnant ponds that are hidden away in the remote stretches of land north above the docks. stretches of land with stalks of goldenrod grown tall. the dried out stalks from last year's blooms.

The continuing heat—someone has called it an African heat.

I stand at the window at the rear of the studio, watching a bird out near the privies. The bird is climbing on the trunk of a tree. It climbs in small erratic movements, then flies further up along the trunk, and then it continues to climb as before.

Is there enough light? Lucie asks. Do you have enough light for the photograph?

The most important thing: the colossal luminosity from the skylight above. The light brings the image onto the sensitized plate.

The essence of a person in a single feature of the face. The existence of a secret character on the surface of the photograph. The skylight is 12 by 15 feet. A well-defined light flows down from above.

From the light to the darkroom where the trays of chemicals are set. The assistant, Edmund Fell, places a glass plate in the silver bath.

My wife at work beside me, fully occupied in the activity of the studio. Expletive: My complete happiness!

And then the pale early evening after the day so hot, the day as though the world was melting in the force of the heat.

The odor of earth. The sensation of dirt filling the nostrils. All the little peasy things that haunt. The fruit has ripened on the dogwood in the garden. It's one of those oriental trees sought after by my mother and tended with care until it bore fruit. And the mullein pinks, wooly with their reddish flowers. The pale light covers everything now in the late day sun.

A game of whist in the evening.

After the whist game sparrows—the subject of sparrows introduced by my mother. She says talk of cold will cut the heat, and then she reminds us that during the severe winter of the previous year the frozen bodies of sparrows had covered Broadway and Fifth Avenue in New York. She remembers that the story had been reported in the Philadelphia Ledger with a description of the frozen birds. For that reason, my mother says, she made nothing of it this spring when the garden sparrows pulled the petals off the crocus. Such a beautiful flower, she adds—and then: The ground shrubs need pruning. She thinks she will get to them in a day or two.

…my aunt talks about the ailments and diseases that assail the human race: boils, constipation, malaria, tuberculosis. The conditions that bring them: sickly winds, bad odors, unhealthy fogs. The means for treating them: to bleed the body, to ingest stimulants, to sit in hot baths, to apply poultices, to strap onions to the feet.

...something about hocks.

...to disable by cutting the tendons of the hock.

...my wife remains quiet during the evening conversation.

I wake in the silence of the room. The atmosphere tenuous. The way the dream I was having is tenuous. The content is lost to me when I wake up and then it comes back. Lucie was pale in the dream. She was weeping and afraid. At first it appeared she was in a wooded area where the shadows of trees threatened all around. But then I could see she was safe at home, sitting with her forehead pressed against the window—on her face still that expression of terror.

Again *he* was pale. Again *he* was weeping. In that same dream I saw my father's fear. At first I didn't know what it was, but then I realized it was the fear of his death. In the dream he was alive, I was asleep, or just about to sleep, my mother was in the next room, I got up from my bed and passed by my father. He was in the north-facing front parlor sitting on a chair, I thought how good it is that he's alive, but then I saw that his face was contorted and his eyes were cast upward. His mouth was open as if to shout, or to scream. When I went near him, he wrapped his hands tightly around my wrists.

of a breath... everything seems to be of a single breath...

Met by the mirror in the hall. For a minute not recognizing myself as me. Exaggerated reaction to my reflection, as though meeting a stranger. Who are you? The question asked to myself, of myself.

Without an answer.

What is the face that life shows? My wife's face is of course perfect, always in my view, always near me, her proximity altering me with the weight of its intimacy, with the mingling of our breathing each night as we sleep. But what of the mutilated face? The Indians say that mutilated people wander forever as ghosts and werewolves. What a strange notion. Werewolves! What of that other face? The face of God sitting among all of life's faces.

To hold on to the spirit that is moving within

towards shadow,

the spectator of myself.

The weather continues unbearable, the heat gives rise to kinds of storms. A major hail storm took place for more than twenty minutes yesterday and hail the size of chicken eggs was dropped.

Today another storm descended on us with a fury, out of the blue, the sky one minute heat-oppressed, but all the same clear, and the next minute blackened by clouds. It was a violent storm of heat and rain and hail, starting up at 4 o'clock in the afternoon; hail fell so fiercely I was afraid the glass skylight would break in the studio. There was sharp lightning and loud claps of thunder; one of the nearby buildings was struck by lightning. When I arrived home, my mother told me that after the storm she went out to the garden to see what had been damaged.

Dear companion of my soul—on a third straight day without sunshine, only rain. Impossible to work as regards photography on a day without sun. I seek a good pastime for enjoyment—someday it might be said of me I was a man who enjoyed the good things of this life. I thought before my marriage I would make a journey back to the West. Or to somewhere so remote it would consume me. Dreams of accomplishment—to set out to travel with a camera. A camera like an eye capable of capturing what I see. Now, in the exhibition room of the museum, I stand in front of one of the museum objects—a naked figure of a man: the sculpture is small, old, has the quality of animation; the sex is depicted pointed and exaggeratedly long.

...returning home purposely out of the way along the docks. The rain reduced to drizzle. Importance of the oyster crops. Five to seven million bushels. Twelve hundred million oysters consumed every year.

...later with my wife I describe the naked figure that I saw in the museum.

A diary of the weather. Sun today. Sun all day today. Clear today. Rain today. Wind today. High gusts. Clear again. Long walk in the rain. Long walk after the rain. The river water rising because of the frequent rain. Peering down into the water from the edge of the wharf. Walking with long strides, the kind of strides often taken in a walk. In my mind the image of a man in the distance carrying a Dubroni mammoth plate camera, 1& 1/2 feet across and 2 feet in length, and weighing over 50 pounds; the camera is strapped to his back as he walks, he climbs between two points on the mapped-out territory, the point to his left and the point to his right, between them the peaks of the mountains.

One eye open and one eye partly closed in the photograph.

Again some distant threat of rain... wind... already wind gusts...

And then the sun is back. Brilliantly back.

Heat? Record heat. I bow to the dominance of weather in this record heat.

...along the city front in the neighborhood of Market Street. Steamers docked along the wharves. Their flags fly with the letter "C" to announce they belong to the famous Clyde Fleet. The large slate-covered buildings, the various depots, and the Clock Tower. To the Noblesse! To the hour! To the passing of the hours!

From an ancient spirit... To life!

The eyes turned inward towards the soul...

Where did the words come from?

A conversation with my aunt about the nature of the soul the general idea of which concerned identity: she was ruminating if in the afterlife her soul would be recognizable as her. The conversation followed an encounter she had had with death earlier that day in front of our house on South Eighth Street.

The little bird and Aunt Lavinia. No. Aunt Lavinia and the little bird. The bird discovered dead. Its tiny breast pointed up. No. Its tiny yellow breast. No. Its tiny yellow breast streaked through with orange. It had a short straight beak. Prompting my aunt to speculation on the genus and the species. It was a finch. A bullfinch. No. She knows from Godey's Lady's Book the bullfinch is short and thick like most of the species of the genus Loxia. And the length of the bullfinch is six inches and three quarters. This bird was at most four inches. The bullfinch's beak is half an inch long; black, short, and thick. This bird's beak was neither black nor thick. The bullfinch's rump is a beautiful white. And the dead bird's? Impossible to know. The bullfinch has a robust breast, the upper part of the abdomen carmine, paler in the young, the pinion feathers black, the large coverts of the wings a glittering black. No. With certainty not a bullfinch. This bird was slight. Not even four inches. Upon reflection three inches. Found by my aunt on one of the cobblestones in front of our house. Dead. Its body as though sleeping. That is on its back with its head turned to one side. At first my aunt did not recognize that it was a bird. It looked like an abstract shape on the pale gray of the cobblestone. She almost stepped on it. More speculation on the bird. How did it come to be lying there? How had it died? There was no blood. It was intact. No. Not intact. It lacked life. The spirit was no longer in the body of the tiny bird. It was dead on our cobblestone as though sleeping with its head turned to one side. Which is not the way birds sleep, birds sleep upright on their perches. Their bodies crouched. Their feathers puffed. Their eyes closed, but their bodies upright. All the more pathetic then to see it. My aunt did not touch the bird, but she had no doubt the body was still warm. The death was new. There were no signs of stiffness. My aunt took the image in as a shimmering in the sunlight. No. As a shimmering in the sunlight at the bird's forked tail. My aunt said: Death is at our door. And then was given suddenly to tears. Inexplicable the way her heart was heavy in her chest. She had to hold herself back. Resist the impulse to reach down. To touch the body of the bird. Her certainty that it was warm. Still warm.

Optimism of the daybreak. The moon still in the sky. The sun not yet up, but the sky getting light. Light. Dark. Light. Dark. Distractedly contemplating the puzzle of the way things begin. The quality or fact of being real. The sense of expectancy. A foretaste of pleasure. Or else the sense of everything disappearing.

Moon of the early morning, moon of the sky, moon of my childhood, moon of my memories, moon that will one day take me to my death. Last night two knocks came at the door. Yes, I wondered too who was knocking.

I hear my wife in the morning. Lucie rummaging in the attic room among the family's outworn clothes.

I go out to walk, following a silent instruction for walking: on Walnut left to Front Street, cross the footbridge, go down the stone stairs, turn right at the water, turn right at the water to find the entrance, the easy indulgence of the morning, the light from the sun almost blinding, the day already hot, there's no end to the heat, the smell of the river, the waves breaking against the wharf, and not far in the distance, half-way across the river are Smith and Windmill Islands.

Smith and Windmill Islands: the fusion of rock and man.

G entlemen, I accept your invitation to be part of the worthy venture, one suitable, too, to [my] temperament. My wife has the portrait business well in hand: the ladies, the children, the men alone or with their wives, or sometimes with their dogs—interesting how frequently it seems that a man wishes to have his portrait taken with his dog. A praiseworthy task you have set out: to retain for history a book of photographic images of the city's old buildings—the houses and public buildings, these man-made structures, erected over a hundred years ago. How old it suddenly feels to me now, this city of Philadelphia...

The fusion of rock and man.

the house of Engle's. he's a tanner. the house sits north of the Town Hall. the Town Hall also to be photographed. Engle's house is well constructed. a modest design. three stories. the house is old but has no history. its construction is its history, its excellence. my exposure will provide a view of one side and the front at an angle, the camera far enough back to take in the entire structure. the short-post fence that encircles the house will be fully visible.

19

the wine shop on the corner of Chestnut and Seventh with its clapboard awning over the entrance. Mr. P— who owns the store wanted to be photographed in front, but I persuaded him that it was the building alone that I wished to record. I invited him to come around to the studio where my wife will sit him for his portrait.

the Arcade Hotel at 615 Chestnut. it stands on the lot of ground formerly occupied by Justice Tilghmann's mansion house.

the Academy of Natural Sciences.

MacKnett's Tavern, the oldest in Philadelphia.

the Chestnut Street Theater, the old wooden row houses, Sully's Residence, Brown's Iron Building, the Apothecary Shop at Fifth and Chestnut.

what memory gives me... there is only that which can still be written and I'm no longer certain of what can be written.

a quieting of the spirit

the evening darkness

moon of my sky, Lucie.

I'm like the dog on his haunches again watching the moon but silent as though his voice had been taken from him.

my thoughts tonight are old-time thoughts. and the house we live in is haunted by two centuries of living and memory. memory entering and sitting down and letting me look back.

you occupy all my thoughts, Lucie... but I'm still bitten by a wilderness landscape that has kept with me all this time until I'm sick from it, dying from it, the way that death cannot be turned around. in the old-time hour. or in the solitary hour. in the hour when I played as a child in the cold-shed out back used to store ice.

you occupy all my thoughts.

contour of your body at night. simple whiteness. all that is of you that has become mine. I lean over you

and everything happens with a kind of simplicity

no longer separated from the world

the objects in the room sit quietly all around.

A moth flies in through the open window attracted to the light from the gas lamp; its flight is clumsy and its plump body falls to the surface of the white sheet.

I brush the moth away and tell you there's no reason to be discomforted.

You turn down the light and in our bed we fall asleep.

Lyric night, image rounding. The flood that comes out when the mouth opens... mouth to mouth... in the dream mouth to mouth...

In the morning we leave for Bethlehem, north of Philadelphia, to view the Moravian farmlands—the trip made with my wife, my mother, and my aunt. Lucie stands beside me in the sun. My mother is poking in the mulch with her rolled umbrella. My aunt is talking to the cows, or to a particular cow, one that seems to be paying her some attention. The sense of the earth and the down-to-earth. The persuasion of the spirit to hold one's thoughts in a natural way. The earth, as it must be, in correct perspective to the cosmos. Everything marked out, defined and circumscribed: the symmetric fields, the orchards, the animal sheds.

Our poor lives only lived once, says my aunt.

Live for each other. I saw the words written on the frontispiece of a book. Or was it *Live for one another* with its broader implication? *Live for one another.* I believe that was it. A Christian sounding sentiment: Live for one another.

The sky turns gray tinged with yellow. The feel of rain in the air. We stop to look at the barn bay and the empty interior where the horses are quartered. The view inside is partly obscured by the darkening light. Outside, whistles like signals...the birds in the trees. We walk in silence. Taking comfort in walking in silence.

When we return home I observe a contented ease about my wife, her arm touching mine, her feet stepping down from the carriage.

We approach the house, the broad rectangular structure, the flat surface of the ground, the house built on this street named South Eighth Street.

The domestic cat stretches out.

A heavy wind, but no rain.

The sound of the wind has come into the silence.

I stare at the high-built chest facing the bed with the open chamber at the top. The little darkness in the chamber.

The room is cooler now.

There, I say…

Our ordinary words.

Our ordinary lives.

To seek the mysterious.

In our ordinary lives.

...when you want to go into the Mysterious you must be bound by ropes so that the agents of the Mysterious might come and unbind you. the ropes will be kept in a neat pile nearby so you can be bound again before you depart...

Fluidity: a man, a horse, or tree.

Attenuated light.

And the words of the psalms: *Hungry and thirsty their souls fainted within them.* Their souls faint within them. And all those little sounds like mice. Unease and then a quieting.

Our earth-bound fate.

The night is only the night with its darkness.

The sun when a cloud passes in front of it, the dimming.

Attenuated light.

And the night with its darkness.

My feelings are high this morning. Breakfast is served where it is always served: as a buffet on the sideboard. The sunlight plays on a corner of the table. Sitting at the table at breakfast, the morning always begins at the table at breakfast. And then walking to the studio, sometimes with my wife, at other times we arrive separately, she's engaged with the portrait business, and I more often with subjects outside. Today we walk together, taking the roundabout way by the Delaware, the breakers out there, and something moving a small distance along the shoreline, wait, I see it now, it's one of the channel catfish throwing itself against the rocky shore, it repeatedly lurches its body forward to reach higher up along the stone surface, and with its mouth all the time grabbing for some substance that clings to the rocks.

To take the spareness of the vision into light. At work in the studio. Light floods the photograph.

The sharp line of the edges, the clarity of contrast, my wife is silent as she works.

We work the entire day.

My wife continues silent.

At the end of day she slides a small box of albumen prints towards me on the work table near where I stand.

These are my own investigations, she tells me—

What I see are close views, close in the extreme, the features of a human face, the eyes appearing as the one thing that matters. The subjects have been told to stare directly into the lens of the camera. The effect for the viewer is one of fixation on the eyes.

...the impression of softness and material uncertainty.

...the impression of softness and material uncertainty and the split between the essential and the merely accessory.

The subjects on her photographs staring.

The living captured by the lens.

My wife's forehead is damp.

...her subjects staring at the lens.

My wife is modest about her photographs

...the soft focus like a fog.

It gives the stillness of seeing, she says.

The stillness of seeing.

The end of the day's work.

We return home with the stillness of seeing.

In the evening we attend a performance at the Chestnut Street Theater to see Miss Susan Denin play the role of Mariana in a revival of Mr. John Sheridan Knowles' play "The Wife." The subject of the play was borrowed by Mr. Knowles from Shakespeare's "Othello," though he has renamed his characters Leonardo and Mariana. As we ride in the carriage on our way home, Lucie repeats the lines that Mariana speaks in the scene of her soliloquy: "I dream'd each night, I should be Desdemona'd ... But my Othello, to his vows more zealous / Twenty Iagos could not make him jealous." But in this Knowles' play, Lucie says, Othello is not Othello—he is Leonardo, and he never doubts his wife's chastity. In any case, she adds somewhat absently, we are almost home. She looks out the window of the carriage, leaning her body against mine. The gesture familiar, intimate, easy...

...a short while later in bed

...she holds one foot pointed

...like a dancer's foot

...the luxury of the senses

...unpacifiable

...and when I bend near her,

...her arms pull under and up through mine.

In the night a word comes back to me: abandonment—the child is told he'll

27

be abandoned in a wilderness, where wild animals will come and take him away. we're only teasing they will say when they see the expression on his face, but in his mind the child has already been left in that wilderness.

Obliged to spend the day at home because of trouble with my eyes. The day spent without sight. My eyes covered with a poultice made with a mixture of plain black tea and borage leaves. First I sat and rested for a while upstairs in our rooms, and now I'm sitting in the garden. It's the peak of the season; there's the smell of althaea roses. Seeing in silence without sight. Awareness of my tongue resting against the roof of my mouth. Awareness of my feet planted on the ground and then trying to visualize where everything is in the garden, to form a picture in my mind of what's standing directly in front of me. My mother comes out to the garden to change the poultice. I believe it's the althaea roses in front of me, I say to my mother. Yes, a profusion of them, she replies. The sensation of light beyond the wet cloth… my impatience to be rid of the poultice.

But the next day I'm well again. At the lake with my wife. Do you think it will rain tomorrow? Lucie asks me.

We stand a distance from the shore.

On the pebbly lake beach.

The water of the lake.

Its advance as silent and as present as an animal.

Do you think it will rain tomorrow? she asks again—I'm so tired of the rain;

it's good it cleared today or we couldn't have come to the lake. How strange the lake water felt when I waded into it, she tells me, the bottom was muddy and soft and my feet went sinking down. At first I was put off by the way it felt, she says, but after a few minutes I found that I liked it—the water was cold even in this hot weather. My cousin Jane has written to me from New York, Lucie tells me—Jane says she is lonely there, William. Her husband John is working all the time and she knows no one. They are living in a boarding house for the time being and Jane doesn't like that either because they have to take their meals each day in the dining room with the other boarders. Jane says no one speaks during meals which inhibits her and John from speaking. Anyway it would be impossible for them to have any kind of real conversation in front of the others. What frightful things in this book I'm reading; I think you should read it, William. Your mother says it's an important book. If it rains tomorrow you won't be able to photograph for the old buildings project. I think it's a good project, William. How else is it all to be remembered? I hope you'll photograph the Rock House at the junction of Shoemaker Street and the Railroad. It strikes me as a worthy structure sitting on that huge expanse of exposed rock.

...she looks out at the water with her arms crossed high on her chest, and then she turns to me with her arms still crossed high.

There are no trout in the lake, William. We might have fished if there were trout.

...in our bedroom in the evening, the delicate musculature of her arms.

...and then in the morning I'm on photographic assignment in the setting of the Asylum.

The season is changing.

The trees will soon be bare of leaves.

The grounds laid out in gardens and walks, a view absent of people, the building seen from a distance, the building isolated in the midst of trees.

Inside is a gallery of faces, photographic canvases with streaks of light from movement.

All the faces and the gazes

I've been asked to photograph.

Moist lips. A clubbed hand. The terrible visions I would like to forget.

Aberrant conditions on display in the Asylum's gallery of photographs. The dead hand attached to the living body. Contracture. The convulsion that leads to a state of immobility of the limbs. The plaster cast of the limb. An entire room filled with such casts.

A room in shadow.

The dim light.

In the lecture room the patients have been administered a small amount of ether.

Foam emerging from a mouth.

A disfigured face.

A young woman is brought out for the clinical study. A doctor urges her forward. She obeys first with reluctance, but then she begins to speak: I experience happiness when he wraps his arms around me. Who is *he?* the doctor asks. Why it is M of course, she answers. I can feel him near me and I start to shiver. I am shivering because of what he will do to me. He looks like a dog. But I can see it's a mistake; it's myself who is the dog. I feel canine teeth have grown in my mouth. But then later these teeth recede and I become a woman made of glass. My steps must be so tiny, so cautious if I am not to risk shattering. Once, when I was falling asleep, M insisted on crawling into my bed. I begged him not to tickle me because I would shatter. I will shatter, I said. But he wouldn't stop. He only repeated the word: shatter.

Her disfigured face.

Once agreeable to look at.

Go, go—I don't want you near me. Those are her words when I stand to leave.

A residue of thought.

The life not spoken... not credited.

On the way home I see a beggar.

The bony hand of the beggar stretches towards me.

The day ends in fatigue, the fatigue gives over to relaxation. Strange the way it comes, the nerves first stretched to breaking, then released.

Stretched to breaking, then released, the night brings meteors!

We stand watching out near Chestnut Hill.

We arrive in the early evening and we'll drive back in the carriage late at night.

The shooting stars a little after 10 PM. The night grown milky in color. The heightened silence. My wife's eyes study the sky. Her face is milky like the wash of light in the sky. The sound of the horses waiting, still bound to the carriage, the occasional shifting or stomping of hooves. In the sky, wings. Vapor trails. An eye. An enormous egg...

...hands. the milky whiteness.

It was thought the world would end during a previous meteor storm.

The sound of the horses' hooves and the wheels of the carriage turning on the pavestone.

There is little left of summer now.

My spirit is easy, Lucie says.

The lamp is burning in the side entrance when we return to the house. Another lamp burns at the foot of the stairs on the way to our rooms.

Swooning into sleep.

The intimacy of our sleep.

The world as though over a distance.

Between us there is no distance.

As though our bodies are shadows.

Entering each other in sleep.

...the season is changing.

...the trees will soon be bare of leaves.

...fall asters and chrysanthemums. the job's tears are dead. there are late blooming gloriosa.

...the days are growing shorter. I turn down S. Eighth St. to Pine and walk west on Pine past the Pennsylvania Hospital. The building stands stately though dismal in the dim light of the street lamp. I give some thought to those inside. It's only the poor who are brought here. The rest of us are treated at home. A faint stench. Perhaps only imagined. We are making progress. The advance of science. The wind starts up turning the night cold. All the same, it's good to be out in the air.

The streets are quiet, the nights are getting colder. When I return home I find Lucie writing in her notebook. Was it cold outside? she asks. I answer that it was. Winter will soon be here, she says. She closes her notebook to put it away, but then she opens it again and reads aloud.

...so much of what I love best: nature and color and light and dark, the uniqueness of each human face, and all the great beauty in this world, I have thought about... A sweet-scented jar on her desk and books piled up. *The Lifted Veil; The Professor; Live and Let Live; Love of Cats.* An armchair next to the desk.

Some talk of a house with a garden owned by Mr. and Mrs. Evans who purchased it from the builder, Benjamin Loxley. It's not nearly as large as our garden, but it's just nearby on 329 Pine. And during the summer months they take up residence in one of the suburban "cottages" where they can flee the city's heat.

She shows me a drawing of a bird in her notebook. There is no notation to go with the drawing.

She tells me the doctor was here today to treat my mother for a cold and neuralgia. He bled your mother, she tells me. She says, I saw the lancet and the bleeding bowl. It's strange what must make us well. When he came down from her room, he gave instructions for her meals.

34

...our voices at night... backdrop of the silence of the house. Your mother found the book she lost; it was in the sofa, down under the cushion, Lucie says. She had been looking for it for days and was relieved to find it. That's very good, I say. The holidays are coming, she says—our first together. And then: I want to feel you near me, she says coming closer. Where else am I but near you? I ask. The night-clothes set aside. The movement of breath... breathing where she is breathing...

In the morning from the window, the trees in the garden standing in the icy rain. A rain that will soon turn to snow. The streets will soon be covered white. Watching out the window. And my wife at the wash-stand.

A breakfast of coffee, buckwheat cakes, ham, boiled eggs, apple butter, preserved grapes, bread, and cakes.

A bird flies by the window. The presence, then the shadow of the bird.

It's November. Thanksgiving is almost here. And after Thanksgiving it will be Christmas and then the New Year.

The image of a door opening into a room. And then it closes.

In the morning Daily Ledger there's an article about a child who drowned in a well. The words 'the well' are repeated several times in the article. The child's body "floated in the well," the article says—most of the body was submerged beneath the water, but looking down into the well one had the impression that only the head was floating.

And then an article about Sicily where the sun is very hot.

An expedition of the spirit. In the studio. A silent communication between the subject and the camera.

Orders placed for photographs. For portraits. Edmund Fell working quietly.

My wife is also working quietly. A rustling sound, vaguely like a whisper. Her eyes behind the lens of the camera. Edmund Fell assisting her.

Eyes that will give us the photograph.

She has written in quotations in her notebook: "*Aura means wind, breeze, and breath.*" And then she has written the words: *caution, extreme patience.* Below that she has written the words: *I should like to photograph a person with the aura visible as a surrounding field. Like vapor. The face as revealed by the lens.*

The title inscription on the photograph: *Relief Ensemble of the Four – Four Women Standing.* But the fourth is missing.

It's not a mistake; it's the intention of my wife.

Photograph of a child with a dead pheasant on its lap. Her notes say: —*it was the first animal to be killed by the child when out hunting with his father. Directly afterwards the child and the bird were brought to the studio to be photographed.* There are two views of the child. In one he is looking down at the pheasant. In the other he is staring into the lens of the camera. In both the bird is stiffly draped across the child's lap; the child holds onto the bird to keep it from falling. All that changes from one photograph to the other is the position of the child's head, and yet this small change produces two distinctly different moods. In the first, looking down at the bird, the child appears soft and far away; but when he stares directly at the lens of the camera he seems to be consciously attempting to look severe. The light of the exposure has washed out the color of the child's hair; it appears white; most of the other tones in the photograph are gray; there are few sharp blacks; the focus is a little soft; the child's hand on the dead bird is the point of interest. The thumb is spread apart from the fingers as the child grips the bird. There is tension in the hand, the forearm is slightly raised, touching nothing, only the hand touches something, the hand gripping the bird.

And then it is night, and then morning again. I wake having slept deeply and well.

My wife's voice in the early morning light.

Did you rest well? Did you sleep well?

Her face a little colorless.

Come, Love.

Gazelle... and desert wind.

Or horse, or lion, or mythic bird, or lamb, or wife, or husband.

i animali

All kinds of life.

Let me uncoil you.

Air touches me.

Like a finger that runs itself lightly from one place to another on my face.

A movement of her hand.

And then a movement of my hand.

Logs burning in the fireplace.

We have all the time in the world.

The time that is most real.

Impossible not to cry out

like an animal

like a beast of the wilderness.

We are on Market Street to see the Horse Parade—the street lined with people who have come to watch. There is still evidence of spirit in the city's horses as witnessed by those who march in the parade. Each horse is held in tow by its trainer, unridden, without saddle and with only a thin woven bridle, led along in the parade on a silk-like rope. One after another the horses pass us by, starting out somewhere near 2nd Street and proceeding west across Market; all manner of breeds represented, all those we have of domestic horses, and more than one pure-bred Arab with slender legs and heavy flanks, at least fifteen hands high, and several of them bay with black points. The occasional resistance shown by a horse, a sudden quick fierce stomping, the animal angry with ears flat and pulling back on the rope. And then with a gesture of mastery by the trainer, the horse brought into line, responsive to the pull of rope. I would like to see the horses in your West, Lucie says. In my West, I reply, but I've not been West since I was a child—though I would like to return there to photograph. As we talk, the splendid animals are passing by, their hearts beating in their massive chests; their eyes turned slightly in, in that somewhat mad-looking way of horses' eyes; ears pricked and alert; tails combed and hanging down. She confides she imagines the ropes coming loose and the horses unbound galloping all along Market Street. When a wild horse is roped, I say, it becomes exhausted and drops to the ground and from that moment the horse is no longer wild.

work for the blacksmith.

dreams of the slaughterhouse. rivers of blood. blood flowing all the hours of the night. it was red at the heart of it. it was a nightmare sustained throughout the night.

what woke me? there was no sound. only the terrorized expression in Lucie's eyes. kneeling on the floor across from the bed. in the middle of the night, the room lit only by the scant light coming in through the window from the almost full moon. she did not want to be lifted onto the bed because of the blood. I could see it when I lit the gas lamp. and Lucie refusing to be lifted onto the bed not wanting to get blood on it...

blood everywhere. a continuous flow.

it means nothing, she says when she finally consents to let me lift her... it is impossible.

I cannot breathe when I think of it. I am suffocated when I think if it. dawn in those hours, and the knowledge of all that is wrong. what is distant comes close. all those hours she stifled screams. I pull her up and then I press her to me. both of us kneeling until I raise her to her feet. the blood looks black in the night, her nightdress soaked in black blood, and the floor too soaked black beneath where she's been kneeling. when the gas lamp is lit everything can be seen: the terrible red that continues to flow in profusion; the terror in Lucie's eyes. she had wrapped her morning robe around her which falls to the floor when I lift her. on the floor a pool fully visible where she had been kneeling. like a child she holds herself now. her resistance is gone. it's a short distance from the floor to the bed. I must get mother, I tell her. *it's all right, she says, the cramping has stopped.* I'll get mother and then go for the doctor, I tell her. *it's so close to the holidays, she says.*

a short while later I return to the room with my mother before I go for the doctor. Lucie's head on the pillow, her eyes watch us. her lips tremble when she tries to speak, her body shivers although a fire has been lit in the fireplace and the quilt has been pulled up to her neck.

fragile, variable, mutable nature.

look at me, the doctor tells her. his voice is calm. the tone is mild. *it means nothing at all,* Lucie says to the doctor.

fissure
rupture
wound
bloodspot

shadows are thrown on the wall by the light from the gas lamp

and all the while the blood soaks the sheets and the mattress; when I lift her so that the sheets can be changed, I see that the blood had formed into a deep puddle beneath her, it cannot not absorb into the sheets or the mattress as quickly as it runs from her body.

the doctor bleeds her to stop the bleeding. he uses the lancet and the bleeding bowl. *was it just a few nights ago I had a dream of blood?* Lucie asks the doctor. *I had meant to ask Aunt Lavinia was it a bad omen.* "bleeding her into unconsciousness will reduce the circulation," says the doctor, "and will encourage her blood to clot." *in my dream there had been a little circle of animals, all with their throats cut,* Lucie says. ice is brought from the ice shed and her lower body is covered with ice.

"there's nothing to be done," the doctor tells me, "the early expulsion of the fetus sometimes causes hemorrhage…"

…and then to Lucie he says, "it's all right for you to sleep."

she says, *I dreamed of a small bowl that had two little feet, they were two human*

41

feet on short little legs.

she retches from the loss of blood, the blood still flowing from her, and now also flowing from the open vein as the doctor breathes it.

breathing a vein. breath. "breathing" a vein. breathing.

breathing a vein, that obscene expression.

my wife's body is now so chilled that the ice, which hasn't stopped the bleeding, is removed. my mother covers her with blankets, a hot stone is placed near her feet.

my mother's face is like ash tending to Lucie. like fire ash. that image before me.

"it is all right to sleep," the doctor says again. and blood running from the lancet cut on Lucie's forearm obediently into the doctor's bleeding bowl.

it requires a precise cut. the hole. like a pin hole. blood draining from a hole. close the eyes once again, and then she opens them

to see the bleeding bowl.

what a delicate bowl

it's a white porcelain bowl with hand-painted flowers, more like a dressing-room bowl.

what are those lines I see? Lucie asks the doctor. *streaming in front of my eyes. everywhere I look I see them.*

and who are those little men half-dressed with their knives?

Lucie becomes hysterical and starts to scream, on the pillow her dark hair is wet and matted with perspiration, and then she stops screaming and from that moment remains silent.

I watch her dying. I'm capable only of watching her die. her breathing becomes labored. and after a while she cannot see. she becomes so frightened when she is unable to see. she tells me that of everything that frightens her, the thing that frightens her most is the terrible darkness. she is still conscious and still alive, she might be saved, I tell the doctor. but the doctor is helpless to save her, despite his bleeding bowl, his lancet, his calm exterior betrayed by the sweat on his brow.

she is alive, but she is dying, the doctor says.

in my mind I hold her back to life.

I hold her to the earth.

through the night she remains alive.

43

the following morning she is still alive, but living only by a thread, she is conscious but blind.

by the afternoon she is dead.

in ancient times the earth and the trees of the burial place

in ancient times burying the dead by covering them with brushwood

in ancient times when the dead are well cared for they enter the earth and are happy

in ancient times the happy dead

the first day dead

the bed is stripped of its sheets. they have removed the blood mattress. only the mahogany bedstead is left. and the table next to the bed. the empty water pitcher on top, the vase next to the pitcher, the white of the curtains, the wood floor with its stains, silence, light coming in through the window.

the bed without its mattress or its sheets

the voice inside my head. or is it in my soul? the voice of my soul trying to tell something about what is living and what is dead. does the soul wander out when life has left the body?—leaving the body transformed by the absence of the soul. first they thought the soul was in the head, and then they thought near the heart. somewhere deep inside the chest cavity. the final escape of the soul made up through the chest or else out through the mouth. out through the mouth in one last exhalation. one last exhalation and the soul is unseated from the body.

the terrible blankness of mind. the room is emptied of its life. the occupants gone, one into the ground, the other towards madness. the face, the lips of my dead. I cannot say her name now, it's impossible to think I cannot say it, but the word in my mouth creates a feeling of suffocation, as though a weight has been placed on my chest, constricting my lungs. and a cloud of breath appears on the looking glass, the image obscured. I am in a knot of waiting, as though waiting for something to be decided, or waiting merely for the sake of waiting, waiting because that is what has been left to me. I'm sitting in the interior of our rooms where there is only emptiness now, my mother comes in and then she leaves, remaining silent. so silent I question if she came into the room at all.

and then I'm alone.

alone to be viewed in my standpoint.

reality, or figment of imagination?

misapprehension.

or reality?

the imagined thing

and what to make of it

this imagined thing

a fabrication

in which I see her strange

and out of character.

strange and out of character, this fabrication of Lucie: she has returned to the bed, the bed has been restored to its usual condition; the mattress, the white sheets, the white quilt and pillows in their pillow casings, white again, everything. Lucie is sitting on the bed wearing only a chemise. she is naked beneath it. it is too cold for that, I tell her. she laughs when I say it. the chemise slides off her shoulders, leaving her shoulders bare. her arms reach up to me. one leg is crossed over the other, the leg is bare up to her thigh, but when I try to cover it, she becomes angry. what an extraordinary night, she says, and then she says, there is a spider in my ear, and she pleads with me to pull it out because she is frightened that it will climb up into her brain. it will be useless to try and get it then, she says, and then she laughs again and her voice becomes suddenly tender. You must not look so sad, she says, I was only playing dead. why did you bury me? and her voice becomes angry again, why did you bury me? it is my wife here in our bed, bringing her hands together in a position of prayer. you must pray for me, William, she says, and then she rolls back onto the bed and stretches out her arms to receive me. she gives a little cry. it is my wife, Lucie, who looks dangerous now, in that way we have been warned the dead are dangerous. my wife laughing again, that unsettling piercing laugh. what is keeping you, she asks? nothing, I tell her. nothing is keeping me. it is the least I can do now. and I go to her. aware of the danger. to be set in motion with my wife who is dead. the touch of whose lips will remove mine. the touch of whose skin will reduce me to ashes. or who will tear me open with her nails. who will bleed me until the bed is soaked again with blood. until the wood floor is permanently stained. my wife who now must do all manner of harm. and she says, prayers, William, remember.

or is it madness? my mother helps me dress, she ties the necktie at my throat, fastens the tie-stud and the cuff-buttons, helps me into the jacket of my mourning suit, and then she walks with me to the front parlor where the coffin is on its coffin stand, in front of it only a few straight-backed chairs, the rest of the room has been cleared of its furniture, someone has placed a Bible on one of the chairs. there are late autumn flowers all around; the clocks have been stopped at the hour of death; no more movement of time; my mother and aunt are in their black mourning dresses. my aunt's dress fits full, my mother's fits close. Lucie's father arrives and comes over to acknowledge me; all the voices are spoken quietly; my mother is talking to Lucie's cousin, Jane, who will sit with us through the night. now the rain has started and they're talking about the weather. Jane has just come into the room and has wet shoes, her wet cape has been taken and hung in the entry. the rain will be over by morning, my mother says, or perhaps turn to snow. the door has been left open between the parlor and the hallway that leads to the front door. the light is dim in the hallway, the lamp has been lowered way down. in the morning the pall bearers will come to the house and carry Lucie out.

when my mother helps me dress it is as though I am the one who is dead, or reduced to a child again, now the boy who had once stood in front of her, the fragments of a thought, or a half-thought, half the mother of the son, the crack of the mother's womb.

I tell myself to listen, then I'll hear you, all that's coming, it's not worth any part of you.

the suffocation of the earth. I must disentangle myself from the suffocation.

not into the ground. she will be afraid to go into the ground. my mother tells my aunt the gloves of the pall bearers will be white.

another of the cousins arrives, reporting that the rain has turned to snow, a light, wet snow that does not stick, but all the same when I look out the window I see the ground is turning white in the dark night and then the others join me at the window and we see that the street lamp is reflecting white flurries. a remark is made how chill it has become, how raw and damp, and someone says that winter is certainly here. and everyone stands there for a few minutes continuing to talk about the weather, the way it turned so quickly this year after the long Indian Summer and now it's already win-ter. I think of the burial ground in winter—the frozen ground that the grave digger will have to break through in order to bury Lucie—Lucie hates the cold and now she will lie in it amongst the dead.

and I have all the irrational thoughts of a madman, madness, the coffin will not be carried to the church, it will remain here in this house with me, here in the front parlor, no, it will be carried upstairs to our rooms, to our apart-ment of rooms where I will request that it remain, carry it up I will say when the pall bearers come, set it down here, no, set it down there, no, set it down anywhere, let it stay for a while, no, let it stay longer than a while, carry it up and leave it, let me look at it.

2

Philadelphia, Pennsylvania, 1859, 1860

[Handprints – the way objects reverberate with the presence of those who have touched them.]

The silence of death.

A dream in which no one speaks, or only certain words are spoken, and the sense of the dream is lost when I wake up. Remembering only that my wife who is dead was riding in a carriage looking out the window saying she was seeing through my eyes. *William*, she said, and I could feel her breath. She was breathing as though her blood had been restored. But she was quiet and pale the way she had been quiet and pale in her last hours. Asters and snakeroot are growing in the garden.

In the medicine garden Agrimony is for coughs, Wooly Betany for headaches, Celandine for skin, Sage for stomach, Tansy for fever, Feverfew for terrible headaches.

The statue of the medicine angel: her head tilted a little forward, her eyes cast a little downward, her hair pulled away from her face and hanging long down her back; she is modestly dressed, she holds a bowl, her hair is pale, the features of her face are sharp, the late November snow is piled up around her feet.

It's the first day of December and cold, there's a harsh wind, but sun—my mother has walked with me to the Christ Church Cemetery on Arch Street at the edge of the city. The trees are colorless and bare; snow has accumulated at the bottom of the headstone;

My son, my mother says. She says the words hesitantly, no longer certain of what to say. My son, she says; or sometimes even, my darling son. I mention my preference for the older graves with their simple stones that have no well-defined shape to speak of, and have only the most unadorned engravings.

When we return home I rip the black crepe from the door. It's meant to signal visitors not to ring the bell—to tell them instead to knock softly to protect our nerves from any sudden and harsh sound during the first month of our mourning. Let the bell clang, I say. Let whoever wants to ring it, ring it. Let it sound. Let it jar us from our beds. And then I hand the tattered crepe to my mother.

There's the smell of lavender in the house, my aunt says it brings calm into a room, she says that breathing it in gives the spirit a sense of peace. Which spirit is that? I ask. All of our spirits, is her answer.

A dream in which no one speaks, it was last night, or perhaps early this morning, in the dream I was digging into the earth, digging and digging until the shovel hit the box and then digging again until the box was fully uncovered and I could pull it up from its hole in the ground, and I pried and pried until the lid gave way and I pulled it open so that my wife could breathe.

Become a voice (Sappho). Speak to me or allow me to speak. Or is it madness? Am I now mad? Weeks have gone by; it's almost Christmas Day. My mother found me this morning, sitting on the stone bench in the garden. Everything was gray and brown and snow was on the ground. The only green was that of the small balsam pine planted before last season. It's too cold out here, my mother said, have you had your coffee and some breakfast?— everything is still hot on the sideboard. I followed her into the house, into the dining room where a fire was burning in the fireplace. Biscuits had been laid out on the sideboard and boiled eggs and ham. I filled my plate, feeling suddenly hungry, it was a peculiar hunger without desire for food or taste. It was as though I had been emptied out, entirely emptied beneath the layers of my skin, down to my bones, emptied even of bones, hollowed out and in need of being filled. Earlier in the morning I had climbed the stairs to our apartment of rooms, Lucie's and mine, the rooms that are set apart on the third floor ell. Everything stood plain and stark inside. The wash basin was empty; no one had come up to fill it because the rooms are now empty. Her soap had been left next to the basin. The scent of bayberry filled the room. Lucie's clothes were still in the armoire, or folded on the narrow shelves of the closet. For a while I stood in front of her writing desk staring at its rounded drawers, and then I pulled one of the drawers open and looked down at the inks and pens and sheets of paper. I looked at them but didn't remove them and then I closed the drawer and left the room. And I went back downstairs and out to the garden where my mother found me sitting on the bench.

the sense of rushing down. what were our wedding gifts?

I am like the old man who desires only to sit in the graveyard.

Pilgrimage to the Delaware. The cold, choppy water, the winter river brown, covered with foam like sea foam. A sense of desolation along the docks. Curiosity about the water. The brown chop of the river. Sea men who have purpose to their life, loading and unloading, nets filled to bursting. Commerce. The coal depot. The torch factory. The varying lengths of the brass parade-torches, the parades that last into the night.

Easy to imagine an apparition in the falling snow—on the wharves, my wife in the distance. Her hair falls light against her dress. Fair. An apparition of the mind. There is no real visitation. Only a presence that is felt, and that only from wanting.

Irrevocable death, nothing left behind, or only memory left behind.

Memory, which is not a real and an independent thing.

Standing on the rock pier as though exiled. Left not with the desire to die, but to join with the dead.

In the biting cold.

So, so. The old German who owns the Dry Goods store on Broad Street says, So, so. He pronounces it as a Z—Zo, he says. And it means we'll see... we'll see what will come... what will be... what the future will bring... where we stand in the world. We'll see what can be challenged, what will topple and fall, and what will continue to stand. The rest will come easy or hard, it can only be seen when it is seen. Zo. Intimations of a future. The sun will rise in the east. Night will fall. There'll be stars in the night sky. The earth. The breeze. The myth. And nothing can be done. I'm caught in this present. Bound to it. Zo.

Before the first light. Darkness. Outside, the elements. And then a yellow dawn.

We are in the days between Christmas and New Years—they come and go one after the other. In other years my aunt has referred to them as charitable days. At the breakfast table I make the remark that Lucie's father looked unwell to me when he stopped by on Christmas Day. Did you notice it? I ask my mother. My mother's voice is mild in response: It's just the effect of his grieving, she says. I reply, Yes, I suppose it is.

It's the Tuesday of the New Year's week. The days that lead to the new year. The temperature is below freezing, but the sky is clear. In the early morning I walk up South Eighth Street and across Chestnut to Sixth, and then I climb the four flights of stairs to the studio.

The iron headrests stand against the wall. An arrangement of studio portraits hangs above them. My wife used to talk about the placement of an object, or else a piece of fabric that she thought would add interest to the composition; or about some other detail she wanted to add to a backdrop. Last night I saw her soul. It was perhaps an illusion. It was not a likeness as in a photograph, nor was it as she had been in life; it was simply a figure, unclothed but not naked; that is, there was not the sense of nudity about the body, nor was there the sense of flesh. And yet it was clear that it was a female figure. The figure stood in profile with its back against the wall next to the entrance table with the mirror above it. I was in the apartment of rooms, in the small sitting room that had been Lucie's. The figure stood there for a moment and a feeling of longing filled the room. I had the desire to approach it, but an apprehension too. I remained perfectly still in the archway of the open door. And then suddenly the figure moved, as though propelled forward across the room to the opposite wall where it disappeared. Was it her soul? What does sense dictate? All the same, it was beautiful, this thing I saw. And it was this vision, this nude soul, with its absence of flesh and its bloodless lips that gave me the courage to come here to retrieve the boxes filled with her photographs.

She called her photographs investigations. Her notebooks too are in the boxes, and her jottings on the long, loose sheets of paper. I open one of the boxes and find beneath the lid a photograph of a bird. It's strangely beautiful, but morbid. The body is trapped between the window and the window's partially open wooden shutters. I wonder had she found it there or placed it? It's a large bird, black, one of the crows or starlings. It's difficult to tell which because much of the body is pressed behind the shutters. The wings stick out from behind, looking tattered and ragged. I'm still staring at it when Edmund Fell comes in. He startles me. I startle him as well. He says, it's cold in here, Mr. Martin. And I realize I'm shivering. His eyes glance at the open box, then at the photograph in my hand, and then he goes to light the fire. I follow him to the fireplace with the photograph of the bird in my hand. Do you know how Mrs. Martin came to take this picture? I ask. No, he says, he does not.

I ask him, will you bring the carriage? I would like to take these boxes to the house. He says, yes, he will see to it at once. The fire starts quickly, soon the flames are licking up around the logs, and the area directly in front of the fireplace is getting warm. We stand facing each other. His face glows a little red in the light from the flames. He is not old, he is in fact a young man, he has told me he and his wife have their first child due any day to arrive. His hair is overly long, and there is a thickness to his jaw. He has one leg shorter than the other which causes him to limp. I fix on his limp as he walks away.

Thoughts all night long that would not stop. All night long in a kind of luminous thinking. And then to wake and find myself in this time, in this present. When I woke I believed my wife was still alive. I said out loud: I thought she had died, but now I know she is alive. *Brain illness*—to be an invalid in the mind. *I have become an invalid in my mind.* My mother and aunt walk on tip toe through the house. They've not said it but I know I disturb them: my general impassiveness, my refusal to engage, yes my disengagement, my general refusal almost to conduct myself civilly. I want only to eat. I eat like an animal. And no matter how much I eat, I'm always hungry. Yesterday my mother made the suggestion that I involve myself with current events— there is talk of little else than war, she said; it fills up all the pages of The Ledger. Then she repeated the words: There is talk of little else than war.

Lucie's cousin, Jane, visited today; again to pay her respects during this period of mourning. She brought her child with her, a little girl. I was sitting in the south parlor. The child ran to me and sat next to me on the sofa. Unasked, she saw fit to inform me she was seven years old. I told her I was not in a frame of mind for conversation. She immediately became quiet and fussed with her doll with full intention to remain. The doll wore a triangular cap on its head; its eyes were permanently open. The fire in the fireplace began to smoke and I got up to adjust the logs. I thought of the night I had spent last night, thoughts that had filled me with fear, it was the excess of fear that sometimes comes late at night. The night had been windy and the shutters banged against the house. I had gotten up from the bed and looked down to the garden, straining to see through the pitch blackness, but I could see nothing. Then in afternoon, in the south parlor with the child, I stared out the multi-paned window that faces the garden. My eyes felt strained, as though swollen. I looked up to the shutters to find the place where they had been banging during the night in the wind. The child was quiet. The sky above the house was washed white with sun; I lowered my head and placed my palms over my eyes.

The feeling of paralysis, the sense that I will never move again, that like the child's doll not even my eyes in their sockets will be capable of moving and I will only be able see what is directly in front of me, the subject of my vision thus left to the whim of whatever position my body has been left to rest in.

My aunt passes by me. There's the rustling sound of her dress. And then it's quiet.

My son is not well, I hear my mother say.

My son is not well.

He needs only to rest.

The improbable death. Women are fragile. The fragile organs imperfect. Salty humors. A secret place inside. An animal inside, a member deep inside. All nerves and sensitivity this thing, this member. I examine the contents of the boxes that Lucie left behind; four boxes in all, containing the work that was her own: her photographs, or else her ideas written down as notes; there are also notations she had written at the bottoms of the photographs. There's the recurring image of a woman in the various tableaux. She was one of the French women, Edmund Fell told me—Mrs. Martin often photographed her.

One of the French women? I am amazed how much she kept from me, all of it tucked away in boxes in the studio. All of it kept secret. It is a woman's trait: secrecy. I'm surprised at the extent of her seriousness with regard to photography: her sense of purpose, the importance she attached to her concepts and methods.

A title, or an explanation, sometimes several pages of an explanation, an *observation upon which she expounds: The aura of a nightmare. A woman came to the studio. She was afraid; I could sense in her an underlying attitude of fear. She asked me to make a pretty portrait for her husband. I sent her away with her lovely likeness in a frame. Unknown to her I captured this other for myself. A little overly dark in the moment the sun had gone behind the clouds. There was a striking change to her face when I captured her during those moments of cloud. Everything I sensed in her seemed to be suddenly revealed on the glass plate. A dark frightened image.*

The note on another photograph says: *A man with his collection. A warning or a foreshadowing. The pin of the collector stuck through the body of the insect.*

One of the photographs is strangely posed: a woman is seated; a man is standing behind her with his hands on her head. Sharp contrasts of light are displayed on the albumen print.

There is nothing more I want. Only to sit here. To look through the boxes.

It's nothing but imaginings, her bedclothes fresh, her body breathing, life contained in her body, and I'm holding her and saying that I must hold her while it's still possible to hold her, that I must remember, that I remember.

In the morning warmth is circulating through the house from the fireplaces, all of them lit, in all of them the flames strong and high. It's New Year's Day. On the sideboard in the dining room are oranges and eggs, the smell of a goose being cooked, a pear pie, and a sponge cake with butter cream. My mother says it's true that we're in mourning, but there still must be a proper meal on New Years Day. My aunt makes the comment it's 1860—already 1860! I take a cognac with my coffee for the New Year. My aunt is talking about her head—for the past several days she has had the sensation of her head snapping, a clearly audible sound. She wonders can we hear it, the snapping. My mother listens for a minute—I hear nothing, she says. My aunt says it is near the top of her head, and then, Oh, my aunt says, my head just snapped again.

Snow is falling. I'll go out for a walk, I say—and then I add that when I come back I'll make my resolutions. My mother looks surprised when I say it. I take note of her surprise. ...but that is what I've always done, I say.

How is everything, William? Tell me the problems of your life. The voice inside my mind. Hurry now, tell me. I ignore the voice. I remain quiet. The morning is cold and the snow continues to fall. I walk south on 8th Street to Locust and then east across Locust in the direction of 2nd Street. I feel the frigid temperature of the year that is only beginning—I feel myself becoming light-headed and I have the sensation that the cold has fully penetrated me. My breath is visible in the air.

To fall in fright, to be frightened, to be afraid, to yearn for. The haunting likeness. The element that will transform, that will reduce to ash.

I encounter the mummers' parade on 2nd Street. They march each year on New Year's morning. The parade moves slowly. The sounds of their bells and horns fill the street. They are casting out the old year by marching and begging and mimicking the dead in bondage. The custom was brought here from Scotland. Some of the mummers are bound to each other with a hugely exaggerated chain. *By flesh. By death.* They are all masked and with their metal soup pots clanging—carrying bells and glockenspiels, bell-snickling, a roving band. As the mummers pass by me, I think: Oh, so they have come up this far into the city now. And I have the sense I'm being swept up into them and into the sound of their voices:

Give us whiskey, give us gin, open the door and let us in.

The refrain repeated over and over again.

...to fall in fright, to be frightened, to be afraid, to yearn for. The haunting likeness. The element that will transform...

Give us whiskey, give us gin, open the door and let us in.

One of the mummers steps away from the others and stands in front of me silent, as though he has a message to deliver to me, but he says nothing. His gray hair is drawn back; he wears no mask but his face is painted white; one of his eyes has a tic, an uncontrollable movement of the muscles, I stare at the movement of his eye, and as we stand there together the other mummers continue to move slowly past us.

In one of Lucie's photographs she had depicted a tableau of women walking single file like the mummers. Each woman is reaching her hand out to take the hand of the woman behind her. Most of their faces are shown in profile, but two of the women are facing forward, Lucie had captured their expressions as regretful and melancholy, and there's the suggestion of motion in the photograph, as though the women are moving away from this earth.

We must run along now, run along…

We must run along, the mummers say…

The parade is moving on…

But the mummer who has stepped away from the others remains standing in front in me.

My wife… I say those words to the painted face that stands before me. The snow is falling only lightly now and the sun is beginning to shine, a radiant light on the streets of the city, shining on the buildings, reflecting on windows, glinting and golden and polished. And this mummer, this masker, who stepped out of line, and who continues to stand in front of me, has long stopped clanging on his metal pot and holds it out to me instead as if it is a begging bowl. And he continues to stand in silence before me. I had a dream, I tell him, I dreamed that my wife had died and that I was calling an absent. Calling an absent. These strange words come into my thoughts: when I call for my wife it is calling an absent. But now I realize, I tell him, that my wife is not dead and it was only a dream. It's not real. It was not real. Just as the painted man who stands before me is not real, his eyes are intent on me, but the eyes that look at me are not real. Then the mummer speaks to me in a voice disguised, as though his words can only be spoken when his breath is taken inward. The words come as gasps on an inward breath. Your wife, he says. But the words and the gaze are not real. And I have the realization that it has all been a dream; that my wife, my real wife, is sitting at her dressing table painting her face white like the mummer's face. And on the dressing table there are roseberries which she has picked from my mother's garden. The mummer stares at me in silence, and all the while he is staring at me my wife plays out her misfortune again on her knees on the wooden floor—she plays it the way a scene in a theatrical performance is played, repeated many evenings in a row. And now the mummer's face is strangely near mine; his features contorted as though by sorrow, as though by heartbreak, how affecting to see so much sorrow. I say it out loud: How affecting to see so much sorrow. And the tears well up in his eyes, his eyes which are sunk deep in his face, and the tears roll down his cheeks, and I pity this man and his grief, this man whose wife has died while mine is alive, and the noise of the bells becomes too much to bear: all that singing and those horns, the banging on the metal pots, a deafening noise to drive away the dead.

3

Arkansas, 1860; The Unorganized Territories 1860, 1861; St. Louis, 1861

if by chance your eyes...

There are the little ewes crying with cold feet. An eagle circling in the morning sky.

From Philadelphia to Baltimore, from Baltimore to Cincinnati, then on to Louisville, and then St. Louis, which links the East with the West, and now down to Arkansas along the Oklahoma border.

I have set out to travel with a camera, one suited to travel and harsh conditions.

The eagle circling in the morning sky.

The ten foot wingspan of the eagle.

Quivers of arrows. The eye of the eagle given by God the ability to see at great distances. And I am taken up by my mind as though my body is lifted.

I have returned to the West, where they're telling a story, where they're passing the talking stick, using the talking stick each in turn, their hands clasped firmly around the neck of the stick. *HA!* the storyteller begins. *HA!* The way things come into the world. That which is coming. *The wren said to the man, "Do not be afraid. Climb on my back and shut your eyes." Before dawn he flew away from the village.* With everyone listening, *HA!* the storyteller begins.

HA!

Wild men such as the wild men of the woods. The dancers costumed for the winter ceremony. Emerging from the secret room. Wearing cedar-bark and neck rings. Five mouths through which the spirit wriggles. A female deity's mask, the half-dazed dancer, the god, the woman, the winter dance.

Here the glass plates are slow to prepare in the makeshift darkroom, slow to prepare and slow to develop, the image sometimes appearing like a specter rising out of the dark. Despite the bright light the image is often obscured from heat drying the plate. Part of the old Choctaw Indian has been lost on the albumen print that I'm holding, but what is visible is the way he supports his head with his hand, his fingers are at his temples, his head rests on his hand.

I have set out with my camera to leave the place of my wife's death.

Trading one death for another.

I return to the lower Red River where I saw my father slain.

Violent noise, loud shouts, chaos of movement, outcries and confusion. But there was no real confusion; there was only cold purpose.

...my memory of the painted outlaws coming towards us, lines painted on their white faces to make them look like Indians...

...dust driven up from the hooves of the horses.

...the moment the hoof beats hit their hardest the devils appeared on the rise of the earth before us, all bearing down in full view of my father and me

Forget. We forget.

And now an eagle circling in the morning sky.

The passage by steamboat to St. Louis, which links the East with the West and down to Arkansas along the Oklahoma border, where the False Washita and the Red River meet, and the yellow of the water.

Somewhere it's written that the Yellow River brought forth a map and the Lo River brought forth a writing.

But today I have neither map nor writing.

The river in motion.

To stay one's course.

The duration of that which always is.

When the steamboat comes to shore I take accommodations in a hotel in Little Rock.

Where just outside the town of Little Rock

there is a circus and menagerie united in a tent show.

Brought here by Mabies for the amusement of the people.

A circus and menagerie united in a splendid and liberal design.

As advertised in the Arkansas Gazette:

> Mabies' Traveling Circus and Menagerie United!
> Educated Mules and Trick Ponies
> Sig. Woodruff, renowned Lion Tamer
> Burmese Cow
> A wilderness of Birds and Monkeys
> American Clown, I. Huyck
> Great feats of light and heavy balancing
> Herr Jennings, the man of iron
> New and amazing! The mystery of The Hermaphrodite!
> The Ambiguous Being, Half Man and Half Woman.
> Available for viewing and talking to.
> All of which will go through with a variety of chaste and
> pleasing performances
> Will exhibit on Monday and Tuesday, the 9th and 10th of July, 1860.
> Two performances each day. Afternoon and Night.

When the hermaphrodite's eyes come to rest on me I have compassion for his wretchedness. His eyes are liquid. He searches my face with his eyes. It's done quickly and then he casts his gaze down.

He can be conceived of as an aberration or a mystery.

The poor pathetic creature how am I to talk about him?

I am in the viewing tent with the hermaphrodite and the cowboys.

Inside the tent where he's displayed.

I stare at him just as the cowboys are staring.

The hermaphrodite never looks directly at our eyes.

How old are you now? one of the cowboy asks him.
I have just turned eighteen, Sir.
What's your name? another asks.
My name is Laurent, Sir, he answers.

Raise your arm up.
The hermaphrodite does nothing.
You can raise your arm up if you want to.
The hermaphrodite raises his arm up slowly and then lowers it again.
Raise your other arm up now.
Again the hermaphrodite does nothing.
You can raise that arm up if you damn want to.

He stands on a low platform in the tent, wearing a white shirt and dark trousers; the shirt is of a soft, almost transparent material; his long black hair is pulled back from his face; his stature is slight; the cowboys stamp their feet when he raises his arm.

Fear of ghosts. It was a child's fear of ghosts. With my father there could be no fear; to be a man was all. My father was large, that's the way he looms in my memory. He said that everything is as it is intended to be in nature: the mountains and the rivers, the valleys, and the traces and remains.

Everything as it is intended in nature.

But not the hermaphrodite.

A mountain lion screamed and it sounded like a woman screaming.

Performances chaste and not chaste.

One of the cowboys stands out as being younger than the rest. I don't git it, he says. His remark brings coarse laughter from the others. One of them spits. You don't git it? Pay your extra quarter and you'll git it. For an extra quarter you'll git to see what's there to see. The cowboys line up and wait to enter the curtained-off area at the rear of the tent. But first the hermaphrodite is led there by Mabies and the circus protectors who carry guns. Someone says something vulgar and the young cowboy's face turns red. I have paid my quarter and wait with the others to be enclosed with the hermaphrodite behind the curtain.

To take into the mind and to keep there. The strange ways of nature. The hermaphrodite's face is covered by his hands and he is naked except for his white shirt unbuttoned down the front. He is half sitting, half reclining on a short-legged chair. One of the cowboys spits. My eyes interrogate the body on display in the shabby tent. The circus protectors face us squarely, still with their guns in their hands. The hermaphrodite's body

78

is displayed in what might be the manner of a medical photograph if such were to exist. The anomalous genitalia bared as though for a clinical examination, as though for the gesture of being pointed to. The viewing is limited to only a few minutes, but during those minutes all the cowboys have started to spit. There is the heat, the dust, and then more dust from the cowboys stamping their feet. The cowboys are still spitting as they walk out from behind the curtain when the viewing is over.

Because my father desired it, my mother and I had moved with him from Philadelphia to live in Arkansas when I was not quite five years old. One day my mother felt light-headed and was overcome by sadness and began to weep. But then the weeping stopped and the sadness was replaced by a vision of beauty. A presence, or a rapture. She said it was difficult to say which. All she knew was that her sadness had been replaced by a vision of beauty.

Indistinct sounds until they became audible. First in the distance. And then drawing close. If you lie down with your ear to the ground like I did—for no other reason than to hear the earth—you will hear the hoof beats of horses. That was what I heard. The sound was a kind of fascination, to have my ear to the earth and to hear the sounds in the distance coming near. I hear horses running, coming closer, I said to my father.

I'm a much lamented man, says Mabies, half his face stiff from a palsy. The hermaphrodite, now dressed, is standing holding his hand over his heart. I don't know what I'd do with it, Mabies is saying, but I grant it's okay for you to take his picture if he agrees—I might find some use for it—as long as you're done with your business before the performance in the afternoon. I have in mind to take a small series of chaste portraits, I say. The conversation goes easily as though the tent is the season's summerhouse. I ask the hermaphrodite if he's willing. He moves his eyes in the direction of Mabies.

Now in the early morning light making ready. The morning holds excitement for me. I arrive burdened with the photography equipment and when he sees me the hermaphrodite lowers his eyes.

In the tent he's wearing the same white shirt of soft fabric he had been wearing the previous day, and the same men's black trousers. His hair again is pulled back making his face look severe. The light is not as bright as I require, but in the time it takes me to set up the camera and the portable darkroom to develop the negative plates, the sun has moved into position above the net opening at the top of tent. When everything is ready, I take the first likeness.

The first of these images shows the hermaphrodite fully clothed, wearing black shoes and white stockings, black trousers and the same transparent white shirt, sitting on the low chair he sits on for viewing in the tent; his cheek is beardless, his hair hangs long, his shirt is partially unbuttoned from the throat, the throat shows white, his hair shines black and his eyes are black like his hair.

Then the long difficult process crouched like a dog to develop the plate in the portable darkroom.

Do you like the thought, I ask him, that because you will have been photographed you will always be alive?

I have prayed all my life only to die, he answers, to be erased from this earth.

A natural octave higher and the voice would be that of a young woman, an octave lower and it would be unmistakably a young man's. As it is, it is constantly shifting, the identification of gender at any given moment given largely to the ear of the listener. Both his voice and his person are more at times masculine, more at times feminine.

I would have preferred to hide myself, he continues, but I was sold by my parents when I was a child. My father despised me, and my mother, I think, did not care much for me either. When I was very young there was no way I could fully grasp the reason. But then I was owned and my purpose was to be displayed.

Why have you consented to be photographed? I ask.

Mabies wanted it.

One day he will die, as we all will die, and the reason for his life will have been lost; everything will have been centered on the way the world perceived him.

But what do *you* want, I ask him.

I have wanted only to be relieved of myself, he says. I have wanted the knife to cut away the difference of my flesh. There was a doctor who once examined me, Mabies called him in because I was sick and in pain, I had stones to pass despite my young age, and so much pain I could not stand up. I saw the doctor's face when he examined me, his shock and revulsion when he saw me, regardless of the fact he knew. He gave me something for my pain and what he gave me worked. For the other condition, he said, there's a rare surgical procedure; he mentioned the name of an eminent physician. I thought at last I would have my knife and felt happy. Of course Mabies was not in favor of the change because the way I am now I draw crowds. But the doctor said there might be money offered for the novelty of the surgery, and finally Mabies said he would allow it, but he said it must be my decision. In the end I refused because the fortune teller told me that if I did it I would die. Strange and a pity to want only to die and when the opportunity is given to refuse.

I ask if he will loosen his hair. He removes the hair-clasp and shakes his head forward, his hair moves like an animal mane, his face appears longer with his hair down and has a sweetness of ambiguous gender.

For a time the cloud-cover puts him in shadow; but then it moves off and the sun pours down on him brightly again through the netted opening at the top of the tent; it's already too warm, hot; and there's a musty smell inside the tent. As though his words are water running, the hermaphrodite continues talking.

I talk to you with a great outpouring of words that come like memory or feeling; words like those that rise up in my dreams. I have conversations with myself, I speak in two voices, one for each of my selves. I wonder what might have happened if it hadn't been true that the operation would cause me to die? What would my life be if I had let the doctor cure me? But that is past and what is past is gone. I can't go back there now. And besides neither of my selves wanted to let go of my flesh.

The sun is still overhead where I require it. I take another photograph and then stop to develop the negative—the negatives must be developed immediately, but except for what I'll give to Mabies all the positive prints will be developed later. The hermaphrodite is still and silent while I take the photographs. But he continues to talk while I develop the negatives.

...that is what it is like, you know, living with two selves, conjoined like Siamese twins, but perhaps it's a gift to have both. Gifts come with their prices. I have thought about a life of solitude with only my two selves, in some far away place, perhaps in India or Egypt. You should go and take your camera. It will give more interesting photographic images than you might make of me. Sometimes I make plans for going there as an adventurer. But going is impossible. I would be stopped by Mabies. Remember, I am owned. I'll tell you a secret about the Wild Man from Borneo, he's just a plain Negro from Georgia by the name of Calvin Bird. A silver plate has been inserted under his scalp so that his Wild Man's horns can be screwed in. It keeps him always in discomfort. He told me that he has a plan to go up North, maybe up to Syracuse and find a doctor who will remove the plate.

...it's all little boats of idle dreams for those who come in to look. The men and women and the little children too (though the children are not allowed to pay the extra quarter). But those who pay stare at me until they've had their fill. Maybe I'll go with Calvin Bird to Syracuse and ask the surgeon there to cut away my extra sex. Which one shall be cut do you think? Which would you have me remain, Sir? A man or a woman? Does it seem a kind of murder? The sharp knife of the surgeon to remove all trace.

The sun is beating full down and the tent is hot. Large beads of perspiration have formed on my forehead. The hermaphrodite glistens too and shows flesh that is delicate and wet from heat. He asks me what's in my mind when I am taking a photograph—at this moment now when I'm taking this photograph of him. I tell him my mind is blank now, or occupied primarily by considerations of light, or the way a shadow falls on his face. Beyond that my thoughts are blank, I tell him. There is no thought. All my thinking takes place before I begin.

I am bothered by the dust and noise, he says changing the subject... and by the circus wagons continually in motion from place to place. When I sleep I sometimes dream of living in a forest where everything is green and where there are the fresh smells of earth and new growth—where I would live as a hermit like the hermits of religion who think of nothing but God from morning until night.

The face of a young man or a young woman, one and then the other. I ask if he can prophesize or is that only a superstition?

83

No, I cannot prophesize, he tells me. Not all monsters have the gift of prophesy. We have a Fire Eater in the circus and he can prophesize. Have you seen him? He was brought from India; he arrived some months ago with the elephants.

One and then the other, now the face of a young woman. No traces of the man in her.

The face of a young woman.

Perhaps I fulfill some intention that has only to do with the dreams of others. What do you think? Do you think that is possible?

I ask her to say more about this.

For them, for those who see me I am a kind of dream. I am what cannot be imagined until it appears and is displayed before the eyes. All the curiosities here in Mabies circus are that. Life would be intolerable without us: without my two sexes; without a man who can eat fire; without the menagerie of animals. I was watching once without being seen; two young boys were looking at the large cats pacing in their cage. The older boy held the younger a distance from the bars. The cats largely ignored them. That's the way it is with the large cats; they are mostly lazy, preferring to recline, and to keep their eyes half-closed on the world. But the boys had both their eyes open wide. And I could see the cats enter the minds of the boys—and I believe from that moment forward all possibilities in life were greater for them. That's what I mean. Perhaps that is my purpose. I believe that's why I stay. Do you think it is a noble purpose?

I consider you to be noble, I tell her, with or without purpose.

But what am I really able to tell her, looking down as I am from a long period of madness?

The long period of madness that follows the moment someone is taken from you. The breath that is held. The line that is crossed in that fraction of time between what is living and what is dead. Even when my wife was dying there had at least been the consolation of the touch of her hand, a few words whispered, then silence...

       And I in turn would say you are noble too, the hermaphrodite tells me.

I watch as she leans back in the chair, as if she is moving backwards away from the camera. Her hairless cheek is smooth. The full sleeves of her white shirt hang long to her wrists; her hands show slender at the bottom of the sleeves. One of her hands is at her chest resting on the muslin fabric of the shirt. Through the lens I see the upside down image of her hand on her breast, and her white throat, which I cannot help but notice is a feminine throat.

I see only a form that is feminine.

She glances at me from the chair.

There is between us an exchange of glances.

To glance. To gaze. To look intently, as in expectancy.

The slowness of the photographic process.

The dim likeness of her ambiguity to be photographed.

The softness of white muslin and then her peculiar expression.

I have only six glass plates to use for the photographs.

After I have used the first three, I tell her three glass plates now remain for her likeness.

　　　…first the sweet, sweet, she says, that's what I have said to myself in a dusty corner.

and then

　　　…but for the remaining three, she says, I will grant the wish I know you have, I will give my body to your camera without need to pay the quarter.

She unbuttons the shirt and it again falls open from her neck to her navel, but the muslin clings to her shoulders and arms. Then she asks me to go out from tent and when she calls me back the rest of her naked body is displayed before me.

Naked and displayed. And still the softness of her muslin shirt. She closes her eyes.

My hand brushes hers when I go near her to make an adjustment.

a slight contortion of her body.

she lifts her hand and with it covers her face.

my hand briefly brushes her flesh.

if by chance your eyes.

the slight contortion of her body.

it's the contortion of a body that cannot satisfy itself. that can only satisfy *itself.*

it's only flesh brushing her flesh.

my hand on her throat.

it's a delicate throat.

for only a few seconds my hand on her throat.

and the ghost waiting to enter.

and my body moving backward, back three times to the box of the camera.

still the ghost waiting to enter.

but it cannot enter what cannot be entered.

I remember the contorted body of my father, the foam from his lips, the blood on his head. I've come back to the place he died but I've seen nothing except the yellow water of the river and the grass that's turned brown in the summer heat. There is the thing in my memory and the thing which is before me now. It has proven impossible for me to find the place where it happened. Impossible to find some remnant of my father. But in the games of my distant childhood I invented a second father, Hatchoo-tuck-nee (snapping turtle), I invented an Indian father, and so I was born twice, it was my second birth, in the Indian custom two cuts of the knife to make the blood flow, and then the lines of white paint on my naked body.

I return to flesh brushing flesh.

moving forward again to the hermaphrodite.

and then again moving back to the camera.

...where the ghost cannot enter.

...and where I must take my leave.

...I must take my leave now, I say.

if by chance your eyes.

if by chance your eyes should fall on this.

if by chance your eyes should fall on this you will know that it is evidence of a life.

lived.

if by chance your eyes...

And then the backwoods at night. The note of the warbler. The clear state-of-being found in wilderness. On the edge of rough country where a soul can come to rest. Where the light has shifted. An abstraction of memory.

...an abstraction of memory. The moment someone is taken. The fraction of a moment that separates what is living from what is dead. My wife's words float as memory. We were on the grounds of Fairmount Park; we had just spread the picnic cloth; the day had been hot. And she had been telling me about her cousin who had hurt her thumb while sewing; the sewing needle had penetrated to the bone. The subject is of no real concern, she had said, perhaps it's too trivial to mention; but it made an impression on me the way the needle went deep into the thumb. Her words float now as memory.

In the hotel room I examine her notebook, which I brought with me. Some-times the writing is indecipherable in her notebook. I struggle with a word;

for example the word "Hour." It appears first to be "Other," then "Horus," and finally I can see that it's "Hour." Scrawls of words she had written quickly, her hand moving to keep up with thought. Now the pages are silent; they summon the apparition. But there's nothing I can do with it when it comes; despite my reaching, the apparition cannot be touched.

In the morning I move from one ghost to another, from the ghost of my wife to that of my father. I'm standing here in Arkansas, where I've returned to find the gravesite of my father. I stand on the shore where the False Washita and the Red Rivers meet. The water is yellow becoming brown and looks dull. I prepare the plate to photograph the river; it will be a long view from the riverbank which is yellow and brown like the water.

I have the sensation of moving backwards into my life, the impression of an apparition moving backwards into its body.

Sometimes I think I'm well again. It happens when?

The Little Rock Hotel.

The hotel at night.

The fading light outside the window.

It's called a hotel, but it's not like our hotels in Philadelphia: here there are only two floors of rooms; the first floor has the common rooms; and the second, the guest rooms. A veranda attaches to the rooms on the second floor front. The heat. The dust. The drawl of speech during the hours of dining. The long, family-style table laid with a white linen cloth and set with white plates.

Miss Trautwine at the supper table is talking about a broach encrusted with black stones that used to belong to her grandmother, obsidian, she says; you know, they are Indian stones. The Indians run wild here: Caddos, Quapaws, Osage, Choctaw, Cherokee; and once there had been the Mound Builders building their earthwork mounds. Mr. Jenks, seated across from me, pipes in with authority that there's modern interest in the Mounds—archeological interest in the effigy and burial mounds, and in the temple mounds. Platters of beef are brought to the table (the beef is boasted as being pure Arkansas beef), along with cornmeal bread served with cheese and butter, sweet potatoes, sweet peas, preserves, and cranberry compote. The conversation turns to the local theater; three nights of Mrs. Pennoyer's performance in "Orphan of Geneva," and Mr. Wallace's as well. How engaging their performances, completely successful, the play already a favorite, the actors were encored the night before and the last few minutes had to be repeated. Miss Trautwine had attended, and Mr. Jenks as well; I have certainly missed something deserving of notice, they inform me. The beef is cooked rare; blood seeps into the plate with each cut of the knife. It's a luxury to have these cattle here, Mr. Jenks says—Arkansas cattle give a more tender meat than Texas cattle. The cowboys run them up as far as Kansas, or all the way west, all the way to San Francisco—those long runs are something to think about, wouldn't you agree, Mr. Martin. And then Miss Trautwine's voice, reporting an article from the Arkansas Gazette: *Negro Clothing, of the very best materials, and at the most reasonable prices.* But Mr. Jenks moves the subject to talk of the Hot Springs Hotel in La Grange, kept by Mr. Mitchell who bought it from Mr. Woods; commodious rooms, he is saying, each one kept with a fireplace, and special facilities constructed for taking a cure. He will be on his way there in the morning. And then reaching for the platter of beef, he returns to the subject of Arkansas cattle; their meat is the most savory, he says, the Texas cattle are too wild and not fit to eat; the Texas cattle are only good to bait traps to catch wolves. The cowboys and the cowboy dances are mentioned, where the men dance with each other, but then the subject is dropped.

To be a wanderer. To go up the Mississippi River. To go back to St. Louis and from there up the Missouri River to the Unorganized Territories. I have only to wait for the steamer. My business is finished in Arkansas.

In my transient room: it's not mine; it belongs to no one; or it belongs to anyone who comes to lodge here for a night; or for two, or longer; along with the bed and the washstand. I open her notebook on the bed.

...written by her hand: *Their faces are always interesting to me... Even that man today with the hard expression. He came in with his wife, but asked that they be photographed separately—he wanted individual portraits. I detected in him something cruel. William was elsewhere and I was grateful Edmund Fell was at work in the studio. I asked him to assist. I believe he understood I was not at ease.*

The way the ghost gains entry. The welcoming. The invitation. The sudden strong sensation that she is in the room. That she is looking for me, searching for me, along the yellow hotel walls. The view down to the street. An unexpected high wind and a torrent of rain; the sweep of the water across the low roofs. And then thunder and lightning. The night sky lit by lightning.

the sensation she's here...

...but all the time I know she is absent. Absent as someone who has gone on a journey and will one day be returning. And I am left sniffing for her presence like a dog.

Breakfast is creamed eggs, thick slices of bacon, biscuits with gravy.

I sit reading the notices in the Arkansas Gazette:

> Piano Fortes, Carpets, Curtain Materials, Window Cornices and Shades, Floor Oil Cloths, Table Oil Cloths, Looking Glasses, Spring, Hair, Cotton, Moss and Shuck Mattresses, Tucker's Spring Beds, &c.

No. 192 Main street

Cotton Yarns

Any quantity of Cotton Yarns of Arkansas Cotton and Arkansas Spinning, received from the Arkansas Manufacturing Company, and for sale at cost and charges, by

Burgevin & Field, on the Levee

1 P. specimen negro cloth. J.M. Black (there it is again, a reference to Negro cloth).

And an advertisement giving the hours of the auction-stands for the cattle and the Negroes.

Whose blood are you trying to hide, Sir? And what may I inquire is "negro cloth?" Where does the question come from and to whom might I address it? I might have asked Miss Trautwine or Mr. Jenks to explain about Negro cloth, but neither of them came down for breakfast. Or if they did come down it was earlier and they have finished and are gone from the lodging. Mr. Jenks on his way to the Hot Springs. And Miss Trautwine and her guardian—where? There is no one at the table I might ask about the cloth.

Silence. The hills. Memory of the hills where my mother and I took the dogs—we took them out alone. It was not significant that we 'took' them, but that we took them out alone. And that we were able to handle them unassisted by my father. My mother herded the dogs together and they obeyed, running in front of us like a half-wild pack. The dogs were docile with my mother—despite their size, their strength, their aggressive natures, the force of their incisors. Memory of my mother and myself as a child making our way into the hills following the hounds.

The bacon is well salted, the eggs are rich and savory, the gravied biscuits have just a slight hint of sweetness.

I have brought the equipment down and loaded it into the carriage. Some of the boxes had to be strapped to the top. I count the boxes and examine the fastenings of those strapped to the top. Everything is in order, I'm ready to depart. To be transported, along with my boxes to the steamer to St. Louis. Will you sign our guest book, Mr. Martin? The book has been opened to the page I am expected to sign; each of the guests before me has written a date and a few words of sentiment about the hotel.

There's a hot wind and dust in the air, the dust irritates my eyes. The monotonous movement of the carriage. The abundance of trees: oak, hickory, locust, cypresses, and dark cypresses; we are moving north to the junction of the Arkansas River with the Mississippi River. The carriage to the steamboat. The steamboat to St. Louis. Some days after I arrive there'll be another steamboat to take me from St. Louis—farther west and farther north—to the Unorganized Territories.

The river stretches out ahead of us; we're moving north against the current. The day is filled with sun; the brilliant rays of the sun cast down on the water. As we start out, the passengers gather on the deck; among them a couple newly married. The bride is plain; her husband stands next to her. The noise of the whistle and the river bells; the smoke pours up through the stack. Someone comments on the beauty of the day—the sun in full force shining down onto the deck. The bride protects her eyes with her hand. With her other hand she touches the railing. She stares down at the water, her features washed out against the wash of the river.

The Indian has been watching, sitting apart from the rest of the passengers, off to himself on the prow of the steamer. His hair is braided and tied with showy strings and he keeps a red blanket wrapped around him despite the hot sun. He is holding a musical instrument; it looks like a toy. It's made from the bone of a buffalo hoof, with buckskin strips tied around the middle and falling down loosely along the sides. When he sets it in motion it makes a humming sound.

In an Indian legend a mother saw her dead children in the other world. They were playing with a musical instrument like that of the Indian who is with us on the steamer; the instrument was in motion, humming. The louder the humming grew, the closer the mother could come to her children.

Birds fly up along the banks. Sometimes we see deer. The river changes from brown to gray. The river seems to flow with greater strength the farther north we go. The steamboat captain says it's not common to have an Indian alone on board. Usually they travel in greater numbers. Last trip there had been more than a dozen on board, at least fifteen or twenty, on their way back from Washington City. They liked to ride up top on the hurricane roof, he says, where there's a good strong breeze; it was a sight to see them, he says, each one wrapped in a blanket.

The motion of the water, the sensation of the steamboat moving past the static land, all along the river banks elms and willows line the shore. My destination seems a false one. My purpose mistaken. Only the motion itself is what I feel to be true. The clear water of the river where I might reach down and drink and forget, as though I were drinking from the River Lethe. The Indian is wrapped in his red blanket with the humming toy in his hand. He's a Winnebago from the Turkey River. His people's prophet brought the chú 'korăki dance after seeing it performed by a band of spirits.

And I grasp at her memory like someone grasping at straws. With my hands, with my arms, with the tightening in my shoulders, with the gripping in my solar plexus, with my loins.

Take water. I raise the jar to my lips. And then I return the jar to the Indian. He is a priest, or a magician, wearing the color red. He tells the story of a hunter who wounded a blackbird, which fell to the ground where it lay wounded. There are no dancers here, the Indian says. The blackbird rose up and... and then the Indian falls silent. Nothing can make him say more. He accepts as a trade for the humming toy one of my stereoscopes, together with a stereo card, the stereo card has a split image view of Little Falls.

The apparition when it comes is like a figure thrown from a lantern slide; it can be seen, but it has no substance.

At night the sky. The stars.

The stars, the resurrected dead.

After four days journey, we arrive in St. Louis.

The streets are stinking in St. Louis from the heat of late summer and the rotting garbage in the alleys that sits unemptied in the garbage carts. Soldiers. Talk of war. Marching soldiers in the streets.

The Lindell Hotel is new. I've taken a room there. Now I wait for the steamer that will take me up country to the Unorganized Territories.

Complaints during lunch that the meal is being served in a haphazard way—the food brought to the table in whatever order the cook has prepared it. A basket of fruit is set out. A man seated across from me reaches over and takes one of the apples.

Small clusters of grapes are on the table with hard cheese.

My room has a bed with four posts and a window facing onto the street that lets in the morning sun. The room is filled with my photography equipment. It follows me as though of its own volition. From place to place. From one city to another. Almost from breath to breath. I wake and there sits my equipment taking up the entire room. Crowding me out. How did it get here? What will I do with it?

The streets wet from the earlier rain.

Muffled voices of the guests in the hotel parlor reach up to my room.

Another night of conversation in the hotel parlor where brandy and cake are served after supper. The long table set with brandy glasses, small plates, and cloth napkins. Everyone gathered around the table. I join them for a while and then go out to the porch, where the moon is breaking through the clouds. Something from the Indians: When the spring comes then my horse and I shall die.

The desire to walk and to keep walking. The sound of the entertainments spills out on the streets. White performers in blackface speaking like Negroes and singing "Camptown Races" and "Old Black Joe."

When I return to the hotel the front parlor is empty—my room is as I left it, my equipment like a waiting wife. But I have no wife, only the equipment and the coming journey, ashes in the eyes, again from the Indians, ashes thrown into the eyes, a sign of not remembering, and the bodies of the dead placed not in the earth, but high in a tree or on a scaffold, to keep them from wolves and coyotes, and to let the spirit fly away from the earth like a bird; vague shadows on the walls until I extinguish the gas lamp.

In the morning I'm told the steamer will set out in a day, or perhaps two; the unreliability of the steamboat schedule up the Missouri.

The wilderness, a rough country carried into waking, the inability to see or feel anything.

A letter from my mother reaches me from Philadelphia before I leave St. Louis. We have another hot summer, my mother says. She describes the excess of heat. And then she tells me that my aunt wants to know if I've met anyone named Owl's Eyes. My aunt had been reading an article in the Ledger where there had been mention of an Indian named Owl's Eyes. Our hearts are with you on your travels, my mother says. And then her appeals and admonitions: we fear for you... the ravaging of sadness... our helpless remaining... we pray the rough lands there will lessen your grief...

Grief. My eyes remain fixed on the word. The descending letter g. The f that rises up. The two framing the rest. At home the door with glass windows that leads out from the south parlor to the garden. The apartment of rooms I lived in with Lucie three floors above. Last night I thought she was present; I saw her plainly. She asked if I knew where the book she'd been reading had gone. Which book is that? I inquired. But she didn't answer.

Finally the passage out. The river of sticks – the Missouri. 600 miles above St. Louis. There's a rage in that river. It's filled with snags and rafts, the rushing water pulls trees down from the shore. They sink and then they float back to the top: a twisted pile of branches and sticks. The earth of the river bank gives way, washed out from underneath and everything plunges down into the muddy water.

The moment when one image is obscured and the next is about to break through. It's the thing I might photograph, to make a photograph of the bluffs, the cliffs, the silence.

Tufa rock. Like a phantom army. The Fata Morgana rising out of the empty space.

Another day. Days. The late fall. The early winter.

What are you doing, Martine? the French trapper asks me—he addresses me by only my last name in his French accent. I'm making a record of things, I tell him. He traces a line in the air with his finger; his finger is thick, short, the knuckles bulge, the nail too long, pointy at the tip and black underneath. It's a good hard nail, Martine, he says when he sees me staring. I can use this nail, Martine.

A distant rumble of thunder at the steamboat landing. And then a crack of sound to split the ears. The air cold, dense, thick, wet. Storms are making it impossible to photograph.

My heart is beating in its usual steady rhythm. The breath flows in and out of my lungs. I feel the strength in my body shaking off the cold.

Jesus died. The words are scrawled across the door of the mission station, carved with one of the clasp knives. *He was taken up to heaven. and then returned to walk among us.*

That it has been written here in this wilderness is one of the miracles of the living God, the priest says.

silent, a night without wind

like spit on the back of the hand

The mission station far behind. And now I'm wintering over with the trappers in the unorganized territories far to the north; that's what the trappers call it: wintering over.

At the post the trappers and their Indian wives; two other women who are also Indian; and an old squaw who sits rubbing a piece of wood.

There are still trading posts like this one, but the glory is over.

All around. The all around.

Sleep comes harder on frozen nights; when it comes it brings a sense of urgency: in my thoughts expressions of life, of curiosity, or contemplation.

here is the place I used to live... in my sleep I'm in the house in Philadelphia. Everyone is home. The door to the parlor is open. My wife is standing at the top of the stairs.

...the trees are naked with their early winter limbs, standing in silence against the cliff rock, and everything silent except for my footsteps. The animal's body shakes, its teeth appear to chatter, it tears with its claws at the metal trap.

the cessation of wind, the day calm

the idea of being wounded, as in a photograph

to be wounded
it has wounded me
I have been wounded

the place where the wound can be found

a photograph too can be wounded

View of four Indians in the snow. The Indians are sitting on their haunches. Nearby there are poles that are jabbed into the ground and hung with a white-tail deer being bled. The deer hangs upside down; the spirit of darkness, fierceness; three of the Indians stare into the lens of the camera. Sitting apart to the left is the fourth, this one wrapped in a light-colored blanket which covers his head like a hood; he is looking out from the blanket with his eyes raised towards the sun.

Something has happened to the print; the winter cold was too severe for the silver wash, leaving black streaks across the faces of the Indians and across the deer, the black streaks on the print mixing together with the stream of blood.

Today a young Indian girl was brought to the Post by the Yaktonais who left her here traded for blankets and knives. She's Mohave: the tribe of the Dreamer. A pattern of blue lines drawn down her chin and across her cheeks.

...the cessation of the raging wind and another buffalo is taken for the winter pantry, the massive bull, angry, set against giving up its mighty life, and then taken down with efficiency and a spray of bullets.

...now in winter every part of the bull will be used for the winter store, but in the spring, when it's hunted for sport, the buffalo will be laid to waste and left to rot except for the tongue.

A combination of trappers and Indians, sometimes soldiers or other visitors come to the post.

...don't go down to your food like an animal, bring the food to your mouth when you eat, remember always to sit up straight, tear the food with your hands, take hold the warm liver of the buffalo, raw, still pulsing with life, and then bite into it. The Mohave girl approaches the table carrying a pot of beans and smoked beaver, and then brings a pot with pea soup so thick the spoon stands up in it.

...the trapper called Bad After Women makes a snorting sound as the Mohave girl moves back to the fire.

Excuse my back, s'il vous plait, eh bien! eh bien! One of the French trappers drunk, drunker than an Indian.

The Mohave girl hangs a cooking kettle from a hook over the fire. Bad After Women follows her movements with his eyes. She adds wood to the fire, and with a stick just once stirs the kettle. The post has beans, wild rice, nuts, potatoes, wheat flour, chocolate and rum. A lone pig for slaughtering. Heavy rags in the girl's hands to keep her hands from being burned. White-tail deer the delicacy of the table.

We can hear the wind as we eat, it rises above the sound of the eating.

Talk of scavenger wolves, outcasts, following the trappers and trying to steal what they can like ravens or crows.

And then the talk trailing off... *barren and covered with snow... remained there until the boat got over the rapids...*

Short, dark, freezing days. I'm a wild man now like the others.

Again these walls, the dark, the night, the winter quiet. My wife's face floats in front of me. We're in the Medicine Garden in Philadelphia, she's looking for a flower called The Christmas Flower, *for you,* she speaks the words. I imagine myself as though I'm someone other than who I am.

...the tracks of a bird, the giant claws where it last stood, a spirit-god, big and powerful enough to destroy a buffalo.

...the brilliance of the sun, the unexpectedness of light, light that is not merely light, but the full force of the sun against the snow to create blinding light.

A party of Blackfeet arrives at the post. There's little trading in the winter storms. The Indians who make it through are invited to

a feast of mush

they ignore the squaws who live here

difficulties of the weather and resistance of the Indians when I take their photographs

The crackling sound cold makes, or the cries of wolves we hear at night, nearby in the darkness, an uneasy silence.

The wind brings the smell of snow into the rooms, a crusty layer of ice sits on top, if I could add sound to a photograph I would add the crackling sound cold makes.

Some of the prints are over-exposed, lucent, as though one is looking through rather than at the image, the bareness of snow, an unwelcoming shape, a woman crossing in front of the fire.

I discover it's not paint on the Mohave girl's face; the lines are facial tattoos made from the dye of the blue cactus.

The tattoos cover her face like a mask.

Bad After Women swaggers drunk around the post, he seeks out the Mohave girl, and when he finds her he bears down on her, talking with his breath in her face. Then holding her shoulders he turns her around and points her towards us with his expression triumphant: he says there'll be a hunt for white-tail to butcher for feasting, there'll be a wedding feast; Bad After Women announces he intends to marry the Mohave girl.

Wintering over

Nothing may come

Barren and cold.

Perfection of weather

Nothing

Wolves or a single wolf?—in the end it's a single wolf. I've accompanied the trappers on their two-day hunt for white-tail so I can photograph. The danger comes at night. Just now awakened from cold sleep in our winter camp by the sound of shouting and the bellowing voice of Bad After Women. I had fallen asleep in my tent soon after covering my camera equipment to keep the temperature a little higher on the chemicals and plates. Now I hear Bad After Women cry out, then he cries out again and a few minutes later I hear the braying of one of the mules. We pull Bad After Women out of his tent. He's bitten on his legs by a scavenger wolf. One of the trappers goes off to examine the mule.

Wolves, or a single wolf? The insistence of the cold. The sky is cloudless. The fire kept burning. The fire was burning, but the animal crept in anyway under

105

the black clear sky. A rifle is fired several times into the darkness. The trapper has thrown a buffalo hide over the mule that was also bitten.

It takes almost a full day to return to the Post. We move slowly because of Bad After Women's wounds. Do you hear the mule? Bad After Women, asks me—the wolf was mad. When we get back to the post, he no longer looks at the Mohave girl, and he no longer talks about anything except the mule. I can feel it, he says—the madness is working itself into my blood. In the morning the mule is dead. Bad After Women has done nothing but weep for himself since hearing the mule is dead.

The old squaw carves and rubs a figure of a wolf – she keeps rubbing it and carving it, rubbing it and carving it.

The sky before storm. Pale and gray without a trace of blue. A blanket of cold mist. They say the snow will be heavy.

In a dream my wife's face floats in front of me. We're in the medicine garden in Philadelphia. The dye of the blue cactus is on my wife's skin. She speaks to me and it's my wife, but now her native language is Mohave.

I'm in the desert with my wife. There is a Joshua tree and a dried lake. There is no water and no rain. She holds out her arms to me, her arms are draped across with branches. These are the wedding flowers, she says, for you, my new husband. I stand before her robed in white, she says that white is the traditional color for the bridegroom.

The meaning of things…

...lost.

...just as the true meaning of things is lost on the Mohave girl, who misunderstands what she is seeing when she sees Bad After Woman return to the Post. She appears to be seized by a madness of her own. The wife of one of the trappers tells us that all the while we were gone the girl inhabited the post like someone whose spirit had left her body, tending to her chores, staring with a blank expression, and sometimes confusing one chore with another. The woman says the girl has been driven to madness by the fear of the marriage that awaits her. And now, already afraid of Bad After Women, the girl believes that this man she will be forced to marry is changing into a mad wolf.

There's wind and snow throughout the night; in the morning it's a blizzard; there's nothing to be done but to hold down for it. One of the women says that the young girl is gone; she left the post sometime before dawn. There's talk of going after her, but the decision is against because it would be impossible to find her in the blizzard; she's been gone too long, her tracks would be covered, it would be impossible in the wind and snow. And now the wives of the trappers have become afraid of Bad After Women who makes braying sounds like the diseased mule and then falls into a fit so that he has to be covered over with a blanket. When the fit subsides he's uncovered, but within minutes a new fit begins. He's screaming he can't breathe, he has no air, he's burning up, he needs the cold snow to put the fire out. He tears all his clothes off and runs naked out the door. One of the Indian women makes a motion towards the door and says the name of the young Mohave girl. She says something that means both of them are mad. And I am remembering how deep the snow can get in a blizzard, and how soft it can feel, and the sensation of warmth digging into it making you want to sleep, and I imagine the Indian girl sleeping in the snow and Bad After Women left to rage in it, until sleep comes, and they will share the same fate, when sleep comes...

...a carving wrapped in deerskin of a Mohave female deity. I had picked it up from the floor to hand to the trapper's wife who was gathering the Indian girl's belongings—but the woman motioned with her hand I should keep it and so I have kept it. The carving kept wrapped in the dressed skin of a deer—the fleshy residue of the animal scraped away and the skin softly grained using a sharpened bone.

Nothing may come

Nothing

...what the eyes choose to see. A revelation of seeing. The awareness that time is passing. That it's already late spring and almost another summer. Another letter from my mother catches up with me when I reach the interior fort on the way back to St. Louis before continuing on the way home to Philadelphia. My mother talks about the way life has become at home now that we're a country at war—the president is calling for the enlistment of every able-bodied man. I place the letter with her other letters, and with my late wife's notebook and a few of her photographs. This one notebook and these few photographs are all I have with me; the rest remain in Philadelphia. I was afraid in this roughness that any I brought might be lost or destroyed.

...the words she has written and her photographs laid out in front of me. The scene recreated, the past rallying again, reassembling on the albumen prints in front of me.

...continuing from the interior post on the way back to St. Louis and from there home to Philadelphia.

...before Philadelphia the journey from the interior post to the descent of the Missouri River... from the descent of the Missouri River to St. Louis.

I stare into the blinding sun from the deck of the steamboat. The impulse to continue staring into it—to sacrifice vision to folly. I resist the impulse. And the arc of time seems to traverse the pattern of my life in the same way we have traversed this land: that is with the explicit sense of right of ownership. Time owns me. I leave the deck and go inside my cabin in the steamer. My wife's notebook on the bed. I turn at random to a page. The words before me: *a bit too facile it gives the impression...* The words appear jumbled and abbreviated; I struggle to read what they say: *moon... fan... the perception not being normal...* And then words that make reference to *a woman hiding the moon...*

a woman hiding the moon. I have copied Lucie's words onto my own white page, the black lines of my words set beside hers.

You see, this is what I've been thinking about. The way my mind has registered delight. Lucie's words.

...and the way delight will be represented in the photograph. The tilt of the young woman's head, the importance of the position of the body, the way it is held bent slightly forward to suggest the movement that in the next moment will bring her closer to the man who is just out of view. Lucie's words.

I look through the photographs to find the corresponding image to the words. It's not there. I hear the sound of the steamboat whistle. Continual surges of steam thrown into the air. The boat is moving slowly.

as if pushing into the wind... pushing towards the man who is not yet in view...

I have been thinking of the possibilities for invention to be placed before the lens...

not a record of a thing, but an impression of it...

the thing that is before you now, that is put before the eyes that view the photograph...

the eyes that view the photograph now. the thing brought back and made alive, brought back into the present. Not into its own present, but into the present that exists in the moment of viewing...

I thought to discuss these ideas with William, but hesitated for fear he would think them odd. And by association think me, his wife, odd...

Her notebook has the smell and feel of dampness from the river and rain. Her words stand out clearly. *This is my favorite picture of my works...* Pasted under the words is a visiting card with the portrait of a woman. A close-up view, the kind Lucie favored. Half in light and half in shadow. The woman's eyes look down. There's a firmness to her lips. Her hair is worn loose and parted in the middle.

My wife has titled the photograph: *This is what the eyes saw.*

To be awakened out of sleep in one's bedroom, in the dim light of the early dawn, the cubiculum nocturnum as it was called by the Romans, the red of the walls and the small winged figures that adorn the headboard, part human and part bird facing in opposite directions.

Half-bird? Half-human?

It is unnatural for a man to grieve so long... these words said by my aunt and repeated to me in a letter written by my mother. The letter that was waiting for me when I reached St. Louis.

I have the sensation of choking in the half-light, in the mythological room with birds, birds or half-birds. What is it that would force me to my knees? So distinct as to be real even though an apparition, the red of the walls, the small winged figures that are neither birds nor humans. She was on her knees. As in a paroxysm of pain.

Now it's raining again. On the way back to St. Louis. Torrential downpours, storms, the water flooding the deck of the steamer. During one storm rain rose to the top of the deck almost more quickly than it could be thrown off and every man became one of the hands to keep the boat from sinking. The thunder came from underneath. At least that's the impression I had of its placement. The storm continued and I thought the water would drown us. The word for water. The power to consume. The river rose up and I thought to let myself be taken, the final breath, the way the lungs would fill with water and then collapse, my spirit in that instant released and my body left to the river. But that is not to be and it is not what I want. I want the grave, the dirt grave, the coffin grave, to be side-by-side with Lucie, my body next to hers in the dry stiffness of earth, no matter if she has gone to bone that is the only final end, I was soaked through by the rain, and then the rain stopped... the gradual clearing...

The news when we reach St. Louis: the state of Missouri has voted to stay with the Union. The newspaper dailies are in everyone's hands. The war is promised to last no longer than the months of summer.

My son is ill... my mother's words. I hear her words in my head, the intonation of her voice; that is what she tells them when they inquire: My son is ill.

111

And something like shame. Hot shame.

A fragment equal to a lifetime, the one who had weight, weight, when she was right there before me, her weight against me riding in the carriage, the weight of her body when I lifted her up from the floor.

Again I'm forced to bide my time in a hotel, this time waiting for the train that will take me back to Philadelphia. My body is shivering though the weather is mild; it's nothing, only exhaustion, nerves, only the end of the journey, the lingering cold of the winter post with its damp rooms that never warmed. Nerves. Perhaps a collapse.

I'm not well, my mother will tell you, but it's only sleep that is needed. The room is one flight up, the bed is comfortable, the quilt is red.

Only a matter of sleep when it comes. And the dreams that inhabit sleep. My hands become a subject of interest to me: the bones of the fingers, the skin creased at the knuckles, what the hands have touched, the fingers that point, that move across the page.

a bowl of fruit is brought to my room

The hotel is quiet as though empty, and yet it was mentioned all the rooms are filled, the other guests too are waiting for the train.

In the morning the sun is brilliant, shining, pouring heat down on the streets, the air is close and filled with dust, the sun is burning in a massive sky, the rest of the journey will be by train, if the train comes, and if it takes us... the war has changed everything.

At breakfast I tip over my coffee cup, my hands slightly shaking, and the black liquid spills out on the table and rolls onto my lap stinging my flesh.

There were place names on the way to St. Louis as though on pilgrimage. Two Trees. A Fork in the Road. My hands have stopped shaking and I reach to take a biscuit. The talk is first of war and then of Indians, then back to war. Missouri is not a southern state someone says. Yes, but it is a slave state, someone else responds. There is gravy for the biscuits, a thick, buttery liquid made mostly of cream. It will be a short war, someone says. There will be battles to come for years, someone else counters. And then a different voice addressed only to me: Perhaps you will tell us about the Indians, Mr. Martin?

It's the voice of the young woman traveling with her father. Her father, a doctor, sits next to her. But, I must not intrude on your eating, the young woman says. No, it's perfectly fine, I say, only I must think what to tell. I clear my throat. The thin membrane of a tale; I treat it with care to keep it intact. And then I say, Yes, well, the Indians. It's true I have photographed them. I describe an open, barren plain that has nothing on it for as far as one can see except brush and brown grass and four men on horses who are riding away, their backs to the camera.

Still some slight shivering imperceptible to the others—it's on the inside and hidden. A slice of ham sits on my plate along with eggs that are boiled, and a biscuit covered with gravy. There is a vase of flowers on the table. On the wall opposite the table there's a painting of a vase of flowers that mirrors the real ones.

Quickly cleaning my plate: the eggs with their yolks, the biscuits dripping with gravy, the ham rapidly sliced, rapidly chewed, rapidly swallowed, and then wiping what is left of the gravy up from the plate with a remaining piece of the biscuit.

Her name is Miss Angeline Stille. Her father is Doctor Isaac Stille. Angeline, she repeats her Christian name—and then she points out that it is pronounced with the same ending sound as fine. Or dine, or mine. But now that you've finished eating perhaps now you will tell us more about the Indians, Miss Stille says

I tell the story of the Indian girl who went out to die in the blizzard snows so she wouldn't have to marry the trapper Bad After Women.

When I get to the end Miss Stille looks solemn.

That's what is known as a simple twist of fate, someone else at the table says.

...in the snow everything was silent except for the sound of the Indian girl's breathing. The light of the moon and a paralysis of cold. Where everything was silent and the young girl came to a sense of herself and the silence and cold merging.

A view through the lens. The face carved from stone.

...stillness portrayed on the photograph. The bodies of animals and birds piled one on top of the other along with branches and twigs giving the appearance of a small tree. The splayed corpse of a fox at the bottom. Its paw and forearm delicately reach around the netting to which they are attached. There are birds of various species, all with their heads hanging down above the fox, the wings are open and loose. The plates of the negatives packed away along with the prints.

...and then the blower doctors come and bring their medicine and the hands of the healers, good medicine, bad medicine, bad medicine can kill you with an illness that has no cure, unless the blower doctors come and take it out from your head and blow it back into the one who has infected you.

...what we have are gradations of luminosity. Exposures of a single view made at different times of day. In one the glare from the sun is so great it seems to burn up the objects on which it shines. A certain formality in the arrangement of the natural objects: hills in the background, a stand of trees in the foreground, some of them gnarled. And dancing in a circle are the Indian medicine men, hooded and wearing garments that look like rags. The hoods have false eyes made out of abalone and turquoise, attached to the outside of the buckskin where the human eyes are meant to be. The dance will drive away the evil spirits. Dances of the Indians portrayed in the photographs, and the desolation in the barrens, in the wilds.

...what we have is a tool for industry. As in the building of the railroads.

War in our country. A slave auction held the other day on the steps of the courthouse. Dust was visible on the skin of a shackled man. A strange contraption held him, half-naked, a kind of knotted rope that looped separately around each of his ankles so that only small steps could be taken, and then from each ankle the ropes extend in an inverted V up to a single rope attached around his waist. The man was fettered to himself. The auction got underway. The noise of commerce. Success is the sale of all of them down to the very last one. Excitement and noise. The smell of blood rising in the veins.

War. Combats. Like the mythic battles between cranes and Pygmies.

Word comes the train will arrive tomorrow, though there is no guarantee that it will take us. It is not unlikely it will be needed to transport union soldiers.

115

I see them walking side-by-side, the doctor and his daughter, completely at ease and engrossed in conversation.

Tonight the last night in the hotel. Outside only darkness.

A memory of my father. A memory of the blood running into his eyes so that he can no longer see me crouching down in the brush where he has thrown me. He has already been set upon and his throat has been slit. The dogs appear. My father always had them with us when he took me hunting. The dogs are jumping up in the air, barking and growling, biting at the legs of the horses of the men who attacked us. They bite at the men's legs until the men shoot them. And then the men begin to mutilate my father's body. I hear them speaking American and one of them has fair skin. I see pale hair and I know they are not Indians. But where my father has thrown me, I'm invisible to them. The memory clearly before me as it was then.

The morning light wakes me, the rays of the sun shining in through the window. But as is always the case here, when I breathe I breathe dust. The wash basin in the room has been filled; I wash my face, my neck, my chest and arms. There will be early breakfast when I go downstairs, and with it morning talk of war, the newspapers filled with war articles, requests for socks for the soldiers, and then in mid-morning the departure of the train.

Two mourning doves land on my window ledge when I'm dressing to go down to breakfast. Or as they are called here: pigeons. They are rather sorry looking birds with drab gray feathers come to sit for a minute on the ledge.

I count the boxes that contain my equipment as they are lifted onto the train. 24 in all. The boxes will share my compartment. The train is half filled with Union soldiers. Wind and dust. Making our way East. The train in motion. Miss Angeline Stille and her father are also on their way back to Philadelphia.

116

We will soon be home, Mr. Martin, Miss Angeline Stille greets me. I answer that indeed we will.

The doctor beckons me to his table when the train stops for the passengers to dine and invites me to have my supper with him and his daughter. They live on Delancey Street in Philadelphia. They had traveled to St. Joseph, Missouri where the doctor's sister was recently widowed. Their plan was to bring her back to the East but at the last minute she refused. They traveled by steamboat from St. Joseph to St. Louis to wait for the train. We are fortunate to be on this train, the doctor says—as the war continues there may be no transport available to civilians. There's the rattling of china as the plates are placed in turn in front of us. Tea is brought to the table. The waiter pours. What are your war plans, Mr. Martin? the doctor inquires.

...demon gods with giant heads without bodies who fly around in storms... ...supernatural beings who live inside mountains who can be heard to be dancing and beating the drums... ... beings with the power to heal and to drive away disease...

The doctor's daughter wears her hair braided in two loops arranged to fall just below her ears. The loops of braids move when her head moves.

What do you think, Mr. Martin, she asks, are our eyes little cameras which retain the images we see? There was something regarding that subject recounted in this morning's news. A woman was murdered and the idea was put forth in the newspaper that the last image seen is recorded on the eyes and that if the eyes are photographed shortly after death the image will be preserved. Do you agree that's possible, Mr. Martin?

My daughter is drawn to the fantastic, Doctor Stille says.

Yes, but much in this world is fantastic, Miss Stille quickly rejoins.

I'm afraid I must discount that theory, Miss Stille, I answer.

And then I have the sense I must go on: There is a difference between recording and retaining; retaining requires a complex process and the use of chemicals. The eyes record, but absent this chemical process they don't retain, or what is retained is retained in the brain as memory. If anything has been seen post mortem on a photograph, it is shadow and nuance. In portraiture particularly the photographer must not discount the influences of shadow and nuance. The facial expression, when frozen, naturally reveals a psychology or an emotional state. My wife, when she was alive, was particularly gifted with regard to nuance.

That is reasoned, Mr. Martin, the doctor's daughter says, but there are also the things that we cannot reason.

I do not discount those things, I say.

The doctor interjects: Speaking of portraiture, may I impose on you to make portraits of my daughter and me when we are settled back in Philadelphia?

Miss Stille's expression does not change; she retains the look of cheek in her eyes, their color somewhere between blue and green: Yes, she says, that would give her pleasure.

"To be shady,—whence all the inflections of shadow and darkness." The words from a book, a small volume of tales by Mr. Poe. Something I'm bringing to my aunt. My aunt has read all of stories by Mr. Poe printed in Godey's Lady's Book.

The sleeping compartment is close; there's a claustrophobic atmosphere. The bench converts to a bed.

The train encounters a delay because of the war; the normal 48-hour journey stretches out a day longer. On the final morning, again in the dining car, the doctor remarks we are nearing Philadelphia. This morning his daughter is wearing her hair undone and unbraided. I see it's abundant—a great mass of hair, untamed like the hair of a Jewess. Despite the morning heat she is wrapped in a light shawl.

We are almost home, Mr. Martin, she says.

I reply that indeed we are. I add that my mother and my aunt are likely to be at the station to meet me. And then for no reason I say that I have been gone a long time and I am feeling a kind of fatigue. My wife, I say, when she was alive, had a special oil for fatigue, something she obtained from the chemist on Chestnut. She rubbed it on my temples and on the inside of my wrists.

Miss Stille draws up.

I have no business going on, but I am wound and cannot stop. It was from a flower, I say, I can't remember which one. Lemon oil was in it. The odor was pleasant. I remember a warmth to the oil. My wife rubbed it onto my temples, but I believe I have said that already. I remember when my wife would use this oil my fatigue would shortly after disappear.

Miss Stille looks at me while I speak, but makes no rejoinder when I stop. It's her father who breaks the brief silence with talk of the war. He speculates on what we'll find. The President is calling for 400,000 men.

It's always the same story in war, Miss Stille says in a little outburst—the women remain behind; the women lose their men; the children, many of them, become destitute.

And then her father to change the subject says, we shall soon be making our good-byes, but remember your promise that you will call on us.

The train still in motion. The sameness of land. The train on the tracks. The vibratory effect of the motion.

And the idea of return—return to somewhere on this earth where there is constancy.

...*here is the place I used to live*... the words that haunt. the sound of the word haunted.

...an image on a photograph, where I have attempted to preserve the things

I've seen. A stand of trees in the wilderness; the beginning of the darkness; an Indian wrapped in a white blanket standing motionless among the trees; waiting for a tryst with his lover; a gloomy courtship in the shadows.

And the way I have looked at it.

...go there and stand with him, the voice says.

4

Philadelphia, Pennsylvania, 1861

Dusk. The Angelus.

Philadelphia

home

the empty rooms

I've arrived home to the empty rooms

I reach out my hands with the full awareness they can only be empty

Home where there is rest. A timetable for entering. The dread of returning—something wanted to keep me at a distance.

Several weeks have passed since my return; it's all the same, a week, a day, a year.

The presence of my wife... she was my wife.

Her words are written in a notebook: *I have had a pleasant day...* The notebook is small and brown leather-bound, three and a half inches by five. The leather is soft. Her hand filled the pages precisely with well-formed, slanted letters. *I have had a pleasant day... this is my favorite of my works... I have arranged the lamp to light only half the face of the woman in the photograph...*

...and then in her notebook words without context...*whistles like signals... or like birds at dusk bedding down in the trees...*

The sense of creeping up, or creeping in. The rooms are stifling in this heat.

The rooms are in the ell on the third floor. Now no one comes up here. Only the structure and the contents remain.

From the window I see birds, flying, rising up, tentative, then flying away, and then circling and crossing back in front of the window; it appears a ritual, its purpose unknown. A remote past. The hot late day sun.

...birds, and the wings of birds lifting.

Only the structure and the contents remain: furniture in the rooms; clothing left in the armoires; the rooms empty.

The sitting room leads into the bedroom. I stand in silence in front of the bed. The desire to lie down on it.

My mother and my aunt when they think I can't hear them.
What will he do with himself?
We must not pressure him.

A book on the side table. "A Life Struggle" by Miss Pardoe. I examine the chapter titles: *Brother and Sister; The Ball; Guardian and War; The Letter...*

...another entry in her notebook... *I read a good deal today... My cousin Jane came around in the late afternoon... the rain was coming down too hard for her to leave and we insisted that Jane stay the night with us...*

Dusk. The Angelus. Bells from the nearby church.

I no longer sleep in these rooms. I sleep in the bedroom on the second floor at the front of the house facing South Eighth Street.

A remote past. The hot late day sun. I leave the rooms and go downstairs and out to the garden..

A new ornament has been added. Something sculpted in white stone.

I have the sense of everything struggling to breathe in the humid air.

To perceive oneself as though from a distance. To listen to what is being said about oneself.

Between that time and now.

Between that time and now... as though from a distance.

The white object is a bird bath sculpted in stone. It's the only white object in the garden.

I must crawl back into my interior.

Inside the house.

I go back inside the house and climb the stairs to my room.

...my feet on the floorboards. Everything's still. There's not a breeze. Lucie's feet were small. Destruction.

...from the front window which faces the street I can see the lone figure of a man standing under the gas lamp. After a while he moves along and turns left onto Locust. The four-poster bed sits across from the fireplace.

...the window at the rear of the room faces out to the garden.

...sometime later a disturbance in the night.

...a barking dog.

...I look out the window and my eyes go to the white stone of the bird bath that is hanging on the rear wall in the garden.

...the dog continues barking.

...barking and howling.

...the moon is visible.

...the uneasy night.

...the arrival of morning.

...the start of the day.

...the morning light.

...radiant.

...the innate wakefulness.

...I go down to the small dining room.

Nothing is out from the kitchen yet except some apples in a bowl on the buffet

Grim Visage — The Horrors of War

An advertisement in the morning Inquirer: *The Horrors of War will be faith-fully portrayed in the Assembly Building tonight and will resemble reality instead of an imitation.*

There continues to be life in the house. Those that live here. The domestic composition of the family. The cat with its back up.

I hear a carriage passing by.

The sound of the carriage and the horses.

My mother expresses exhilaration with regard to her ramble of the day before.

She has finished her sewing for the box of clothing to be sent to the injured troops at the Chester Hospital.

My aunt asks if I will accompany her to the Palmer Street wharf to see the whale that came up the Delaware the day before and was destroyed by the fishermen.

> What kind of whale? I ask.
> She answers, An ordinary whale—
> Yes, I say, I'll accompany you—

In the afternoon we are standing in front of the dead animal.

...it's called a Right Whale according to the fishermen—it lies stretched out from one end to the other of the pier. My aunt is taken with its size, and also with the fact it has a blow hole for breathing; she engages one of the fishermen in conversation about the way it was killed and the number of nets it destroyed, and whether, at any moment, he had felt pity for the creature. No, he says, he had not. But he had recognized it as a force. My aunt stands in front of the dead whale as though posed for a photograph.

...from the pier the islands are visible. Smith and Windmill Islands.

On the way home it begins to rain.

...water from the moon.

...rain.

In the evening despite heavy rain, I go out to take supper with the doctor and his daughter. When I arrive, Miss Stille brings me a brandy to remove the dampness. We take supper in the dining room. The table is round. The window is open.

My father escapes the heat when he can by fishing, Miss Stille says.

The doctor nods his agreement then turns to the subject of the war: the impressiveness of the City Home Guard, five thousand men, and the news from New York: ten thousand have already moved.

There were deer today in the park at Logan Square, Miss Stille says. My father and I saw them when we stopped by after going on the steamboat.

The entire time we looked at them they grazed on the grass just as though we weren't there.

The doctor continues on the subject of the war: The English are already nervous because of the cotton, he says. His thoughts, he says, are little else now than a record of the war. It will be a short war, the doctor adds; it's predicted to be concluded by the New Year.

Whatever time it lasts, I say, it's impossible to ignore that it's here.

My father hauled a large fish out of the lake this morning, Miss Stille says.

And I don't mind telling you he was very satisfied with himself for it. And then she turns to her father and says, Admit it, Father, you were very satisfied.

The doctor attests to the size of the fish.

Mr. Martin, Miss Stille says turning her attention to me, remember you promised that you will photograph me and my father.

It's a promise I'm looking forward to keeping, I say.

But tell me, she continues, is it true that the eye of the camera sees more than the human eye? I read that one can hold a magnifying glass to a photograph and see details obscured to our normal sight.

That's an established fact.

When my portrait is completed, I shall study every inch of the photograph you make of me. The hidden things your camera sees may be the things that please me most.

My daughter is making a study of photography, the doctor says.

I commend her for it, I say.

She colors a little, but says nothing. She makes a movement with her head as if to cast off the remark.

Is it true, she asks, there was a time one had to sit without moving for a full ten minutes to be photographed?

That too is true, I reply.

Angeline, her father says... but he does not continue with his thought.

She turns to look at her father. And then she turns back to me.

darkness of distances

my father hauled a large fish

the need to walk in the summer night

The need to walk. It's still hot. Still hot even by the river at the wharf at Arch Street. I stare at the water, at the empty fishing boats docked and ready to go out before dawn for rockfish and shad, and everything smelling of fish, and the gulls circling and screeching. Despite the hot night a beggar is sleeping under a blanket. I can hear the raucous noises from one of the poor hotels nearby, where men share a room for a night's sleep. I leave the wharf and walk west along Arch Street and pass the cemetery at Fifth. To visit the dead. The desire to pull her back to life. The tremors in my hands. I think about the photograph that I will take of the doctor's daughter. Miss Angeline Stille wrapped in a shawl. Her flesh partly visible as it was at supper earlier this evening: her face white, and her neck, and the base of her throat. Her hair worn loose. Abundant. I think of Lucie's hair before she died. The word again: died. The estrangement of silence. The dead best visited at night. I turn back towards the cemetery and make my way through the unlocked gate.

Let everything rest...

in the hot ground.

Digging deep into the earth

to place a flower on the grave. To wait for the apparition to stand before me. In front of one of the graves next to hers there are flowers formed into a figure like a small human being.

Only a slow grieving

Not an assault on the grave

Not committing Mr. Griswold's shocking act of assaulting the grave of his newly dead wife. It's true it happened years ago, but the rumor persists that he dug up the coffin and pried off the lid and then he threw himself on top of what he found inside. When they discovered him he had fainted. I have not done that!

Treason. Black night. I stop by McMichael's where the late night talk is of treason. A ventriloquist's dummy and today some women caught sending delicacies to the war prisoners. Signor Blitz, the famed ventriloquist, is at McMichael's, his doll in tow, and for our amusement he performs a dialogue with the doll on the subject of what to do with those who conspire with the South against the Union. He has found a way to make the doll's fist pound the table as if completely on its own. And the doll, with its black hair painted slick against its head, and beneath its nose a little black mustache, becomes savage with rage. The crowd at McMichael's rises to its feet during the performance, and at the end, when the doll stands stiff, its mechanical eyes shifting from side to side as if to meet head-on anyone who would oppose it, there is a prolonged applause and an enthusiastic rallying to Signor Blitz and his doll.

At home I find my mother still awake despite the hour. The house is silent. My mother asks if I would like tea. I tell her, no, but that I will sit with her a while. There is much on my mind, I say. She says she thought as much. We speak softly.

I have not asked you, I say, where the birdbath came from. It stood out to me when I saw it as the only white object in the garden.

She says it was purchased from Atison's on Chestnut; it's in the Roman style, but only a copy brought recently into the shop—I thought the garden needed something just like it, she says; and I was thinking of the birds.

Do you find it mysterious? I ask her.

What an odd question, she says. Perhaps it's mysterious.

Where I sit I can see the standing-clock in the hallway outside the dining room. I read the late hour on its face. It has no chime; I've always been glad it's a silent clock.

It's the contrast of its whiteness, I say.

She makes no reply.

Will you send someone to invite Doctor Stille and his daughter for dinner, I ask.

She says she has arranged to send someone in the morning. She will invite them to take dinner with us Friday. Is that all right, she asks.

I tell her it is fine. The doctor has asked me to come round to his consulting rooms, I say. To determine why my hands sometimes tremble.

That relieves me, she says.

He's certain it's nerves, I say.

It still relieves me you will have it looked at, she says.

Edmund Fell told me because of his bad leg they have refused him for the war. He was disappointed. He keeps the studio in good order. I think it now feels more his than mine. Though it remains a kind of base for me. The portraits were Lucie's talent. I have never been much interested in making portraits for family albums.

You must do what suits you, my mother says.

I have always liked this house at night, I say.

The gas lamp casts its shadows on the wall. I have intertwined my fingers in front of me on the table.

Tonight at McMichael's Signor Blitz made quite a show with his doll, I say.

You stopped by McMichael's, she says without expression in her voice.

Yes. The talk there was all of war and treason.

Elizabeth was by to visit today with letters from her relatives in Richmond, she says. The letters were innocent, of course, but Elizabeth said she is nervous having them in hand and I believe she is right to be nervous.

Perhaps, I say. But I have kept you up too long.

Are you satisfied you've said everything? she asks.

Yes.

It was only about the birdbath in the garden then?

It was just to visit with you, that's all.

What have I done to make you reticent with me, William? What are your own intentions about the war?

There is much to consider, but I thought to enlist, Mother.

Treason. Black night without sleep. Next to the bed is a pitcher of water. The doctor said to drink water. His daughter has written herself in my mind. The sense of what might come, what might be permitted. The other evening my aunt talked at supper about the spirit of a baby coming into a room. There was some question about it, she said: no one remembered there being a baby—but the presence was there with its simple thoughts. I don't know why I think of it now. And then my thoughts turn back to the doctor's daughter.

night

the dark sky

sky pointing

birds that point to the sky

rest

the doctor said I must rest. rest.

...taking note of everything that's white in the room: the white mantel on the fireplace; the white sheets on the bed; the white of the albumen prints in two stacks upon the desk. Earlier I removed them from their box and now they stand out in the gray of the room. When I close my eyes, the images of the two stacks remain. I open my eyes and get out of bed to examine my wife's photographs. ...She has written: *September 2, 1859. Two children brought to the studio for their likeness. A boy and a girl; the boy older by perhaps a year or a little more. His arm protectively, assertively, around the girl...* My wife was meticulous in her notations. I turn the knob on the lamp to bring up the light. Interrogation of my wife. The manifestations of the dead and on the face of it the superior power of the living. This written without explanation: ...*the light like a revenant returns.* Followed by the words: ...*in another time*... But when morning comes there'll be no ghost. There'll be only another day spent at the studio, or spent at the Athenaeum where I'll read the newspaper accounts of the war. I gather up my wife's photographs and return them to the box. The box makes a thump when I set it down next to the others in a corner of the room. Night has come as hot as day. Nothing but silence and darkness. I lift another box and empty its contents onto the bed. My body is tired, but I'm unable to sleep. The photographs are sprawled out before me on the bed. The house is still. I'm awake, but fatigued. The others in the household are sleeping. The house has that stillness created by sleep. The morning comes and I find myself still sitting in the chair. In the place on the bed where my body should be are the contents of the box. Like a mourner who sits vigil I have sat the night up in a chair—the contents of the box have become a corpse in my bed.

And later in the morning tending to the business arrangement at the studio—Edmund Fell keeps up the portraitures. I remark favorably on one of his albumen prints: a woman and an infant. The woman is in profile and part of her face is obscured by the infant's head which faces almost full front. The woman's hand grasps the infant pulling it close to her breast. The infant's hand in a fist. The downward glance and the tilt of the head of the mother. Edmund Fell tells me it's a photograph of his wife and his new little daughter, Lucie. The child is just six months. He says he hopes I will not mind that they've named her Lucie..

When I leave the studio I walk along Vine Street with the desire only to keep walking. There's a large dog in the distance. I'm reminded of my father's dogs. When I was a child they used to gather around me, the dogs half wild, their large wild bodies all around me, their mouths open as if to consume me. My mother watched nervously, but my father held her back. Leave him alone, you will make the boy fearful. The dog moves off and I turn south towards Chestnut Street on my way to Spruce and the Pennsylvania hospital. The hospital has been converted almost entirely to a war hospital now, but the doctor has kept his consulting rooms and he wants to examine me there.

A company of soldiers walking north on Sixth cross in front of the Athenaeum. They are part of the City Home Guard.

Continuing south to the hospital. And then entering the doctor's consulting rooms in the left wing of the hospital.

My feet are on one of the open grates on the floor, where the heat from the furnace comes up in the winter. I look down to my feet on the open grate. After examining me, the doctor says that my tremors result from strained emotions. I'm to be treated by rest—my activities are to be kept tranquil. And then the doctor tells me he once defeated the reigning chess champion, Morphy—before Morphy's reputation became so large. We talk about chess for a while and promise we'll have a game. And then out of nowhere the doctor says, I have suffered my own loss—my wife, too, died not long ago. We were older of course and had each other's companionship for many years. But for that same reason my loss was also severe. My daughter has much need of me now. Together we've been working our way through Cooper's novels. May I ask if you've read them?

I tell him I have, but not in many years.

You might want to look at them again, he says; my daughter will ask your opinion.

It would please me to do that, I say.

The doctor thanks me.

And then I tell him: I've brought some photographs I'd like you to see. They're of a condition I once encountered in the West. It was some time ago, well over a year, some months before I met you and your daughter on my way back through St. Louis. At the time of the encounter it was only six months after my wife had died. I thought that they would be of interest to you as a man of medicine, and in any case I'd like to know your view.

I have time now if it suits you, the doctor says.

I unwrap the photographs.

The sound of raised voices passing by the consulting room comes in from the exterior hallway.

As you can see the conditions for light were not perfect, I say. We weren't in a studio after all; we were in a tent—the only light was through a small flap at the top. She posed for me on the same platform that was used for her to be displayed to the crowd. It was a traveling show put together by a man named Mabies. Here, you can see how unselfconscious she was. She was accustomed to the interest of an audience.

Remarkable, he says. To my knowledge no medical photographs exist. You have achieved something remarkable.

They show no more than what was. Mabies permitted them for his own profit, but those that I kept are private. For my own memory and curiosity, or for some good purpose as might arise. If for example they could be of assistance to her. I showed them to you because of your profession and because I have confidence in you. I wanted to know more about the condition. She spoke of a doctor in Syracuse and a treatment. Is there a treatment?

The only treatment would be surgery, Doctor Stille, says. But I would not recommend it. I know of no expert in Syracuse or elsewhere. It seems you think of her then as "she?"

There was a gentleness to her in either sex. I believe I saw her interchangeably as a woman or a man, but it's possible I saw her more in her female side. So there is nothing for her then? Only to remain as she is?

She made an impression on you, the doctor says.

Perhaps one of friendship, I reply.

There is little we know about it. The knife would be experimental.

I see, experimental.

Yes, perhaps even brutal. Perhaps resulting in death.

Well then, there is nothing to be done. I change the subject. What of the war?

Eleven more glass blowers have enlisted. I have that from the

Ledger. It is said that soon Pennsylvania will have more troops in service than any of the other states.

The doctor leaves off with the thought and then moves away from the photographs.

I will enlist, I say.

I would like to see you looking better first, the doctor says.

Yes, I agree that would be best, I say.

And then I take my leave and make my way to the Athenaeum.

Where there's talk of intermittent fever. They say the cause of death was intermittent fever.

The news of the death is presented to me in the reading room.

I've just gathered up my books and set them on the table when one of the library's members approaches me, talking low; he sits in the chair next to mine and apologizes for the interruption. He wants to know have I heard that our friend Henry Benners passed away the night before. No, I say, I didn't know about Benners. Yes, well there it is, he says—the cause of death was an intermittent fever. Then he makes mention of Pierce Butler's arrest, saying in a whisper, we are a country divided, and then he shakes his head: it seems that all the news is bad, he says. But at least the President's message in the paper this morning. Have I read it? If not, I must. He read it at the start of the day with great satisfaction. He says now he must leave me, giving a pat to my shoulder. I return my attention to the stack of books I've taken. The books on the Athenaeum's shelves are arranged by subject and country: Travel and Study in Italy; History of Slavery and the Slave Trade in America; English Fiction; American Fiction. American fiction and books of James Fennimore Cooper. I begin to browse through my selections, selections made for the doctor's daughter: *The Wing-and-Wing; The Ways of the Hour; Sea Lions; Satanstoe; The Water Witch.* After a while, I take *The Ways of the Hour* to one of the side-chairs in a rear corner of the room situated by the open window; the desire for solitude; staring out at the tops of the trees; six privies are down below in view from the window, they are six private compartments arranged in two back-to-back rows of three, each with a little gabled roof. In the civilized world—the thought crosses my mind. I get up and go to the water cooler where I take a tin cup and pour water into it from the limestone container. The low afternoon sun throws a glint of light onto the cup.

...my membership share in the Athenaeum comes from my great uncle and my aunt. My great uncle had no children and when he died he left his share to his sister, my aunt. On my eighteenth birthday my aunt made a present of it to me.

It's still so recent that I'm back and only this morning my mother said again, William, it's so good to have you home.

Then she repeated it, it's so good to have you home.

...*blood from the moon.*

The blood women shed.

White teeth and laughter at the table.

It is something my aunt has just said...

...we're in the middle of the Friday supper at our house with Doctor Stille and his daughter.

...the laughter is Miss Stille's—because of something my aunt has quoted from Godey's Lady's Book, referring to matters of commerce: *Feathers are at the moment heavy... Butter is firm... Cheese fluctuates...* The doctor comments on our economy now with the war. A question about the food directed at me by my mother, and then, you have been quiet, she says, quickly adding that men are always more quiet than women when at their food. After a few minutes, Miss Stille turns her attention back to my aunt. Your nephew has mentioned that you are an adept at Spiritism, she says. I cannot speak for my father, but I am a believer. Oh no, not an adept, my aunt replies, I merely have an interest and we sometimes have sittings here. Miss Stille colors. I'm sorry, she says, I have too much enthusiasm. Nonsense, my aunt says, there can be no such thing as too much enthusiasm—perhaps you and your father would like to come sit with us sometime? I would like that very much, Miss Stille answers and then she turns to her father. I would be curious, he says. We will arrange for it then, my aunt says. When the supper is finished we take coffee in the garden. The stalks have been lit to keep the insects away. Coffee is brought and the doctor is invited to smoke.

In this garden at night it would seem the spirits might come without prompting, Miss Stille says. Do you mind if I walk in it?

It has become like a jungle in this heat, my mother replies.

Oh, but I like it that way, Miss Stille quickly rejoins.

Have you heard the news, the doctor asks, of Pierce Butler's arrest?

Yes, I say, I heard it today at the Athenaeum.

He was arrested for treason. I feel pity for him, the doctor continues, but in such times as these it doesn't come as a surprise—he has long openly favored the South.

Yes, I say again. And then my gaze turns to my mother in conversation with the doctor's daughter at the far end of the garden.

Night. Restless sleep. The sense of relief when I wake up.

The sky and the clouds as they've always been.

The morning sun.

I've come down to the garden again because when I came down before the light was not right for the photograph.

I set up the equipment in the garden to photograph the white birdbath. I want it to show in an exaggeration of its whiteness. Standing in front of it, I remove an overgrowth from the vines that have attached to the stone. The light keeps shifting because of the clouds. When the clouds move past, the light is brilliant; when they collect again, there is shadow. I take two photographs: one in brilliant light and the other in shadow.

...portrait of an inanimate object.

I use the small work-shed at the rear of the house to the right of the garden to develop the negatives. The process is slow.

...for several hours transfixed, tense, excited.

My mother comes out while I'm working and asks if the flowers show well in the photograph? It's only a likeness of the birdbath I'm taking, I tell her. She says, What a strange thing to want to photograph.

...grace to you, Sir. An experiment with light.

Her dear old father.

Her dear old father. Those are the words I hear when I've finished with the photographs and I go back inside the house. *How cold. How startling. Never a gentler man.* My mother, her friend Elizabeth, and my aunt are talking in the south parlor. I nod to them as I pass by. My mother gets up and comes to my side and walks with me to the bottom of the staircase. She asks if I've eaten. I tell her I haven't. I have papers to sort out, I tell her, and then I must go to the studio. She says that she'll bring a tray up and I can eat while I'm sorting out my papers.

The windows in my room are open; the drapes have been gathered to one side. I walk over to the washstand and put water on my face, then I remove my shirt and douse my chest; the excess water runs onto the washstand and onto the floor. When my mother comes into the room with the tray, I'm still without clothes on the parts of my upper body. Elizabeth will be going home soon, she says walking past me. There's ham on the tray, she says, and bread with butter, and iced water with lemon. And then she leaves me.

The way thoughts arise

in one's mind.

I've eaten little. I've not dressed. I've sorted no papers.

As I climb up the rear staircase, I cross paths with the housekeeper climbing down—she tries not to stare at my half-unclothed body. At the top of the stairs is the apartment of rooms. I enter the sitting room that used to be Lucie's. I stand at her writing desk with the gaselier above; through the opposite doorway is the bedroom: the dark red of the walls, the wood floor, the uncovered window. The bed is still adorned by a heavy winter spread— it's a bed that's not used; there's no need to change to a summer quilt in season. I open the door of the closet where my wife kept her clothes: the narrow shelves are empty, as are the hooks for hanging garments. The awareness of my hand in front of me closing the closet door.

On a page in one of Lucie's notebooks

I swept a great deal this morning in the studio, though Edmund Fell insisted I must not. He said that it's his work to do, but I took a certain pleasure in the motion of sweeping, and in its usefulness. And then at around 11 in the morning, a family came in for a portrait: A husband and a wife, the youngest child in the mother's arms, and two at her side. They were all visibly nervous; nothing I said or did seemed to relieve their nervousness. The husband kept his hand clenched when I took the photograph. William arrived just after.

I read several chapters of 'The Lady Lisle' today. And then I went round with William's mother to see her friend, Mary Edson.

From the window I see my mother come into the garden and walk over to the summer asters; she takes one in her hand and examines it. She stands there for a minute and then goes back into the house.

I return to my room on the second floor. The ice has melted in the glass. I pick up the glass and drink; the taste of the lemons has been largely diluted by the melted ice. It's early afternoon, there's still time to sort through the receipts that Edmund Fell gave me: a year of business at the studio faithfully recorded while I was in the West. It was with sadness in his voice that he told me the Army would not take him because of his leg.

I examine the prints from the year past. The prints have winter on them. My hands have started to tremble. For periods of time there is no sign of disturbance and then it begins.

Death kept by memory. It's only memory that keeps the dead. And there's no reason not to lie down now on the bed. The doctor said I must rest. There's no reason not to lie down on the bed and rest.

Periods of silence and waiting.

...because the summer is so hot

The late August sky.

The way time has passed.

The way time has passed... is passing.

...you remember there's the sitting tonight, my mother reminds me—the doctor and his daughter have been invited; your aunt is in a state of agitation though she pretends that she isn't; she wants the impression to be favorable but she will tell you that it makes no difference. My mother stands facing me; her manner is direct. If you will be attentive to the Stilles, my mother says, it will give reassurance to your aunt. They are my friends, I say, it's only natural I'll be attentive to them. I consider the approaching evening. There will be the sitting. It will be overly warm in the room. The doctor will be uncomfortable, but he will not complain. His daughter will be seeking to make contact with her dead mother through the medium, Mrs. Lord. The doctor would prefer to hold back, but his daughter will be intent on it.

...Miss Stille's hair, when she arrives, is braided in those two strange loops which fall just below her ears. The rest is pulled away from her face. The shape of her face is oval. The color of her skin is very white. In contrast to her hair, which is dark. Her eyes are set wide. Her expression expectant. My aunt has seated her next to me. On her other side is her father. My mother sits next to him. On my other side, my mother's friend Elisabeth, and then the gentleman, Mr. George Fisher, who has a strong interest in calling the spirits down. My aunt is planted firmly between Mr. Fisher and medium, Mrs. Lord. Before she begins, Mrs. Lord requests that all around the table hold hands. I can feel that there's a ring on Miss Stille's smallest finger.

The medium begins:

     I shall never forget our experiments with a so-called light when you took a bottle of red liquid.
     Are you certain it was red?
     Perhaps it was not red and not liquid.

     Everything was taking place in the midst of a controversy.
     I know about it. It's an odd place to begin.
     Will you take our questions now? Is there something you would like to say?
     It is known the soul carries the passions with it.
     Tell us what is important.
     Above the door there was a key.

The alteration of the medium's physical appearance. Her eyes are closed, her skin is pale, her face has gone a little gray, her head is tilted back, and her lips are slightly open in the dim light of the gas lamp.

     Can you identify yourself for those of us present? Is it difficult for you? Will you say your name so that everyone here might know who you are?
     It is the name it has always been. There is no reason it would change.

Will you say it?

It is —.

(The name remains unspoken)

Can you tell us to whom the key belonged? It is of significance to someone sitting with us this evening.

What do you think I am?

Is there someone here who is a relation of one of the sitters?

At one time, yes. (The medium's body stiffens.) But there is some-one else close by who is reluctant to speak.

Can you tell us who it is?

It has left now.

Can you then tell us what it is like where you are? There is a doctor sitting with us who has asked.

Ask what you will.

Do you eat? Do you sleep or dream?

There is no need. Who is it you are seeking?

The young woman's mother.

I see two children in a kiss. One has his mouth against the chin of the other.

Are they spirits, or more?

They have attached themselves to the woman in question.

The doctor leans forward in his chair.

The woman is near and waiting. You may ask her to come forward.

Are the children still with her?

Yes.

Will she speak to us?

The children will take her back soon. She wishes you to know that she is not cast out, that she is here with awareness and power.

Miss Stille asks if her mother is safe, if a message might be delivered, if she and her father are remembered?

I wish to remind of the piano and a favorite piece of music. It is that odd piece by Mr. Sweelinck. You will keep me near you with it.

Miss Stille's hand holds mine more tightly at the mention of the music.

I bring no more than can be abided.

The words have come as though in response to the increased pressure of Miss Stille's hand.

But it is time. It is a young light and cannot remain.

Miss Stille's hand tightens again to protest the departure.

Just under three quarters of an hour have passed. The sitting has lasted a short time, shorter than usual.

We cease now   but remember   there is still one in shadows who would prefer to remain as such.

I begin to have a sense of something I would prefer not to...

May the blessings of God rest on you ♰

I look for a moment at my mother and my aunt. There is an odd expression on my aunt's face.

Are you trying to wake me? asks the medium, Mrs. Lord. Yes, wake me...

The medium is coming out of trance.

Yes, I am awake now, says Mrs. Lord.

My aunt asks the doctor to take the medium's pulse because it will be an accurate reading if the doctor takes it. The doctor takes the medium's pulse. It is 78. Her breathing is steady, but a little rapid. You must rest to bring you pulse down, the doctor says to Mrs. Lord.

A short while later we are gathered in the garden after the sitting.

The idea of thought-coincidences. The bed of the nervous system. Descriptions of the nervous material of the brain. The idea of the nerves as the bearers of memory, or the brain as the source of all phenomena.

I walk with the doctor away from the others. My daughter has faith in it, he says. There is no use in introducing science to her. Science is new and faith is ancient. My daughter will take this seriously, he says... it will be best to support her.

We rejoin the others. My mother hands an iced drink to the doctor. My aunt is eating one of the small cakes that have been put out on the table.
I want you all to know that it was good to have my mother near again, Miss Stille says, and then she asks if I will walk with her around the garden.

I wake to perspiration on my face, on my chest, my naked body in the tangled sheets, the quilt thrown to the floor, the windows open, the washstand ready, the smell of soap, the weight of my arm across my body.

The sound of birds coming from the rear window and I have the idea I'm sleeping outside.

The smell of spike lavender.

Flight of the imagination... Miss Stille untangling the sheets... her hands brush my skin...

...fully awake I look down from the window and see several birds at the birdbath drinking. even today the expectation of—

...in a corner of the room the boxes containing my late wife's photographs. her photographs. the seriousness with which she attended them.

...visible remains.

...traces.

...the sky filled with light.

...and I feel everything just out of reach...the memory I'm trying to take hold of...there had been the morning when a fox had come into the garden. I was almost twelve. I said to my aunt if you want I will shoot it. Oh, no, it must not be shot, my aunt said.

...but now it's afternoon and Miss Angeline Stille is holding her hand out for me to help her up into the carriage. As I climb up beside her she brings my attention to a woman in a hat that she finds overdone. We examine the ornamentation on the hat. There are two dead birds on the rim, stuffed and perched to look live. I have no opinion of women's hats, I tell her. She laughs and reminds me we are on our way to the outskirts, beyond Fairmount Park, where we can sit by the Schuylkill River where it will be cooler.

My father asked me to give his apology for not joining us, she says—he was needed at the hospital.

I look out from the carriage window. The clouds are white against the sky.

It will do you good by the river, Miss Stille says. Water is restful. Her voice is calm; she speaks slowly and matter of fact.

We pass Logan Square and I mention there are no deer. She leans in front of me to see. The view of the park is from the window on my side of the carriage.

It was my mother who appeared to us at the sitting last night, she says. There's no doubt of it for me. There was no one else present except for me and my father who would know about the piece of music. And then she adds sadly but without sentimentality, my mother died suddenly, you know; it was her heart.

Was it a comfort then? I ask her. The proceedings with Mrs. Lord?

It was both a comfort and not, she says. What about you? Is it a comfort for you?

What do you mean a comfort?
Having your aunt's gatherings at hand.
Do you mean in relation to my late wife?
Yes, she says.
I have never allowed it, I say. I have discouraged it. Forbidden it.
Oh, I believe I understand, she says.

North of the Waterworks near the river are the public gardens. The carriage takes us there and leaves us. I tell the driver the hour to return. Miss Stille wears a blue dress; her hair is down; she has removed her hat. A short way in the distance, over one of the dwarf elms, there's a small flock of birds flying repeatedly back and forth in that strange pattern I've observed before. They fly back and forth over the tree with the sense of willfulness about it; almost ferocity. The birds continue that way for a while and then fly away. Miss Stille's head has been raised to watch them. When the birds have flown out of sight, she lowers her head. Why do you think they do that? she asks— fly back and forth that way? I don't know, I answer, but I've also seen it in my mother's garden—it's perhaps a kind of stalking. She repeats my words: a kind of stalking. Are you comfortable, I ask. Yes, I'm comfortable, she answers, and then she asks, do you feel restful? I'm never restful, I say. But my father says that you must rest, she says. She is sitting next to me, near me. I have no doubt your father is correct, I say. Her voice in response is slow, deliberate: We can sit here in tranquility, she says. Yes, we can do that, I say. From where I'm sitting I can see the clouds in the sky above the tree, the tree that the birds had been stalking. White, vague shapes, as I had seen them when I looked up before when climbing into the carriage. But today the clouds are heralds of nothing; it will not rain. And next to me the doctor's daughter is alive in her pale blue dress, speaking of tranquility. Her hair is unbound. She lowers her voice: We will be still and quiet and that will bring restfulness. Do you really think that will bring restfulness? I ask. Yes, she says, I think it will. And then for a time we sit together completely quiet. It's the hottest part of the day. Her flesh is alive and responds to the heat. Her skin is glistening. Her skin seems to have grown whiter in the heat. Beads of perspiration form on her forehead and below her eyes. They look like tears. But they are not tears because she is smiling. She flushes a little when

155

the beads of perspiration form; she is embarrassed by them; she would like to raise her hand to her face to wipe them away, but does not want to draw further attention to them. But then it appears she can bear it no longer and she raises her hand to wipe the moisture away. I watch as she does it. Delicately with her fingertips. But it does no good because the sun is too strong and within minutes her face is moist again. She lifts her hand to her face again, but this time I stop her. I prevent her from completing the action and I touch her face with my own fingertips. My thumbs rest lightly on her jaw, my fingertips are on her cheeks beneath her eyes. I wipe the beads of moisture away. She is alive. She is not memory, she is not dream…

the beads of moisture

the curtained windows of my bedroom

on the wall the angel musician

one of the *pifferari*

one of the *pifferari* angel bagpipers.

…it is painted in the Roman style and hanging on the wall in my bedroom. The figure of the angel is a child. His arms are spread across the instrument. His shirt is white and gathered with a small broach at the throat. A flat-style hat appears to sit easily on his head. His hair falls to his shoulders beneath the hat.

dreams all night long that will not stop. Lucie riding up from the dead, having seen it, it's in her eyes.

come sit with me a while, William.

she is emaciated with her frame bony, her breasts sagging, her belly slightly bulging, her hair falling limp down her back. there are two straight-backed chairs where we are sitting side-by-side.

in this house.

we turn towards each other as though we will kiss. her face shows the same emaciation as her body. there is murky light in the room. her lips are waiting for mine.

in this room.

where we sit.

she has placed a finger on her lips.

divinity of trees.

the smell of earth. my wife and I sitting. the two chairs which have been placed side-by-side. I look to see where the bed is. the room is empty except for the chairs.

come sit with me a while, William.

we continue sitting in silence.

the smell of earth. the repetition of phrases. she hands me her diary. the smell of old leather.

where the pages are silent.

a little way in the distance the sound of a carriage.

I keep you dearly.

I hear my wife's voice as it was.

and then the chair is empty.

I wake and feel the sheets. The curtains are closed, but the thin summer fabric of the spread has been penetrated by the morning sun. The sensation of my body in bed, the spectacle of the fireplace across from the bed, the writing table between the two rear windows, below is the garden. Half expecting to see them now in the bedroom: the two chairs from the dream; Lucie sitting in one of them.

in my head I hear my late wife's voice.

I read one hundred pages of Motley today.
That's a good many.
I read straight through the morning.

When I go downstairs the door to the garden is open. The cat has killed another bird and carried it into the house. He is a murderer, my mother says, a small murderer. They are just like the big cats, my aunt says.

And then talk of the flowers and the heat and more sewing for the soldiers.

My aunt is reading aloud from Godey's Lady's Book. A description of the mechanism of the gas lamps.

...the gas is pumped from the Gas Works into the buildings, and then into the lamps from above. By turning the knob on the lamp one is able to turn it off and on. By adjusting the knob one can control the degree of brightness. It is the gas itself that produces the light.

My mother mentions the doctor and his daughter in connection with a performance at the Walnut Street Theater: there's a plan we'll all attend. I sit eating silently, bringing the bread to my lips. The morning egg. The rim of the cup.

The heat is so constant, my aunt says. Has Mr. Lacey delivered the ice? The last she looked the supply was low. It will not do in this weather to be without it.

What night did you say it will be for the theater? I ask. It will be Wednesday evening, my mother answers, and then she asks how I'm feeling, I look worn to her, she says, as though I've not been sleeping—I must eat and rest just as the doctor has prescribed; has he examined me again; it's perplexing not to see any improvement; perhaps he should examine me again. I'm going to the Athenaeum this morning to read the newspapers, I tell her. And then to the studio to review the accounts with Edmund Fell.

159

...yesterday, when I brought Miss Stille home, she had unhurriedly stepped down from the carriage.

...in my mind the thought that on Wednesday evening it will be the theater.

Now at the Athenaeum there's early morning talk that the Union troops are poorly trained. I sit at one of the tables where there's a stack of newspapers and a photograph. A salt print from a wet collodion glass negative. The name of the photographer is not given. There is only a card stating the subject: *The Traitors Hanged in Washington*. Four bodies in black robes are hanging from the scaffold, the robes are tied around their bodies with rope to keep the fabric close, a white hood is on each of their heads. The length of the rope from which the bodies dangle is the same for each in perfect measurement. There is perhaps two feet of space between them. The bodies hang suspended from a bar at the top some twenty feet above the ground. There is a standing platform behind them from which they have been made to drop. The photograph's view is from a distance and the angle is from above. There's a crowd in the foreground made up mostly of soldiers, but there are civilians too; I can see there are women too in the crowd. It is mostly the backs of the people that face the lens of the camera. A light rain appears to be falling, there are several open umbrellas, the crowd may be dispersing, the traitors are hung and dead. I walk over to the water cooler and take a tin cup. One of my hands is beginning to tremble. I turn the knob to run the water into my cup. A new slab of ice has been placed in the tray at the top. It drips down through the limestone. The water is cold. My mouth moistened.

The water dripping down through the limestone.

And a short while later Edmund Fell is also talking about the war, his desire to be a part of it; to fire a musket held high at his shoulder. We're at the studio and he's repeatedly cursing his leg which keeps him from joining. A little before noon his wife brings his lunch. She has their infant daughter with her. It's the infant, Lucie, who has the namesake of my late wife.

When his wife leaves, I admit to Edmund Fell that I've come back for the war.

And then I leave for Race Street and the National Guard recruitment center.

A trembling hand is nothing to the body. Shoved into a pocket to keep it still. It is my hand. Only one hand trembled, but now the trembling has stopped. Both hands are still, calm, certain. Yesterday with Angeline, I placed my hand on her face. She leaned her head forward a little so that her face pressed into my fingers. The desire of the body. The memory of a moment. The desire to bring her close. But now I'm in front of the Armory. It's a three-story building. A flat roof. The round arch of the windows. Broadsides for recruitment cover the walls that flank the door. My attention is fixed. The calm of certainty. The light has begun to hurt my eyes. I close my eyes for a minute as I stand at the door outside the building. Inside, the light is dim. There's the business of war. I am a man of business. I'm prepared to understand the business of war. The only qualifications are that you can stand and that you can shoot and that your hands be steady. I have placed my hands on the table in front of me. There's an ease in the conversation; it's the conversation of men. I'm not afraid of the dead, I tell them. The officers laugh in a companionable way. And I laugh with them. I'm also companionable. At times any man might lose heart. I search up and down the faces of the men. There is quiet. There is almost nothing to be done. Just to hold the pen in my hand. At night there will be stars and marching. Just to write my name. One of the men is saying even an X will do. But a man of business does not need to sign with an X. And at night there will be a cooling down in the weather. And there will be a comet to see when we are sitting on the roof of the ice-house with all the lamps extinguished in the garden. Or when I drive to Fairmount Park with Angeline. On the outskirts of the city. Or if I marry

161

her and take her to Rome, which she has expressed an interest in seeing. Or to be awakened out of sleep again in the bedroom in the early dawn. To find everything red. And the small winged figures on the headboard that are half-birds. The room cold in late November. To find my wife on her knees. To find myself standing there. To find myself kneeling beside her. There is a painting of a battle hanging on the wall behind the recruitment desk. And I have some narrow awareness of the officers waiting. Awareness of a pen in my hand and the difficulty of holding it. My hand will not be still; it will not grasp. I cannot hold the pen. Wind. Eventually rain will come. Accompanied by hail. And also by thunder and higher winds. And now the awareness of a cold wind on my face. A paralysis of one side of my face. And of the room becoming dim. Because it is night. Or because of passing clouds. And the knowledge it will get dimmer still, until I can no longer see at all. And then there is a commotion around me and I hear someone say the word: Collapse. He has collapsed. The word collapse. And then someone else says the words: Bring a doctor. And someone else again, has said the word: Identity. And I find myself falling. Strange to be falling. And also strange is the last image that comes into my head before I lose consciousness. It is the image of the fires where glass is blown. At the mouth of Gunner's Run are the glass works—the glass pits and the fires, not far from the wharves. And it comes into my mind that I'm seeking the darkness of the glass pits. In the glass pits lit only by fire. To practice the delicate art of the glass blowers. And then I have my last conscious thought of being absent.

5

The Four Corners; Canyon de Chelly;
Santa Fe, 1873, 1874

If we think of a human soul we might think of a figure dancing all covered with earth-plot and bark, and with rope-hemp and fur, and a face like a mask, the eyes hollow and slanted, the hands raised like claws. And we might imagine that the dance is taking place on the top of the mesa, or on one of the four sacred mountains. The sky heavy with clouds. The clanging of bells. The beating of drums.

The old well at A____. There are two figures

dawn. it's cold. I wake up cold.

But here in the day it's so hot it can fell a man. The chemicals for the photographs begin to boil. The plates are ruined.

Everywhere rock rises up reaching for the flat surfaces at the top of the mesas. At the bottom a well has formed where the Indian women come to collect water. A small ledge, less than one foot, where they can step down to the water of the well.

...the taste of the years that have passed. I've been and gone and been again. The time traversed. The place crossed through.

Sir: You are hereby appointed photographer to the W_____ Surveying Expedition.

—survey of the Western lands.

—survey of the Western frontier.

—those portions of the United States Territory south of the Central Pacific Railroad, embracing parts of Eastern Nevada and Arizona...

—in the deserts and mountains of Arizona, Nevada, Colorado, and New Mexico…

All through the day we were followed by vultures waiting for us to throw something away. And then I was surprised to hear the calls of mourning doves; the Indian told me the canyons are filled with mourning doves. He said they bring good luck or bad, depending on the direction of their calls. If the calls come from above they bring good luck. If from below the luck will be bad. I think they're coming from above, I told him. And the Indian laughed and laughed. He is Navajo. The color of flat brown rock with a red cast. His name roughly translated means the one who points the way.

Instructed by Mr. W_____ to take supplies and a guide for a journey north to the canyon between the mouth of the San Juan and El Navo de los Pavres, and the pueblos.

The Indian standing in prayer. The look of a phantom. He is my guide, he says, not the guide of the others. He makes a motion towards the slight bend in the base of the canyon, and then to a cavity about sixty feet up that stretches out across the rock wall. Not empty, he says. The words are spoken as a warning. He's wearing the wide-brimmed hat I gave him to let me take his photograph. It's a ruin, I tell him—no one lives here any longer. Not empty, he repeats. They go this way; they go that way, he says.

When I speak long stretches of English, the Indian takes what I say as a series of sounds, a kind of music; unconcerned with the meaning. When I profane he catches the new inflection and intensity. I notice he takes pleasure in the moments when I profane.

We have reached an impasse. He will go no closer to the ruins.

I swear at the sun, the heat, and with my hand I encircle the watch in my pocket. It was a present from my wife, from Angeline. I'm considering offering it to the Indian if he'll go up into the ruins with me. I take the watch out from my pocket. For you if we go, I say. Go. But he refuses to go any nearer just for the sake of a watch and for me to take photographs.

We are standing a distance from the scarps bordering on what used to be a watercourse. White dwellings built into the rocks are visible. The Indian is waving his arm and talking quickly.

> Here, they go about their business, he says.
> Here, they have been dead for centuries, I say.

The word alarms him: dead. The word dead and the names of the dead must not be spoken. A bird appears in the sky. It's a hawk, circling.

> The bird is not a real bird, he says.

I feel the strain, the heat, the dust in my lungs and the dryness. We smoke together for a while. The tobacco leaves in their pure state are too strong and I've combined them with dogwood and cherry. We've rolled the leaves in cornhusks. The quality is good. The first puffs are sent in the direction of the ruins. I tell him the rest of the pouch will be his if he will help me with the climb to the ruins. The pouch is full. He tries not to look directly at the landscape in front of us. As we smoke, I know we have reached an understanding; he will accompany me in exchange for the watch and tobacco.

The rhythmic and repeating call of two mourning doves.

171

The whistling of their wings lifting off, then swooping and navigating around the rock.

We stand facing the wind. The Indian is making prayers.

From Ana: alien; Ye'i: the Gods; igai: white; Anaa'ji: the Way used to expunge evil spirits.

We are at the closest place in front of the ruins that is permitted him. For him to proceed is to step over the threshold of the living into the land of spirits. He says that jealous spirits are watching even now from their place on the cliffs high above; they are standing, as they have always stood, on the rock overhangs that sit in the high dry air; their dogs are standing with them. That sound we hear, the Indian says, is the barking of their dogs.

We have three mules with us on the field trip to carry supplies and the camera equipment. Even before we arrived here, for many days, there's been no grass. The mules have developed sores because of the lack of grass.

A small rock lizard sits just inside the opening of a break in the rock for the time that it takes me to develop a plate. The printing can wait until I am in St. Louis, or all the way back to the East, but the developing of the plates must take place immediately or they will dry. I'm in the makeshift tent that serves as a darkroom. The image of the Indian is on the plate with his long black hair showing white on the negative; it hangs lank to his shoulders and he stares with suspicion in the direction of the camera. His expression appears exaggerated by the reversal of black and white, his eyes like the eyes of an apparition. When the Indian sees himself on the negative, he says he is seeing a spirit.

Mr. W____ said the views must entice settlement to the West. In that sense, Mr. W____ said, with a nod in my direction, the burden of responsibility belongs to you. in the wind-swept desert.

Before I left on the field trip with the Indian, Mr. W____ remarked on my fitness. Fit for a man turned forty-two years. More fit than the younger men.

Outside the tent, the lizard still has not moved. When I touch it with the point of a tripod leg the animal springs forward and in seconds disappears.

We are standing at the bottom the canyon. The elevation of rock wall stands before us. We are a white man and an Indian facing the elevation of rock. The wind blowing dust in our faces.

another kind of silence

the canyon walls rising to 1200 feet

rock and dust

the way the wind has sculpted rock

in the shadow of the ruins

The Indian is wearing his brooding expression. He wants to turn back but won't say it because he has given his word.

Forty? fifty? sixty feet above the canyon bed? The ruins protected in a niche.

The barren landscape has entered the frame. The rock face is smooth; its ledges narrow. I resolve to climb it in the morning. The Indian tells me the dead are sitting upright on the rock ledge; we cannot approach; not even the birds would dare approach. The terms of the dead—to sit inviolate. Without message for the living except to remain at a distance. The Indian is reading the night; reading the stars, or reading the shadows on the cliff wall. Just as earlier he read my face to know I was honest. That he could trust me. And just as he read my foot to know I had endurance. That I would persevere. The smell of the rock wall, the canyon dirt. The pack mules close by. The yuccas here have put their white flowers out—it doesn't happen every year. Earlier the mules ate them. Now one of the mules is stamping his foot. And everything is disappearing into the rock, as if the rock urges it. To sit upright on the cliff ledge side-by-side with the dead. The Indian talks nonsense all through the early night, sometimes in Navajo, sometimes in English, mixing the words of both languages into his sentences. Until he talks himself to sleep. He sleeps with his eyes half open, slits of the whites showing, lit by the fire. His lank dirty hair is tied around with a thick piece of cloth; the color of the cloth is dull in the darkness, but all day long it shined yellow. Gray wolves howl in the distance. In the morning, from the ground, I'll photograph the wall cave before we climb.

the night
the mules
the Indian
the canyon

within the rock

an opening for the soul and for consciousness

The Indian sleeps still wearing his plain woven shirt and odd pants that come a few inches below his knees, and the soft leather boots worn by the Navajo men. I have the sense the white slits of his eyes see through sleep. Utter stillness of the night. The rock cliff dwarfs us. While the Indian sleeps I stare at him, I examine his face and his motionless body; he has the look of the spiritless. But even in sleep a man can feel when he's being stared at—the Indian doesn't stir but for a minute his eyes are fully open. His body poised to spring. Shadows thrown by the fire. The Indian's gaze, slowly, bringing his mind back into wakefulness; into wakefulness where he sees that all remains as he left it. And just as suddenly his eyes again close, back into those half-open slits, and he sleeps.

a distance away. the gray wolves in the canyon. wailing.

It is a place, Mr. W_____ said, where no one will come until we record it.

Silence and solitude; the arduous labor of years on the hardness of rock, the hardness of rock and the forms that are not human. The rock swallowing shadows. The wolves now silent. The snorts of the pack mules. My body is tired and the intrusion of thoughts before sleep. Home. My wife, Angeline. The look on her face as we parted. You are leaving again too soon, she said. We talked of the necessity of my leaving.

The morning without wind. Without the cries of birds. With only the bones of dogs, bleached white, like the bones of the humans.

We stop along the way so I can take views at different distances. In a niche, below the massive rock wall, the white sandstone slabs are visible, the dwellings carved into the rawness of rock, the stone bleached white by the sun like the bones of the dogs.

...and the small black tent I pitch each time we stop. The tent for developing the plates makes the Indian uneasy. If the gods did not want it, I wouldn't be able to do it, I say. One of the mules stamps his front right foot a few times on the ground. The tent disturbs the Indian, its small size with a purpose only to serve as a portable darkroom. The silver bath for the plate. The thin coating—the application even and delicate.

in the day the heat can make the glass plate dry so fast that the image is lost. sand sometimes gets into the negative.

When I close my eyes against the sun I have the impression figures are standing on the ledge of the ruins. As long as my eyes are closed traces of the figures remain, black against the red emptiness superimposed on my lids by the sun. But when I open them I see nothing; there are no figures; there is only the reddish-brown rock and the white dwellings sitting sixty feet above, in the niche in the cliff wall, and the empty space in the niche above the dwellings, and above the empty space the continuing cliff wall.

I close my eyes again to test the shadows.

A flash of lightning darts down into the canyon. A late day storm. Another lightening strike. The Indian silent. We stop for a while and then we go on.

my hands are becoming the color of the rock

And in my eyes mules. Birds. The Old Ones the Indian said dwell here. Towering above with their feet pointed to the left and the right.

The Indian again unloads the equipment. I erect the tent to protect from the light when I prepare the plates. The process, already slow, becomes slower in the heat; in the distance the white of the dwellings.

The Indian passes the boxes which contain the chemicals into the tent to me. He makes no sound while I work. Everything is tenuous, uncertain. The heat can make the plate dry so fast the image will be lost. I make an adjustment in the thickness of the coating. Another adjustment in the time I allow for exposure.

Scattered rocks and bushes. We climb using the ropes. Of necessity the mules and equipment left on the ground below.

All the time we are climbing I have the sense of a presence watching.

We climb the sixty feet. In the distance rock balances on rock—figures of extraordinary height. Elder rocks worn into the shapes of giant men. These rocks are your old ones, I say to the Indian. He answers in a sing-song. When I ask him what it means, he explains, adding gestures: Don't move the stones. Don't take from the dead. Nothing can come of it. And then he stops his sing-song.

He removes the bandana from his head. The bandana drops to his neck. A small flock of ravens flies up in the canyon. I can see them from above as they rise and descend, their bodies large, coal black, the long length of their wingspan. The Indian is disturbed by the sight of the birds. They belong to the spirits who can take your health. I turn my attention to the interior dwellings of the ruins. One dwelling leads to another through the archways of the openings, a figure or a symbol carved on a wall, and then a wall of figures like shadows, silence between me and the Indian. We move from one room to another. The Indian has started again with his sing-song. They can take your mind, he says. Or else they can take your speech. The spirits will take you into the land of the dead. Another lightening strike. But still no rain. The day is like fire, burning my skin, making it browner, redder. The light moves and changes. And then only silence. No wind. No sound of the wind.

Empty of life and yet filled with the presence of life—the reverberation of those who once came and went their way. Stone. Clay. The archways of the living-compound. One can see through the archways from one room to the next. Each leads to another and to others. There are sometimes carvings on the walls. A strange shelf like a mantel still intact over one of the archways. Behind the houses of the ruins only rock. No one can enter from behind.

From the ledge of the cliff I can see the white flowers on the remaining yucca down below.

From the ledge of the cliff that lines the ruins I stare down at the canyon floor below: the sparse presence of cottonwoods.

Sand, dirt, stone.

The mules are tied and standing where we left them.

The wolves are wanderers the Indian says. A delirium in his eyes. At first I regard him with serious attention, but then I see the delirium. The wolves are wanderers, he says again. There are no wolves here, I say. Ai, he says. he points to the wall and says there's a wolf. The shadow of a wolf thrown against the wall of the interior room we are in. They are hiding in their hiding places, he says. Here there is nothing, I say—only a dwelling with nothing. There are drums from underneath, he says. I say nothing. Ai, he says.

Night.

The tops of the mesas.

When I return to the canyon floor I find the mules tied where I left them. The Indian is still up on the cliff wall.

The Indian.

It's dark, the temperature is falling.

The chemicals have gone bad after the day's heat.

There's pemmican to eat. The dried buffalo meat mixed with fat and berries held in the rawhide containers that fold over like envelopes. Pemmican preserved in the containers so it can be eaten.

A sliver of moon in the sky.

All the red has left the sky.

I wait for the Indian to come down from the ruins.

I read a letter from Angeline received before I left St. Louis weeks ago:

...The creek is my own small wilderness, William. Sometimes when I sit there I have the sensation of a door opening onto all of nature, and I know we are part of it and not separate from it and that if we let it, it will lift us up. I can only imagine the wonders you are seeing; I know you will bring them back to me as impressions captured on your photographs, and also in that part of yourself that carries your experiences with you.

I think of her sitting by the creek, her hair a tangle of black unloosed like a storm, blatant in her beauty, and she seems to approach me now at the base of the cliff, stepping out of the rock wall, saying—

—stepping out of the rock wall. At the base of the cliff. She has been my wife for these ten years.

The howling of wolves in the distance.

Sounds in the canyon play tricks: I hear the sound of a howl of a man from the niche above as though from an animal.

The Indian still up in the ruins.

If he doesn't come down in the morning there will be nothing I can do except leave.

The wind makes the fire wild. My body is tired. I want to sleep.

Earlier the images were jarring on the negatives. Dry earth, rock, brush, shadows.

Rock that has formed on the earth over a long span of time.

The breathing of mules.

Incomprehensible because it is immeasurable.

In the night the sense of being watched. The sense that there are figures lining the ledge on the cliff wall. Ready to sound the drum, the alarm, in the shape of birds, like the night.

The night cold takes me by surprise after the heat of day. I fold the letter and put it back into the inside pocket of my shirt, my wife's face has disappeared, brush wood to keep the fire burning throughout the night, there's no choice but to sleep.

When I open my eyes I see the fire is burning low. I throw brush on. At first it burns slowly, but then in a burst the fire rises.

When I open my eyes I see the Indian standing across from the fire.

When I open my eyes I see the fire is burning low. I throw more brushwood on. At first it burns slowly, but then in a burst the fire rises.

when I open my eyes. when I open my eyes. when I open my eyes.

Flanked by the cliff wall and the fire. The dirt of the earth beneath me is no longer warm. In my mind I hear the words of the Indian telling me that the bodies of the dead are sitting mummified by the heat and arid air, that they are sitting where they were placed on the cliff ledge after their spirits left them. Why do you come here? the Indian asked me. What do you want here?

When I open my eyes I see the Indian standing on the other side of the fire. He has come down from the niche and the abandoned dwellings. The fire lights him from below throwing red on his face.

The way that wind can assist fire. The Indian silent. Darkness behind him. Stories of those who walk through fire.

My mouth is dry when I start to speak; it's almost impossible to part my lips; and after parting them it's impossible to give shape to a word. Bad medicine. Bad magic. Care must be taken with one's sleeping soul. Wind catches the flame.

The question of why I have come. A knife in his hand to cut away rope. I rise to my feet when he starts toward me through the fire. His hand that holds the knife has lifted. The scabbard of his knife is made from the skin of a bear. I examine his face coming through the fire. There had been blood running from his feet when we were in the rooms of the ruins. And now from my gun, gunshot to drive him back behind the fire.

If he is a ghost, then he is a ghost who intends to kill me. If he is man taken over by a god, by one of many gods, then he is a ghost who even so intends to kill me. If he is a man taken over by a ghost, then he is under the spell of a ghost and still intends to kill me.

It can be one story or another, one vision or another. I prefer the vision of the old man who woke up one morning to find that he was young again, that he had been given his life to live again. It is always that same story, the story of a life, lived, and lived again.

There is the story of the boy who got lost in the woods. He became aware of his feet on the earth. The smell of the forest. The sounds that trees make when the wind catches their branches. It was a story similar to other stories. It seemed to have nothing to do with this story.

I was taught by my father to walk one foot in front of the other. On the earth. Awareness of the earth on which I'm now standing. When did I rise to my feet? Only a few minutes ago it seems I was sitting with my back against the cliff wall. The black birds of the canyon with their long wing-spreads invisible in the night.

When morning comes everything will look different. I'll rejoin Mr. W____ and the others. Mr. W____ will look at the negatives, his eye will be critical, but he will also admire them. He'll look at the images on the glass. One image after another. Now and then he'll say it looks too hard, too vast, too barren, too old. He'll say no one will be enticed by it, but we will keep it anyway. Even in this place I have found a way to provide darkness to develop the negative. But I leave the printing for later. The difference between what the eye sees and what the camera sees. Each of the moments that have become an image on a photograph. For example the image of the Navajo woman and her child. The woman is sitting on a rock. The child has thin bare legs. His little woven shirt comes to the top of his thighs. She wears one string of turquoise beads around her neck. The child is leaning in towards his mother's knees as if to hold on to them. The child is staring apprehensive, afraid of the camera. His mother's left hand grasps his arm. Just before I took the photograph the child was laughing.

the Navajo herding their sheep

Sir: You are hereby appointed photographer to the W____ Surveying Expedition...

ropes to scale the cliff walls

to take us to the ruins.

the layers of rock and when the morning comes each stratum will be illuminated by the sun on the rock

but now it's still night and the body of the Indian has fallen to the ground on the other side of the fire, the irreparable strike—that which cannot be taken back. and the inability to move backward in time except in memory.

the wind, a ribbon of breath, circling down into the canyon, silence, then the rasp-throated cry of a bird. I find the sound disagreeable. wind warning down into the canyon.

when I open my eyes I see the Indian standing across from the fire. he has risen up from his wounds, now he's chanting a sing-song about the Old Ones still up in the dwellings. there are more than sixty rooms. there are more than one-hundred people who used to live there.

the red sandstone turns black in the night, as though the night is cut from the black stone. the sound fire makes. watching, I cannot see beyond the fire. but I know there's a corpse on the other side where the Indian fell when I shot him. he had tracked back, his eyes staring, a glint of steel in his hand. he refused to answer to his name. when I repeated it he still refused to answer. but when I stand up and go to the other side of the fire there is nothing there.

184

earlier I had asked the Indian to climb the rock wall using a rope so that I could photograph him to show the proportion of the cliff—his image would be far in the distance, I said, small and imperceptible, the camera would not be able to catch his spirit. he would be like an ant or a grasshopper. he listened to me seeming to consider what I was saying. the spirit is taken from the eyes, I said—the theft of the spirit is from the eyes. the camera will not see your eyes.

there is no body now; he has disappeared. there is only the black night, black sky, black stone, stars—I touch the ground.

aware of the sensation of my feet on the ground as I walk over the _____ my feet touching, sinking a little into the _____

I am between the fire and the expanse of the canyon on the other side. it is impossible in the dark to see what is out there.

there right before me on the dirt floor in front of the fire there is an empty spot where I saw the Indian fall, I saw him fall, I saw the blood mass.

and yet there is no body.

when I was a child out shooting with my father there would be times a bird would fall and the body would disappear and the dogs wouldn't be able to find it. they would stand whining and sniffing at an empty spot on the ground and my father would curse. his foul words stood apart from the language I was accustomed to hearing. but when we were hunting we were men together despite the fact I was a child and soon I developed my own taste for cursing.

the body is gone.

the ravens of the canyon in my dream, picking at the carrion of other birds. more like vultures than ravens.

chants sung by those who used to live here.

something from my past, precious visitation: the way a soul enters a room. the final gesture that a soul makes for the living.

but I'm tired now, my eyes are closing.

for months on end what has there been?—nothing but forage, mules, wagons. there has been nothing for months on end—nothing but forage, mules, wag-ons.

when my eyes close I see Angeline. but when I open them there are only the three rising towers of rock that appear to be three robed figures; they have shoulders that slope, heads chiseled in stone square on top of their shoul-ders. there's scuttling in the night on the canyon floor, around the base of the rock. my eyes close again. I dream that I'm sitting on top of one of the mules; the mule feels huge beneath me. I take the pistol in my hand and point it at the Indian guide. he is made out of straw and has come down from the ruins with a knife in his hand. when I shoot blood runs out from the straw. his death is not a real death.

the straw bursts apart, the blood spills forth, the Indian falls to the ground, but there is no body. it has been dragged back to the ruins by the ghosts of the Old Ones. the guttural sounds of their speech...drums...wind...

The early morning air is still cool. Traces of the night are more absent than present. Suddenly, as though out of nowhere, the Indian returns from the ruins; he starts giving water to the animals and seems the same as when I left him. All the equipment is packed and the Indian loads it onto the mules. I feel the temperature rising. Soon it is scorching. When we arrive back at the base camp it's like reaching home.

Mr. W_____ hands me something that looks like bread, a dark substance, made from the supply of flour that remains. Before night falls we examine the negatives of the ruins. I can see he's pleased. I point to the place on the negative where the two rope lines show black against the cliff wall and explain that we used them to climb to the upper ruins. I remind him that the ropes will show white when they are printed. The dwellings will also show white. It was a settlement, I say. The cliff wall rises another 1000 feet above the niche that holds the dwellings. Ladders used to be let down to the base of the cliff so that those who lived there could climb up. It's eight or nine hundred years since they've been abandoned. It's something to think about, Mr. W_____ says. And then he moves the subject of the conversation to the composition of the rock face and the geometric planes; to measurements of distances and altitudes, and to the camera's inability to measure. I talk about compensating efforts and point to a negative showing the Indian guide looking like an insect on the face of the rock. And here in this one the same view without a human figure. I mention the ability of photography to deliver different states of time. He finds the idea worthy of note, but not of primary interest. He picks up the plate and examines it. Well it's docile enough there now, he says. I'm not certain it's docile, I reply—oh, it's true the Indians in the region have become quiet because we have treated it as war. In any case it's a kind of ghost delivered on the photograph.

> Tomorrow you'll go to Santa Fe, he says.
> Yes, I reply, and begin wrapping the negatives in flannel.
> Well, goodnight then, he says.
> Yes, goodnight, I reply.

Instructions from Mr. W_____: Proceed to Santa Fe for the purpose of obtaining views about military headquarters...and then continue East to the Survey's head-quarters in Washington.

Angeline, there's nothing but desert and rock. You will see everything when I return home and print the negatives. Forms that rise abruptly from the earth. Ancient ruins. Indians. It is said the Indians are superstitious, but then who can really say what's superstition? I have had dreams here that did not seem like dreaming...

The old church at Santa Fe.

The beams called vigas and the roof-supports.

The Church of San Miguel. When the streets were walked by the Tlaxcalans.

River. Ward of Analco. The Tlaxcalans.

At night I sit on the wooden stairs of the flat-roof inn. There's the sound of cattle and talk of the fighting between the ranchers and the herders.

...there are pigs on the streets here, allowed to run free. The public place, the Plaza, is filthy today from the wagon trains that have just left. It's rough, and a little lawless, but compared to where I've come from it's civilization. There is a telegraph office, Angeline. I sent a wire to you an hour ago. I will wait for your reply as a means of touching you...

I entered the city with the mules hauling the wagon loaded to breaking with boxes of plates and equipment. The Indian entered with me. I looked like an Indian myself. My hair is grown long and I wear a band of cloth around my head to keep the sweat from my eyes. A bath was provided at the inn. It brought me more to myself. Moving out from Fort Wingate the main party will be collecting specimens and taking measurements.

Angeline, many questions are being asked about the survey. There was a gathering given in my honor last evening at the home of Mr. and Mrs. Dubich. Theirs is the only brick house in Santa Fe. It makes me think of Philadelphia. There was violin music and a piano. Mrs. Dubich asked if I would give a short presentation.

Today I took photographs of the Church of San Miguel. Saint Michael the Archangel, conqueror of Satan. The church is on the south side of the Santa Fe River: the area that used to be called the ward of Analco. Analco is an old Aztec word meaning on the other side.

I photographed the old church today, My Wife. It's called the Mission of San Miguel, named for Saint Michael the Archangel. The word angel, like your name Angeline derived from angel. The church is over 200 years old. A long history for this country. Though the ruins are many hundreds older. And the rocks of the region millions. The bell from the bell tower rang all the while I was taking the photographs.

A long history. The bell from the bell tower. I made exterior and interior views.

The exterior of the church has a triple tower diminishing in size each layer up. The huge bell in the bell tower is bronze. Some say it was cast in Cerrillos, while others say it was brought from Spain.

As I listened to the bell I wanted you to listen with me. It rings more sweetly than our church bells in Philadelphia, and with greater sonorousness. The sound seems to echo throughout the entire city.

The triple tower surmounts the entrance. The church is narrow and very long. There's a painting above the altar that shows Saint Michael hurling Lucifer down.

Angeline, The church is said to be haunted by souls of the dead who refuse to leave. All parts of the city make claim to hauntings.

Inside the church I burn magnesium wire to produce sufficient light for the views of the altar.

The souls of the dead. When do we not have them with us? They are always with us. But you well know that. You have lived as my wife these full ten years accompanied by my dead. The altar of San Miguel is adorned as it was two centuries ago: the colors muted with occasional deep reds and ochre. The dominant painting over the altar is Saint Michael, the Archangel, hurling Lucifer down. When I was in the canyon ruins I found several prayer sticks. I didn't know what they were until the Indian guide told me. Angeline, I believe you have understood necessity.

The magnesium throws its light enabling me to seize in my view the double set of railings; the first of them has its gate open towards the pews; and directly in front of the pews is the altar railing. There are carved beams on the ceiling and framed paintings of the saints on the walls; the old Spanish frames are hanging at odd, exaggerated angles. A small cross sticks out from the top of each of the frames. I have used the stereoscopic camera. The magnesium throws a light like a flash of lightening.

A painting of Saint Theresa of Jesus hangs over the altar. She is shown as young. Her hands are clasped. Her eyes dominate the portrait. The background is dark, as is her robe; the darkness is broken by a white cape worn across her shoulders. And by the white flesh of her face and her hands. One bare foot is exposed at the base of her robe.

I will be home soon. I love you hard; it is a hard love. You understand.

I have tucked a human figure in my view. It's one of the Christian Brothers kneeling in prayer in a front pew. He is seen only from behind and wears black so that his figure disappears into the dark wood of the pew.

The magnesium stays lit only for the time it takes to expose the plate. Afterwards the church is again in semi-darkness. The Christian Brother approaches me as I'm putting the equipment away. He asks about life back in the East, he's originally from Boston, but he's not been home since he joined the Order. He was assigned with the others to establish the educational work here in Santa Fe. He tells me that initially some of the others resented being assigned to this wild and dangerous place. At the time he had been a little resentful himself; he found he had to struggle for the sake of his soul with his resentment. But now he has come to love it here despite its roughness. That is the work, he says, to educate, which in turn civilizes.

The souls of the dead.

The church.

The souls of the dead are said to influence the city.

The noise of the city. Only days ago the canyon silence. That last image of the mules standing packed and ready for the journey out. Strapped onto their backs the barrel-shaped crates containing the photography equipment and supplies. The glass plates wrapped in flannel to protect them. The images reversed in negative of the cliffs and the canyon.

This morning in town there have been complaints of bush wolves on the outskirts preying on the sheep. Someone said jackals. Someone else said bush wolves.

I photograph a view of one of the narrow main streets. The sun is strong; the street is empty except for two figures in the shadow of a building. They are at a distance and therefore show small and a little indistinct. Many of the buildings, not the adobe, are three, sometimes four stories high. The streets are noisy in the day, but even noisier at night. All night long there's the drinking and the prostitutes.

All night long.

The drinking and the prostitutes.

The names of the prostitutes called out in the night:

...Queen; Spanish Queen; Rose; Gold Dollar; Peg-Leg Annie; Little Dot; Belle; Emporia Belle; Scar-Faced Lillie; Oglala Shorty; Jack-Rabbit Sue; Four-Ace Dora; Razorback Jennie; Annie; Big Annie; Sallie Purple; Squirrel-Tooth Alice; Hambone Jane; Galloping Cow; Big Minnie; Rowdy Kate...

To be breathed out. Dead. As in the flowers of the dead.

6

Philadelphia, Pennsylvania, 1874, 1875

When the book broke apart I was able to read it.

There is the bed drawn in white. A chair facing the bed as though for a ghost to sit watching.

Photographic portrait of a woman with her arms above her head.

The light thrown by the gaselier. Figures forming in the darkness. Repeatedly dark.

The suggestion of a bed, darkness, a figure or figures, a single figure.

A phantom arm. Phantom legs. The body disappearing on the albumen print.

The hot air balloon descends too rapidly; injuries to several of the gentlemen on board.

Clumsy in flight and in the way that it lands: a kind of frantic fluttering and then falling.

A hand pressed over the mouth.

Plangency of the night.

A hand pressed over the mouth in a kind of wonder.

We're the husband and the wife.

We're looking at the photographs.

A full hour or so spent with the photographs. Faces. It is a theater of faces.

Obtained by offering bribes. Tobacco or a piece of fabric.

The faces are not handsome, she says. She removes her hand from the photograph.

I take hold of her wrist.

The husband and the wife after the long period of absence.

The bed made up with white sheets. A quilt. Pillows.

The dark wood at the base of the night stand.

She says something about happiness.

She says it in a sing-song.

Inscrutable.

The easy indulgence.

The place where her neck meets her shoulder.

A dreamy spaciousness.

...hair when she loosens it.

...errant.

The sound of rain hitting the windows. It's raining again! Do you hear it? I hear it, I say. I can still taste the dust in my mouth and it washes. I push the drapery aside and tighten the sash. Only for a few minutes, I say. And then I loosen the sash from the drapes. I think there's a heavy rainstorm now! An early fall rainstorm. We might have been soaked. I think there's lightening! Thunder! Were you afraid of the thunder? I couldn't open my eyes.

At night the fire burned in front of me, a bird sometimes rose up in the darkness.

The hour when the gaslights on the sidewalks are extinguished and the streets are unlit except for the light from the windows.

There is a sameness. The streets were the same today when I walked them; the same signs on the buildings: *Confectioner and Fruit Dealer; E.G. Whitman; Landreth's Garden; Field and Bird Seeds; Tea Warehouse; J. Howell & Company...*

The wind starts up. An early fall wind pushes against the bedroom window. The spread is taken down. The bed linen white. There is a rainstorm now, do you hear it? The wind and the rain beating at the windows.

My wife in her nightdress. My wife of ten years. Angeline.

My wife's body beneath her nightdress.

Words not intended to be spoken.

...when I was in front of the fire, I say, between the fire and the cliff wall, when the dirt of the earth beneath me was no longer warm: there was an endless solitude of night, the floor of the canyon beneath the stature of rock—the elevation of cliffs, the black spread of the sky with its stars. When what I was seeing was the opposite of what I was charged to convey in my photographs. They wanted the land to appear safe. But the land cannot appear safe. We are held in its balance. Among the monoliths. The giant rocks that stand looking straight ahead like men. When we climbed we thought our ropes would be enough, but our ropes were often not enough. I wanted you to see it. But only for a moment to see it so it wouldn't crush you.

I have always been careful with you, I say. Tonight I don't wish to be careful. You remain silent. The night and storm converging.

We met on a train, you say.
No, I say, we met at the hotel in St. Louis while we waited for the train's arrival.
Yes, you say, but it was on the train that I felt I came to know you.

You are tired, I can hear it in your voice.

...when I was a child, I say, I had a dream about my father's death. A red fox brought the news. And once the news had been brought, I saw my father. His head on the pillow. His body stretched out on the bed. His arms extended long at his side. He grasped my hand. He couldn't talk. He could only grasp my hand.

You touch my face with the tips of your fingers.

With rain of such force it could not be otherwise, you say.

How barren the land is behind her, you say. That Indian mother nursing her child. Was her face really so dark? Or does it only look that way in the photograph?

It was dark, I say, and it also looks that way in the photograph.

The wind and rain against the window.

What to make of them?—the sounds that come with wind and rain.

A vicious horse. What is that about? A vicious, biting horse that charged a woman. Just as she was passing by on Chestnut Street the horse ran at her and knocked her to the ground. The woman has brought a lawsuit against the owner. What is that about? I touch your face. My hand to guide you. There is a rainstorm now. Wind and rain at the window. Talking. We might have been soaked. Talking. If we had stayed out we might have been soaked.

The window of our bedroom. The house belongs to you. To you and your father. The rooms are small, but sufficient. The hallways are narrow. Windows on one side. Rooms on the other.

The oval of your face.

The field of focus.

You look just like that

You look always just like that.

The night is calm now and silent. You have arranged the room for sleep.

My thoughts break off.

The rain soaking the earth.

To again be home.

Before sleep.

My thoughts break off...

...but what was I thinking when I was thinking? The way the fingers move across

the page grasping the pen. Being taken forward. It is no time at all. Barely a mo-
ment. They are starting to become a problem Angeline says, referring to the deer
in Logan Square. There are so many it is practically herds. Herds. I repeat the
word: Herds. Or this, Angeline says, pointing to an image on the photograph be-
fore us: the image of a Navajo boy sitting with his mother on a wooden bench. I
used to read to you, I say. Do you remember? In the early days of our marriage.
And you would turn scarlet while you listened to the passages I was reading. Do
you remember? Shall I read to you now, or when you approach me? Or when I
see you again after the time that has passed? My mouth on your flesh. The place
where your neck meets your shoulder. Your body half on top of mine. I'll make
you turn scarlet...

My thoughts break off...

Home...

Before sleep.

To again be home...

In the morning I go to my mother's house to visit with my mother and my
aunt. A painting of my grandfather hangs over the lowboy in the downstairs
hall. I take the painting down and look at the back. There is no signature. In
him was the blood which flows in my veins. My grandfather, I say, I have no
son; there will be no grandson. There is the smell of black coffee. My mother
insists I have breakfast. My aunt tells me that she's been reading about the
Indians. No, not your Red Indians, she says, I'm talking about those in the
Far East—they have wisdom; wisdom that is being brought to us only now.
I cannot stay long, I say, I'm on my way to the studio. I'm on contract to deliver the prints of the negatives. I'll be kept busy printing for the rest of the
season, perhaps for as long as a year, in order for the sets to be distributed

to Mr. W____. He needs them for his albums that are being compiled about the Survey, and for the corps of engineers and Secretary of War. The front door of the house; the stairway dado; the smell of the coffee; black liquid in my cup; the eggs on the sideboard.

Is it time or is it death?

It is only the time that it takes to walk to the studio.

The Navajo called it *Tseyia*—it means inside the rock.

The frozen moment. One in a succession of moments.

A single image of a raven soaring in the canyon.

And the time that has passed flows back into the subject on the photograph.

I am moved and moved again. There is work to be done. A certain resistance sets in as I enter the studio.

How striking the light is. The impression of fire. The early morning sun shines down from the skylight. For a few minutes everything is red.

Edmund Fell greets me when I arrive. He tells me that the printing is underway. The walls of the reception room are covered with old photographs.
All the old likenesses, Edmund Fell says.
He adds that the patrons like to see them.

If there is someone they recognize, he says, Oh, it's so-and-so, they say—they say, all the years that have passed and he's exactly as he was then.

And then he repeats what he said about the likenesses: that the patrons like to see them.

At that moment there's movement from out of the darkroom. Oh, it's Lucie, Edmund Fell says. I draw a breath at the sound of the name and a young girl comes moving towards us. This is my daughter, Edmund Fell says. The girl wears an apron over her dress to protect it from the chemicals. She is almost fourteen, Edmund Fell says—she has her own ambition for photography. She has been assisting me for a year now. Lucie, tell Mr. Martin about the adjustment you have made to the sodium chloride. The name spoken again and again I draw breath. With all due respect, Edmund Fell says, she lives with the namesake of your first Mrs. Martin. Yes, I remember now, I say. A strange earth-colored stone with a face carved into it hangs from a piece of ribbon down from the girl's neck. I ask what it is and she says it's a charm. Your late wife is an influence on my daughter, Edmund Fell interjects. The girl's face colors, but her gaze remains fixed. She's drawn to your late wife's work, Edmund Fell says. You're drawn to the late Mrs. Martin's work, isn't that true, Lucie? It's true, the girl says. What is it you're drawn to? I ask. For a moment she's silent. And then: The way she treats of men and women, she replies. In her photographs the late Mrs. Martin gives us portrait images of those who seem not to be themselves. You mean in the tableaux vivants? I ask. She replies, They are representations of others not themselves. Yes, I say, they are representations but they have a humanity.

Photograph of a woman robed in white, full-face to the camera; her eyes are open wide, but her expression is otherwise tranquil; there' a dark spot at the base of one nostril, above the lip, that can be assumed to be blood.

the way she treats of men and women

to have a humanity

images of men and women

We turn back to the work at hand.

We turn to the negatives. To the bones of the vertebrates. To the geological interest: the cliffs, the rock formations, the structure of the dwellings.

If you are going to print, I must prepare the trays, Lucie Fell says. And then she disappears back into the darkroom.

The passing of time,

a short passing...

The passing of the day.

...when I leave the studio the late day has grown cold, the streets will soon be lit by the gaslights, later the gaslights will be extinguished and the streets will be in darkness except for the light that is visible from the windows.

...the fires left behind.

...the headstone resting in weather. The ground blown with leaves. The purpose of the stone: to remember. Already old. The stone old, dry—no longer bleeding.

... and it's always one story or another story, like the story of the birds told by the Indians—the birds have gathered to decide who should raise the human infant... The hawk has too many enemies. The eagle's nest is perched too high. The woodpecker's nest is too crowded.

...it's the meadowlark who lives on the ground who will raise the child.

...or the story of the old woman who each night swallows the moon so the dead will appear in the meeting lodge.

...in the evening supper with my wife and her father. The doctor is eating, chewing—when he swallows it brings a rise in his throat. He holds his fork in one hand, in the other a piece of biscuit. With the biscuit he pushes shards of lamb onto his fork.

The three of us at the table, the doctor at the head, my wife and I on either side, my wife is preoccupied during supper with the news of Signor Pedanto and the unfortunate accident of his hot air balloon. He had made the ascension from Wind Island, Angeline says, but at Willings Alley the balloon caught a snag, the aerostat struck a flagpole, gas escaped, and the balloon descended rapidly causing injuries to the gentlemen on board. The doctor listens but makes no comment, he remains silent with his mouth closed in the midst of chewing.

My wife touches her glass to mine: *For my husband, she says...may you always be happy.*

And then she takes a small portion of plain cake and pours a little honey over what is left of it.

On the cobblestone outside the window the sound of horses.

I think there's a rainstorm. Do you hear it? The wind and the rain. We might have been soaked.

The light is quickly fading, the streets are cast in gloomy darkness,

The bed made up with white sheets. A quilt.

Pillows.

A murmur of words.

I have her before me.

The oddness of words.

Scatter.

Afterwards we'll sleep.

The oddness of time.

Time and its movement.

...hair unbound.

...visible breath.

Palpable flesh.

Afterwards we'll sleep.

...but importance should not be given to dreams, to that alien landscape, some strange projection of the mind, only of one's mind without a reality of its own, insinuating itself with the suggestion of a real existence and symbolic meaning... and yet at the same time the mysteriousness...

the dream

those little hands that reach for you at night, from the under-corners of the room... the hands of small women... and of children who have died...

expressed as wind... as air moving...as the movement of air...

The memory of a dream when I woke up; I couldn't remember it at first, but then it returned. In the dream I had been listening through a door to the voices of two people talking. They were talking low and I couldn't make out their words; there was only the barely audible sound of their voices, a conversation from which I had been excluded. These sounds, which I knew in the dream were not for me, became like a magnet, pulling me to them with an overwhelming curiosity. Until I couldn't hold myself back and opened the door and burst into the room. It was my father sitting alone.

He said: Be silent!

Be silent and think about these things. It's morning. Another rotation of the earth upon its axis. All that we know that those who came before us didn't know.

It's morning, be silent.

The streets when I walk them.

The morning is quiet.

The spectacle of the soul, of the million of souls.

Led by that which is leading.

Again the daily routine. The entrance door to the building. The odor of chemicals that defines the studio.

The reception room. The operating room. The room outside the darkroom.

...the girl, Lucie Fell, is standing with the print in her hand. It's one of several that I entrusted to her. I have exposed until there was high detail, she says.

...she is timid and talks low. I have to strain to hear her. She says, My father has gone down to the glassmaker to see about the plates for the negatives.

Black paws. The black stains on her hands from the silver nitrate used to sensitize the paper.

She hands me the print and I examine it; it is one of the long views of the canyon; the ruins in the niche are not visible because of the distance and the dark shadows, but the gigantic scale of the rock on all sides is fully represented, the rock structure with its massiveness and strength, neither welcoming nor unwelcoming, displaying only the fact of its great dimension, inimical to human life, disadvantageous to all that is animate, except for that which is animate within the rock itself, or in the fine sand baked hot, or in the wisp of cottonwoods that in themselves look like stone, dwarfed beneath the cliff walls, and also dwarfed are our tents in the foreground, pitched where we made our camp, the tents are so small compared to the scale of the rock they go nearly unseen, and someone will have to point to them before the viewer will be able to see they are there in the photograph.

It is the objective the eye had when taking the photograph. I sense her desire to fully grasp what I'm saying; partly to please me, but more because she has her own interest. The requests will be continuous from Mr. W_____. Over six hundred this month alone, not counting the stereographs.

The paper exposed and then removed from the frame. The girl washes the print the way I have demonstrated. It is my practice to stop the washing exactly at the moment the milkiness disappears and not to wait, as others do, the additional seconds. And then to treat with gold chloride to prevent fading. The print must be agitated continuously, I say. Yes, she says, her father has taught her the same. And agitated also with a gentle motion, I say—it will take a while, no less than five minutes, but usually several minutes more. It requires judgment and is largely determined by the aesthetic objective of the photographer. The assistant, when there is an assistant, must also be acquainted with that objective. Your father will guide you; he's been employed with this kind of printing before. She peers into the fixing bath. I say, now is the time to remove it. The time that will come when all other time has been erased from memory. Or the way time determines reality. Unbridles it. I watch as she removes the print from the bath. And then I examine it. It's a harsh place, I say, but it has beauty too. Edmund Fell returns and calls out the name of his daughter: Lucie.

It's late in the day when I leave the studio.

The wind has started up.

There is a sameness. The early winter wind pushes me as I walk from the studio. Along the same streets, the same signs on the buildings: *Confectioner and Fruit Dealer, E.G. Whitman, Landreth's Garden, Field & Bird Seeds, Tea Warehouse, J. Howell & Company.* I walk to Penn's Landing, and then to the piers.

One of the horse cars on the pier: a carriage drawn by the horses.

I approach the dock stalls. There are others approaching the dock-stalls. But the others give the impression of having business or purpose.

The temperature is cool; the air is damp. The wind has made the water choppy. The boats that are moored rise and fall with the chop of the water.

Gulls are scavenging, some are strutting along the wooden railings, others are circling in the air, they are after scraps from the fishing boats, carp and flounder, dead or half alive, an overflow from the catch that have become loose from the nets. One of the gulls drops something from the air which falls onto a jetty of rocks out in the water a short distance from the pier.

I become aware of a woman in the distance, at the far end of the pier, facing out to the river—she stands close to the edge with her back to me, near to the water; then sensing my presence she turns around. The gray of her clothing gives the impression I'm looking at a shadow. Those who had business here are gone, as though vanished, perhaps their business has engaged them in the freight depots, or in the anterior rooms of the warehouses, the immense grain buildings that line the shore of the docks. The woman's eyes appear to be fixed on me. I wonder what reason she has to be here; alone, so close to the edge of the pier; she might be distraught and intend to step off; or she might simply be standing without reason, just as I am standing without reason; she might be out for a walk, or for air, or simply to watch the water. All the same it's not to be done; it's not ordinary for a woman to be alone here. I think of Angeline; she will be waiting; I've promised to be home for an early supper. I take a step to leave but stop, still struck by the woman. She appears in distress. I start to take a step towards her and again stop, afraid I'll alarm her. It comes into my mind that she's an apparition, like those that once used to come of Lucie; they were products of my mind, though they've not come for a long time. An apparition. Perhaps the woman is an apparition. A ghost. The thought that the woman is a ghost strikes me as ludicrous the moment I think it. Yet, I've thought it; even now whispered it, and said aloud the name Lucie. It's been thirteen years since she died; more than ten since I married Angeline. I feel a constriction of the lungs, the experience of tightening. I must bring it to a halt or it will overcome me completely. The woman looks nothing like my late wife. Her eyes remain fixed on me. I have the impression she's asking for help. I call out to the her: Do you require assistance? She remains silent, but shakes her head no. I shall go back then, I say. I shout it to be certain she hears me. She makes no reply, but remains as she is, as though waiting for me to leave.

Thrown to the hounds...

I take my watch from my pocket...

...thrown to the hounds like the hounds in my father's stories. Hell-bound hounds who make their passage through the air and then appear as if out of nowhere in front of their prey. They will chase you down, my father said. You can't see them, but you will know they are there by the sound of their baying.

I would have walked farther, longer. I pass through and dust rises. In clouds as though it were smoke.

In the land I've just come from my eyes were forced shut by dust.

Made wet by rain. It has started to rain.

The smell of burnt air, even in the rain, from the recent fire at the Tatterstol stables.

A solitary reflection on the nature of myself, out of the ordinary and strange, and then the suggestion of something else, something irretrievable except as shadow, and the fleeting sense of a presence, only in my mind, attesting to the uncharacteristic nature of my mind, the idea of a normal life, of what it might consist, the way it might be lived.

What is it?
I've asked myself all day.
What is it?

Were you walking?
Yes, walking.
For how long?
I don't know, perhaps an hour, or maybe two.

I've returned from the empty land, the spare beauty, the moon that hangs over the basin of the land, the hollow in the earth no longer filled by an ocean.

The civilized self and then the other.

The wolves of the canyons left behind.

And that which was not intended to be spoken.

The pathetic imagining.

...*my good wishes for your health.*

The malevolence of ghosts and angels.

Or else that expression the ladies use: *She is over the moon with happiness.*

I walk past the row houses with their brick fronts, stretching one after the other.

Trees line the streets. They might be chestnut trees.

There had been that conversation I had earlier about the uses of photography: the games played with Tintype, dressing up for the camera as though for the stage, the role of fantasy, or the preservation of what is real as it exists now in life; and I made the comment that my objective is the preservation of something more than the archive assignments, rather preservation of a wilderness apart, to treat the aesthetic of a wilderness apart.

The sky is gray. The wind has caused a drop in temperature.

May I see the photograph?

The darkness and flames, the art of the glass blowers, the darkness of the glass pits, where the glass is blown.

No false moves. An inner word of caution. But caution why? What reason is there for caution? What to be cautious about? Nonetheless a good practice. Always to be cautious. No false moves, which are a form of recklessness. To be reckless: to be careless; to be irresponsible; to exercise a lack of proper caution. The day is done. The light is fading in the sky. Returning home. My footsteps on the sidewalk. The short walk home. Angeline will be waiting. I'm on time if I hurry. For memory's sake—what is remembered? What is best forgotten?

There is first a hush and then the storyteller speaks.

Let me hear it, tell it to me before sleep, let me place it with the others, with the hands of my imagination.

At home Angeline is reading, waiting, she's lit a fire in all the rooms, she's concerned her father is still at work at the hospital and now the weather has turned cold, he'll be chilled when he arrives, the walk is a long one and she knows he will not take a carriage, she'll make tea, we'll sit near the fire, forgive her please if she seems faraway, she's been reading "Elsie Venner," the tea will be ready soon, it's a new black Assam, she wishes her father would stop working at the hospital, he should see only his private patients because the work at the hospital is too strenuous, he's been looking tired, his skin is turning gray, she's been so worried, and then she tells me she visited with her friend Elsa Roberts in the afternoon. They played a game of Chinese Checkers on Elsa's new game board, the pieces are marble, they were beautiful to play with, the winner is the first to move all ten pieces into the opposite triangle. She lowers her voice, last night she had a dream, she was living in a house situated on the water like the immense barn-like ship-houses along Front Street, only in her dream it was not a house for ships, but for people, and she lived there, it was uncertain if I lived there too, or for that matter her father, we were not in the dream, she was alone, and the house was on the water, and the water was so close that when she stood at the window she could reach down and touch it. It was not the ocean, it was a river, our Delaware, or maybe the Schuylkill, though probably the Delaware and not the Schuylkill because the Schuylkill is farther away, and she can't help thinking now it might be a good thing to live by the river and see the water. She might have a dog, it would be a family dog, like the dogs I had when I was a child, although I had several and she would want only one, and she would go walking along the shoreline accompanied by her dog. In her dream the water lapped up against the outside wall of the house, she could see the waste from the ships, so it couldn't have been the Schuylkill, there are no ships on the Schuylkill and the water is clean. There was a lighthouse in the dream, it was wakeful and lovely, and a tree called Listen's Tree, haggard and old and riven by storms, it was one of our Delaware oaks and marked the half-way point between the river and the ocean, and there is no question now the river was the Delaware because from the window she could see Smith and Windmill Islands.

She says she tasted salt in her mouth and had the sense of the river entering the sea. She felt the presence of the river and she couldn't stop thinking about her dream. She woke up remembering it; she remembered it all through the day.

But now she's fussing because her father has come home and he's wet as she said he would be and the wind has exhausted him on his walk home from the hospital. She brings him a brandy to brace him, and a tray with hazelnuts and almonds because the fat in the nuts will prevent him from catching a cold, and there will be a hot soup at the start of supper, which makes her think of the sea turtle soup she had when we visited New York, sea turtles that were served in their own shells. You can have that here in Philadelphia as well, her father says. Yes, she replies, and oysters there as well as here in the oyster saloons, though I think we have more here and fresher too. But her father has left the subject of oysters and is complaining about the recent meteor showers that failed—he says that according to Mr. Daniel Kirkwood in the Philadelphia Ledger there will not be others in such number until the close of the century. I won't be here to see them then, he says—but perhaps you'll remember to look at them for me, Angeline. My wife cries out, Father!—and then she tells us the Benners have just set sail for Europe. They will spend all of their time in Italy looking at churches and paintings and all the other old things, it's the wrong season, but they wanted to be in Venice in winter, how quickly the time goes, it's almost the holidays.

The strangeness of not sleeping; that is of not being able to fall sleep. The night. A wife in the bed. The necessity of removing myself from the bed quietly so as not to wake her, her breath as though stopped, imperceptible, but she is breathing: a light feathery breath that is noiseless, with my face close to hers can I feel it. The house is set for sleep, but I'm not sleeping. All animation has given way to absence, or perhaps to the presence of a different kind of life, one suited to stillness and silence. This is the house of Angeline's childhood, her girlhood, her young womanhood. I've lived here ten years, but I don't regard it as mine. It belongs to her and her father, and now in the night I feel like I'm an intruder in its rooms. My eyes adjust to the dark like an animal's eyes. I climb the one step up to the dining room. It's only a single step, but it sets the room off by itself. On the wall there hangs a painting of the wharves. I think of the woman who stood on the pier. Do you require assistance? I shall go back then. The oily blackness of the water. Gazing across the two islands in view: Smith and Windmill Islands. And then the sensation someone else is in the room. Perhaps the night's spirit. But the ghosts here are strangers. I never knew them in life. I stand at the front window. The street is empty. The moon is full, or almost full. I can't see it, but I can see its reflected light. The room is cold. The furnace is off. There's only cold air coming up through the floor slats. And an unlit fire in the fireplace. And the empty wing-back chairs sitting in their corners. Today another letter arrived from Mr. W_____ with a large order for prints. The prints are to be delivered to the Congress and the Appropriations Board whose opinions make a difference. The work of the studio will remain for some time turned over to printing.

Barely the moment that no longer exists. The nights I sat there with my back against the canyon wall. The fire in front of me. The dwellings empty in the niche above. The braying of the mules. And then the silence. The memory pressed into the earth of those who had come before us. But look, my hands have started shaking. I try to stop them from shaking. To conceal them from myself. This morning at the bank on Arch Street the condition flared again and my hands became unpredictable in the middle of the money transaction. Now I turn back to the window and the light of the moon; its pale light falls like ash on the cobblestone. Again I sense a presence. I turn and see a figure on the stairs. The figure stands mid-way down on the narrow staircase. For a moment it's unclear to me just what it is. And then: William, Angeline says. I realize the figure is my wife. It's all right, I say, I couldn't sleep. I'm coming up now.

I'll come up now. I'm coming up now. My wife remains where she is on the stairs until I reach her. It's too cold down there, she says, you are frozen, she turns and climbs and I follow. I'll cover you with blankets, she says. She keeps her voice low. She is cold too. Her body is shivering.

221

You are cold too, I say to my wife. Your body is shivering.

And a few minutes later she has piled blankets on the bed, and I am underneath the blankets and she is lying next to me and there is warmth filling the space beneath the blankets, our bodies are warming, she has turned on her side, and I can feel the warmth of her breath as she begins speaking, and she keeps her voice low, not all the way to a whisper but low, and she speaks as though telling a story to soothe me to sleep, and our bodies are touching, and I can feel her warm breath, and her arm that she has brought across my chest so that she can hold on to me. Not only did they play Chinese Checkers today when she visited with her friend Elsa Roberts, but she saw her friend's birds, canaries kept in cages, there are so many of them they have to be kept in several cages, most of the birds are bright yellow, but some of them have streaks of orange, and they were all singing, it was extraordinary to hear it, this concert of birds, and to see them jumping from perch to perch in their cages. Elsa is troubled that the colder weather is here, it has only begun and will soon be much colder and the birds are delicate, last year she lost several, it's a hard climate to keep them but she cannot bear to part with them; in New Orleans, where she is from, there was not this difficulty in keeping birds, here she must take all kinds of precautions, but it gives her such happiness and her husband is not bothered by it. Her husband is a dentist, his name is David Roberts, his office is on Spruce Street below Fourth, he opened his office there when they came up from New Orleans. And speaking of New Orleans isn't that where Edmund Fell is from? Then my wife lowers her voice: Is his daughter a big help with the printing?—and then not waiting for my answer she says she would like to give a party for her father's birthday, she's been giving it much thought, she's worried he continues to work too hard and insists each day on walking back and forth to the hospital. But it's such a quiet hour now, she says—the mind can move freely when it's so quiet...

...the mind can move freely when it's so quiet and she remembers that there's something else she wants to tell me. It's about a person and a warning. A warning or a strong presentiment that when a certain moment comes,

222

some appointed time far in the future, an evil fate will befall that person. Perhaps an illness or an accident, perhaps even death. But the time is not here and the moment far off in the mind, and there seems always time before the time that will come. But it's never forgotten, it's something that always looms in the mind. Then at last the day arrives. The moment comes and nothing happens. Nothing that was feared and dreaded. The person is still alive. Unharmed. Not only alive and unharmed, but something agreeable is brought by the moment. So you see, she says, and she gives it significance with her tone, the time that has passed has not brought the malevolent thing that was always imagined.

She asks if I'm sleeping, I tell her I'm not. If you're sleeping, she says... but then she doesn't complete her thought... I was so unhappy when you were away , she says instead, and now you're back and here beside me and there's no need for me to think of anything else. But there's so much work for you to do, all the prints to be made, it's good you have extra help in the studio— though the girl is young, she's only fourteen, but still it's good that she can be of help. Your body is warmer now, she says. It's always the wind that makes everything cold. I prepared the windows against the wind, they are closed tight and covered by the fabric of the draperies. Today after visiting Elsa Roberts, I stopped by to see your mother and your aunt. Your mother predicted a long and bitter cold winter. I told her I already felt it, that the wind had gone right through me on my way over. And now I've kept the fire burning low so we'll have some warmth. I feel the hours going by. I can't see your face. I can't tell if you're awake or sleeping. It's all right if you are sleeping. I waited for you to return and now you are here, within reach and close to me again. I don't want to fall asleep, I don't want, for those few hours, to relinquish the presence of you. All the time you were gone I imagined your return, as if imagining it would hasten it, but nothing made the hours move faster. It was time that had to be endured. And it doesn't matter now that you've been back for many weeks, that weeks will turn to months, that winter will come and the trees will give up their leaves, that their branches will be naked unless covered with snow; and it doesn't matter either that it was not the first time in our marriage that work called you away. It has called you away many times and I should be accustomed to it, but I shall never become accustomed to it, and each time you leave you say you're not gone, that you're still with me. I go outside and stand under the sky to feel the truth of what you've said. I can feel you best when I'm under the sky. And each time you return you say you were never gone from me at all. But the fire's still burning low now, the chill is gone. I want to tell you about Elsa's new baby. Though I know it's true you don't care much for the subject of babies. He's only a few days old, his head is a perfect shape, his eyes when he opens them are intensely dark in his small face, focusing mostly at random, but occasionally, it seems, fixing on his mother's face and staring. He's a new soul come into the world. Elsa used the phrase 'my son' and it was evident that she enjoyed using it, though what she said was a lament. She said: My son doesn't look like me. I said it was too soon to tell, his features were still too new in his face. When I saw your aunt today I mentioned Elsa's baby and she said that each soul is an old one returned—that it is not many souls and many lives, but one single, indivisible life seeking its own perfection. I told your aunt I was not certain I understood; it seemed a lofty thought; and if it is true, then who are we really? Your aunt didn't answer. But then when she spoke she talked about the sounds that can be heard within one's own body. They can be heard by using an exercise practiced in India. She's enamored with India. And with her new friends. Especially the Russian woman. She said the Russian woman's ideas have been brought from India. Your aunt would like to go there. She feels too old now, but all the same she would still like to go. And then she told me about the discipline of the mind practiced there which enables you to hear the sounds inside the body. The ears are closed with the hands, and the eyes are also closed, and a certain meditation is employed, and then the body's sounds surface to be heard, and they're like all the earth's sounds, like the ocean's roar, or like the humming of bees...

Angeline stops talking and I hear water hitting against the window. It's raining. The smell of pine. And the late fall rain. And I hear a voice say: Oh, my child, have you been weeping all night long? The smell of the bedroom. The wrinkled sheets. How long have you been walking? A bird will fly to you. They say it's impossible to die in your dreams.

In my mind the image of a woman. From an image captured on a photograph. The photograph's not one of mine. It's something from the doctor's library: a photographic medical journal containing prints of patients with disease. The photograph is of a young woman in a suspension device designed to treat her curvature of the spine. She is seen from the rear, naked from above her hips, her arms are pulled up above her head and tied to a pole at the top of the device to stretch her back. She wears only her underskirts and they hang loosely from her hips. There is a plaster of Paris bandage around the middle of her back. But above the bandage her naked flesh is seen only from the rear, ripples on her skin where her arms meet her shoulders, ripples from the arms pulled taut and raised. Her hair is dark and gathered in a net. Except for her dark hair, she is very white and the photograph gives an unnatural impression of whiteness.

The rest of the night without sleep.

The shutters banging.

A bird will fly to you.

Were you weeping?

Time placing time.

Don't forget silence.

Use language fairly.

Wind against the windows.

And then shadows in the rising morning light.

Their movement is noiseless, thin; buoyant and easy; undemanding and agile; there is nothing abrupt, nothing that would break them apart.

The bedroom window partly open, a shaft of morning sunlight falling on white sheets.

I put myself in order for the day.

The sense of picking up a thread

and following it

the day begins like all the rest

sun, air, the approaching cold that's not yet arrived

earth, streets, the horse-drawn carriages, the beaten beasts

I watch myself walking as though it's not myself walking
as though it's an another self walking

and the apparition of a skull comes back from memory

rising on the surface of the negative as I developed the photograph

it's from the Casa Blanca ruins

something dug from dirt, from ruins, along the jaw bone and the hollow cavities

sunlight on the rock

black shadows in the cavities

the memory of something from the Indians

ashes in the eyes

fires and cold weather

there's been nothing here in Philadelphia this season but fires and cold weather

twenty-eight horses died trapped in their stalls

ashes thrown into the eyes

but now I've arrived at the studio

where there's sunlight on the cobblestone in front of the studio

Inside, the girl is preparing the darkroom. The Casa Blanca ruins rising on the photograph. I'll use an acetate, I say. She says the skull frightened her when she first saw it on the negative.

The time that has passed, that is passing, minutes, parts of an hour, an hour, more than an hour.

The girl approaches me with a question about the first Mrs. Martin: She says, My father told me the first Mrs. Martin made many photographs, but here in the studio there are only these few—I was wondering if I might be permitted to see some of the others?

The memory of her voice.

My late wife's voice as it was then:

Shall we have tea; is it time for lunch; let me see, oh, let me help you; I have read many pages of Lady Mortley today; the sky all gold today; as if to remind me...

...remember, it was early winter then just as it's early winter now. The trees were bare; there had been snow; the ponderous movement of the others through the house: your mother and your aunt; the doctor who was attending; the nurse who had been hired... it was such a short winter... what was flesh is gone...now there's only the spirit...

And then there is silence

and a vision of black.

A vision of black about a man who has no feet. The man is myself and I can't feel my feet. I say to my late wife: I can't marry you if I lose my feet. And then the figure of the doctor as he makes his pronouncement: They've turned black; I can't save your feet. Hacking away at my bones until they've been split off from my body.

Vision or memory? Words that let go from my mind.

Where do they come from? What are they?

Stalking like memory.

On the way home from the studio, I stop at my mother's house and go up to the apartment of rooms where I've left the boxes containing Lucie's photographs.

The rooms are dimly lit; I bring up the light on the gaslamp. I'm standing in what used to be Lucie Beale Martin's sitting room. Strange when I think of it that way, with distance and formality: my wife, the late Lucie Beale Martin: I had ordered the boxes with her photographs to be brought back into this room and placed on the floor. Through the open door, I see the red walls of the bedroom; the bed; the dark wooden planks of the floor; beyond the bedroom, the room that used to be my study.

Who cleans these rooms, I ask when my mother comes up to look in on me. My mother replies, They are cleaned by the same person who cleans all the rooms.

No one disturbs anything, my mother says, the rooms are only cleaned.

My mother standing in the gaslight.

From the window I can see the garden.

If the boxes were moved at all, it was only to clean the dust away, or to sweep behind them, my mother says.
I tell her it is all right. I'll look through them now.
Shall I bring you anything? my mother asks.
No, I say. Nothing.

I'm aware of my hand touching the cover of the box, of my hand moving the box away from the wall,

I remove the old daguerreotypes from the boxes. I find they've turned black. At first my confusion. The blemishes of jet black against the lighter black of what might be a dark sky on the first one. Nothing but black extending out from one side to the other of the frame of all her daguerreotypes. She sometimes worked in daguerreotype although it had already become outdated. Black so that nothing can be seen. The sheets of silver brazed to the copper have tarnished. The images are obscured.

In the other boxes I find that her albumen prints made from wetplates are intact. A portrait of a woman and her child, the color has been applied, a rose tint to the cheeks and to the backs of the hands, and a hint of blue to the eyes, and to the boy's jacket, the fingers of the mother are being held by the boy with both his hands.

The digressions of memory. The interiors of thought. What has been or what will be. Or what remains to be overcome. Like some last barrier to overcome, preventing the entry of spirit into flesh. Now there is no sound, only silence, and the sense of being suspended in the silence; suspended in the empty space of what has been forgotten; and what is remembered is a thin thing, worn away and eaten by time; or else the memories that come unbidden, or unrelated to the rest: a flock of migratory birds sitting in a circle on the ice on the river; and all that's in the midst of life, the rusted iron benches and old pieces of sculpture, or the chalk-white statues made from plaster casts; or the lives of the men and women who came to the studio so that my late wife could make their likeness for the family albums.

A corridor of thought.

And sitting before me are the darkened images on the metal plates.

I separate the tarnished plates and place them in a separate box to bring to the studio where I can clean them. It uses cyanide to clean them; the cyanide will bring them up new, one-by-one, as they were when they were made.

And then I leave the rooms to go home, home again to my house, to the house I have now with Angeline and her father; I walk by way of the wharves again, I don't think it will rain; it will continue to be damp, but it won't rain; and the gulls are on the wharves as they always are, despite the fact it's getting cold. Where is my mind now? What is it fixed on? Ideas that come when staring into the water. The water looks dirty, soon it will be covered by ice, and I have the idea that I'm going to see someone rising up in the water,

231

someone coming to greet me, or only a body perhaps, perhaps the body of the woman I had seen standing on the pier; and it will be her face coming up to the surface, pressed against the surface of the water, and she'll speak... *I'm still here... the water is cold... lift me out... lift me out so I can be warm...*

Fog covers the wharves.

The day is finished.

It's night.

It's night and I'm home and I can see my reflection on the bedroom window.

I reach over and lower the gaslight.

Cats are bawling in the yard below.

My wife's breath on my neck, she has turned onto her side, her body near mine.

I bring her body on top of mine.

...a bird of night, the sound of it's wing-beat, a measure of violence.

I feel my wife timid, we've been married a long time, there's nothing to hide, in a while I groan as she slides down from my body.

The intake of breath.

In the dark

In the night.

And the sleep that will follow.

The girl greets me when I enter the studio in the morning. It's been too dark for new portraits, she says, but my father and I have been making prints for your albums. We're making good progress. I've been sensitizing the paper with silver nitrate. Would you like to see the prints now? My father's in the darkroom. I'll let him know you're here. As she talks, I'm still holding the box in my arms that contains my late wife's tarnished daguerreotypes. The girl is staring at the box, then she realizes she is staring and looks away.

> These have tarnished, I say.
> I'll clear the darkroom, the girl says.
> It doesn't need the darkroom, I say.
> May I assist you? she asks.
> No, it's not safe. I'll be using potassium cyanide to clean them.

I pour the cyanide solution over the plate and when the tarnish is removed the image is revealed. The subject is a man standing next to his collection of butterflies. The inscription reads: *And I am in the presence again of the one whose arrival I've been awaiting.* One-by-one the other images and their inscriptions appear: *This is the place I used to live... We may be consumed by what is strange and far away... The woman who has made her body tell a lie...*

Time places time. Moves it along. Protects the bodies of our dead. Leaves us the language of the faces in the photographs. The faces are frozen as though it was stone that had been photographed. Or marble with its singular hardness. They stare back until the gaze is averted or the eyes are closed. *There is no need to sleep, the voice says, stare at the faces in the photographs...It takes great compassion to photograph the dead... in the midst of all the rest... images like reality but not reality... memento mori...*

Thoughts move me along, the images brought back, as though it's the lives in the photographs brought back.

...the dead brought back.

Would that please the dead? To be brought back?

...but now the work at hand. the girl stands before me holding the photographs.

...photographs of the canyons and the cliff walls.

...in the dark between cliff walls of rock while underfoot the coarse dirt of the floor, rock which has been pulverized into dirt, and the sky here with its greater expanse, the waste and the wild, at the edge of the rock cliff, and where down below is the floor of the canyon, and the sky is awash in a colorlessness of night, looking out from the cliff rock, there can be no misstep, the mountainous rock and the colorless sky.

...and then the day's work is over and I go home to Angeline and the night and the grand day that's approaching: the day of the Indians.

It's called Solitude, Angeline says, this small tract of land that leads to the ravine. It's the next day, almost the day when I'll photograph the Indians, and we're at Fairmount Park. The name of the ravine is Sweet Brier, Angeline says, it's named after the mansion. There was a tour brought us here during the time you were gone. Now I'll be your tour guide. I can tell you everything we were told: There's a rustic bridge to cross a short distance from here, and then the river road and another rustic bridge; and from on top of that bridge you have a broad view of the Schuylkill. It's still early in the day, William, we still have time to walk a while; it seems a nice way to prepare for tomorrow and the Indians. When Angeline stops talking, I remain quiet in thought, though I admit there's no specific thought. The sky is for the most part clear. The carriage that brought us is waiting a short distance off. The driver had cautioned as we were getting out that the ground was damp and the air brisk. But we like brisk air, Angeline had said. And then we had walked to where we are now. We continue to walk, moving even farther away from the carriage. They should have arranged for the Indians to come here to Fairmount Park so they might feel at home, Angeline says. The Indians wouldn't feel at home here, I say, they are from a region of desert and rock. Their landscape is not like here. I know, she says—I know from your photographs. And then she says she hopes it won't rain. What a disappointment it will be if it rains. She says she wants to see the Indians walking in the parade though she knows it won't be the way that I have seen them. But it will be something all the same, she says. It will let her see for herself a little of what I have seen.

The day is moving so slowly, Angeline says—why does time always move slowly when one is waiting for something?

She tells me about a child she had once seen: a boy wearing spectacles with a very thick glass, and a device in one of his ears to permit hearing. She said she caught sight of his eyes at the periphery, where she could see them without distortion of the glass.

...she complains it is cold, getting colder.

...she says, The boy had lovely eyes.

...and then it is night.

...the way the night passes.

...and finally the frenzy of morning.

...it's the day of the Indians.

A delegation of Indians from the Black Hills of the West will be paraded across Market Street before they travel on to Washington in an attempt to reach an agreement with our president about their land.

As we approach South Eighth Street on our way—where we will stop to pick up my mother and my aunt—we see a man carrying balloons for the parade. The balloons are large and there are many; half are red and half are white. The wind has started up and the balloons become unwieldy, at moments taking the man off balance.

Rock rising into the sky.

We know the bird is not a real bird.

The eagle soaring. Rock rising into the sky higher than the eagle.

And men becoming shadows in the parade, crossing rock-pavement, walking on the cobblestone of Market Street, small brush trees at the bottom of the canyon, rock shadow, nothing but a frame of mind for it, something catches the spirit and for a minute everything stops, and then the Indians resume their walking, tied to cottonwood, the sun on the horses, birds that fly into the canyon, in another season, cassiope flowers fragrant shaped like bells, and the impression of a door opening, the Indians are walking, they are the great chiefs walking, a numinous community, birds, animals, rocks, humans, the offspring of a falling star, the secret name, the name that is known only by the Indian, he has stood before his heart, or stood with his heart in front of him, for the span of a lifetime, during the movement of a lifetime, the light of the movement from one place to the next, his words are reaching me with intimation in a sing-song, he is Red Cloud walking, Chief of the Oglala Sioux,

walking as though sleepwalking

or standing naked in mud

he moves to come forward, but then sinks into the mud

first lightening and then thunder, unaccompanied by rain

walking as though sleepwalking

unaccompanied by rain

the fire torches have been lit, the men start barking like dogs, distorting their faces.

the old woman vomits up the moon

searching for the dew

the Grey One of the Gahe

shadows at the north end

between north and east

rattles

they are the imperial chiefs of the tribes who are walking

dancers uncoiling in the pithouse

in the summer house

walking with their eyes closed

in trance-light

they are the chiefs of the tribes

inexorably bound

in vision-light

inexorably bound

they are matter and spirit walking

they are the chiefs of the tribes

shadows at the north end

they are matter and spirit walking.

The Journey Out will be the title of the first plate.

Mr. W_____ has arranged for the chiefs to be photographed in the studio directly after the parade before they continue on to Washington. There are staged depictions of their land on a studio backdrop. The backdrop is incongruous to reality—a setting that bears no resemblance to the Black Hills. Mr. W_____ has laid out his intentions: the photographs are to appeal to the imagination; they are to stir and to fascinate; to arouse curiosity and at the same time to satisfy it; satisfaction is to be taken from the idea that one is glimpsing a race of men who are not as we are.

I lift the cover from the lens and Chief Spotted Tail shifts his gaze to the right. That's the way it will come out on the photograph, with Spotted Tail's eyes in full slant to the right. Chief Red Cloud looks down, his eyes half-closed, as I expose the plate. When I bring the exposed plate into the dark-room to develop it, Lucie Fell has everything ready. Her father will in the meanwhile pose the Indians for their next photograph.

Waiting in the reception room are Angeline, my mother and my aunt, along with Angeline's father and Mr. W____, and some acquaintances of Mr. W____, invited to see the Indians. Their headdresses are magnificent, I heard my mother say when I went out there a while ago—and then my mother said to me: Imagine, all those years ago. And here things stop, my aunt was saying to Mr. W____; my aunt had him in her grasp, plying him with her ideas, Mr. W____ that most pragmatic of men.

Now as I'm about to leave the darkroom, the girl, Lucie Fell, tells me: I looked out and saw them. I think one of them saw me too.

How would he have seen you? I ask.

Through the crack in the door, she replies. I had it open a little so I could see while you made the likeness. One of the Indians turned his eyes towards the door and he saw me.

It's not of any consequence if he saw you, I say.

It made me feel strange, she says; his eyes were gazing at my eyes, as though he had expected to see me; I felt he was waiting for something from me with that gaze.

You aren't supposed to keep the door open, I say.

It was only a little and only for a few seconds, she says.

We'll be finished soon, I say. Are you able to prepare another plate?

Yes.

And when you've finished come out from the darkroom away from the chemicals.

My father says it's all right for just this once, she protests.

Nonetheless, they are not good for you; in a few minutes your father will fetch you and the plate.

We have stood the Indians up against the backdrop. They regard the camera's lens as a living eye. They're wrapped in dark blankets. Chief Long Horn has covered part of his face with his blanket. And then the sound of laughter from the other room and voices suddenly loud in conversation. The Indians turn their heads in that direction. They are the voices of those waiting who wish to honor you, I say to the Indians.

He was killed by a nail that went into his foot, I hear my aunt saying when I go into the reception room to see about the noise—he didn't die immediately, but it went untreated. When my aunt sees me, she asks, William, is it time to meet our exotic guests?

They will be coming out soon, I tell her, and I will thank you to talk quietly.

Angeline comes forward and takes my arm. My mother is standing with Angeline's father.

Is it going well, Angeline asks me?

Yes, very well, I reply.

I would like to help you, she says.

You are always a help, I say.

I mean more directly with your work, she says.

But that would be impractical, I say, you have no interest in the darkroom, and you've told me you find the chemicals foul.

Still, I would like to help, she says—are they really coming out soon?

Yes, soon, I reply.

Before I can leave, my aunt takes me aside and asks, Will the Fell girl be coming out with them?

I don't know, I say, she's not easy around people.

We have stood the Indians up, put them on their feet so to speak, so to speak arranged them for the photograph. They're wrapped in the dark blankets of winter. On their heads are the headdresses for the hunt: the headdresses are small with only a few feathers; a few more feathers are held lightly in the fingers of one of the chiefs. Edmund Fell steps away after making a final adjustment and joins me next to the camera. The light is changing; it will require a longer exposure. A longer exposure and the need to hasten. Empty shells of birds arranged in a corner, sawdust and straw, it's a spirit of the forest who can confuse you, or give you the power to heal, or make you ill. Baths that are taken by rubbing the body with grasses known to bring visions, inside skin and feathers, the wings slightly lifted as if about to take flight. And everything is silent now, the silence of taking the photograph. And the great Chief Red Cloud follows my hand to the lens as I lift the cover of the lens for the exposure. All movement has stopped and what is posed now will remain. And I have it in my mind, as I've had it there before, that the Indians may be right about the photographs—that they capture the spirit and once the spirit has been captured it cannot be taken back. There are the three chiefs in front of the camera, their breathing arrested, their images will soon be fixed upon the photograph. And the preposterous backdrop becomes something *other* than what it is, hinting now at being a real wilderness, and in front of that wilderness the strange compliance of these chiefs of the tribes, and through all the duration of the exposure I can feel the gaze of Chief Red Cloud, just as Lucie Fell described it, and I'm certain it was Chief Red Cloud she was describing when she said an Indian had looked at her; Red Cloud, Chief of the Oglala Sioux. And his gaze is spacious and seems to encompass the entire room. The dark silence of his eyes, the noise from the street, the sound of a street-song, someone singing and playing an accordion, and the incongruous song is coming from the street and rising into the studio. Edmund Fell has removed the cover from the lens. We are in that moment of the process when the subject must remain still, and then in a moment release from the pose. That's very good, I say, and then I say, There will be one last photograph. I hand the sketch of the pose to Edmund Fell, and I walk away to stretch my body before developing the plate. My eyes go to the albumen print hanging on the wall outside the darkroom. I go over to look at it while Edmund Fell arranges the Indians for the last photograph. It's hanging above the work table that Edmund Fell's daughter uses. It's an albumen print made by my late wife, one of her wet plates. I had brought it to the studio for Lucie Fell to see when I brought the daguerreotypes. It was one of my late wife's experiments, morbid and beautiful, a dead bird trapped between the pane of a window and the window's partly open shutters, and impossible to tell if it's a crow or a starling, the way the body's pressed behind the wood. Crow or starling? The words are in my mind, that's what I'm thinking: crow or starling, or a bird of fate. The words are on my tongue, but they remain unspoken: a bird of fate. And just then the silence is shattered by sound: the sound of a crash and glass breaking in the darkroom and then the screaming of Lucie Fell. I run into the darkroom and in seconds I'm screaming too. For water, bring water. The water is brought by Edmund Fell. And he is first frozen and then on his knees next to his daughter. She had lost hold of the plate and dropped it into the silver nitrate; some of the chemical splashed into her eyes. But she is now morbidly quiet as her father carries her out of the darkroom into the outer room where we had been photographing the Indians. The chiefs of the tribes are watching. And my family and the others who had been waiting have now run into the room. Doctor Stille is at the girl's side. It was my fault, she says. The dark discoloration around her eyes is almost immediate, and on other parts of her face, too, in a few other places where the liquid has made contact. It was my fault, she says again. But now Doctor Stille has been handed his bag by Angeline and takes the tincture of ether out from inside; he pours it onto a white cloth and then puts it near to her mouth and nose so that she can breathe it. She becomes silent almost instantly under the effect of the ether. And for a few minutes she remains silent. But then she makes small sounds, and speaks some words as if in a delirium. She says that she would like to open her eyes, that she cannot open her eyes; that she feels nothing, but that she's certain they are burned. The doctor has said to bring a carriage, quickly; she must be taken to the hospital; there is a young doctor there who has made the eyes his specialty and he must treat her. And again soft cries from the girl through the ether, and I'm watching Edmund Fell with his child, and at that moment she seems to me, as she has seemed at times before, to be the child who perhaps might have been mine; who except for misfortune might have been Lucie's and mine. And I know that she has never been more a child than she is at this moment; though it is also true, and I know it, that she will never be a child again. And it is as though I have breathed the ether too and I am led into my own darkness. It is as though the ether has been administered to me.

7

Philadelphia, Pennsylvania, July 27, 1898

[It's here, but I don't have it.]

Today (Lucie Fell)

I give a description of a man who has been robbed. I still see his face as it appeared on the negative plate and then on the print. I was in the darkroom. I remember everything about the darkroom: its narrowness and its shelves, the corked glass containers, the window at one end of the room that was covered to block the light. There were shelves in front of me and shelves behind me. All the chemicals we needed for the photographs were held in the glass containers. I mixed only certain of the chemicals, as taught to me by my father, Edmund Fell, and by Mr. Martin. Mr. Martin said photographers must also be chemists. There was a table in the center of the room. The room was rectangular shaped and so was the table. The table came almost all the way to the shelves on both sides with only a small amount of space for me to stand, or for my father, or Mr. Martin to stand. There was a tray on the table that took up the space of almost the entire surface. It was filled with the chemicals for developing or printing. There was another table, much smaller, beneath the window where the prints were washed and fixed. You may think it disturbs me to think of it now, but it does not disturb me. I always loved the darkroom; I felt of use there.

There were times after the negative had been laid over the albumen paper and exposed to light to develop the print when I wanted to pull it away before it was finished. I wanted to see it as it was at that moment and to fix it there that way because at that moment it was something other than the thing itself.

When we worked on the prints from the famous W___ Survey, Mr. Martin had no tolerance for anything except that the work be carried out to his specification. I wished always to please him and to show him I could do excellent work. I believe I accomplished that. He often told me I had a talent for it. I was young then, only fourteen.

But I have set out to describe a man who has been robbed. I feel pity for him because I have been robbed too. I will describe his face. The first photograph Mr. Martin took of the Indian was a close view of his face. It made me think of some of the portraits taken by the late Mrs. Martin, Mr. Martin's first wife, Lucie Beale Martin. I thought I saw her influence present in Mr. Martin's work, in the way he represented portrait images apart from his land-scapes, the documentation produced from the Surveys. I never mentioned it, of course. I knew that he would not want to hear it. But the late Mrs. Martin's influence was without a doubt there. It was as though Mr. Martin borrowed Lucie Martin's eyes whenever he took a portrait. I wish I could borrow them now. Even for only an hour. But I know full well that is impossible.

My father was Mr. and Mrs. Martin's assistant in the studio before Lucie Martin died, and when I was born I was her namesake.

The Indian was old. He was one of the chiefs and everyone said it was remarkable he had been able to travel so far—all the way from the Black Hills in the region of the West known as the Unorganized Territories—with the other chiefs to talk to our President in Washington about keeping their land. Mr. Grant was our president then.

The Indian's eyes were closed and his head was tilted slightly down. I thought at first it was a mistake on the negative that his eyes were closed, but when the print was developed, I realized Mr. Martin intended it. The headdress had been removed and without it the Indian's hair hung straight down. His hair was long and it reached to his shoulders. I saw it was gray when I opened the door and looked outside the darkroom. I remember being surprised that Indians have hair that can turn gray.

That was a full ten years ago. From the first I was attentive to Mr. Martin. The illumination on the Indian's face was in shadow at the nose and the cheekbones. The nose was shaped like the beak of an eagle. Deep lines of age were visible on his face. Similar to the lines of age I've felt on Mr. Martin's aunt's face. Since the accident when I came to live here, I've considered her my aunt too. Her face and the Indian's were both deeply lined with age. I realize that a man who has been robbed looks much the same as anyone else. He was the same Indian I had seen through the open door of the darkroom. He had seen me too. I mentioned that to Mr. Martin. The Indian was in full headdress with feathers. Mr. Martin told me that they were eagle's feathers. A metal band sat across his forehead. Pieces of animal skins hung down from the headdress. When I came out of the darkroom, I moved a little distance into the room so that I could see the Indian plainly. I could see the other Indians too, and my father who was changing the plates, and Mr. Martin who was arranging the placement of the Indians for the photograph.

I have not called him Mr. Martin in many years. I call him William now which seems to me as it should be. In the studio the profession's term for him is The Master.

Now William has begun to have lines of age on his face too. I can feel the lines when he lets me touch his face to see him. His wife Angeline's face is smooth as silk though I don't often touch it. I saw her only once with my eyes. It was when she first arrived at the studio the day of the accident when the Indians were being photographed. She was beautiful that day. There is no reason for me to think she is not still beautiful.

The Indian saw me. We stared at each other before I went back into the dark-room. I had the impression there was something he wanted to say to me. The doctor, Angeline's father, told me later it was something I imagined. There are many things, he said, that are mixed up in my memory, or are inventions of my mind that grew out of the terrible shock.

The day the Indians were being photographed was the day I was robbed of my sight. I regard it as theft though I know it was my clumsiness that caused the accident.

To rob. To take by stealing. To take something from someone injuriously and unjustly.

I don't agree with the doctor. I did not imagine it. The Indian stared at me as though there was something he wanted to tell me.

The Indian's face was the final image to my sight—the last thing granted for me to see. His face on the negative, and then on the print. There was no misstep; the print was perfect. I remember I said to myself it is exactly as Mr. Martin wants it.

I was young then and my face was full and round. I wonder if it is still round. Mr. Martin—William—says I have a lovely face.

It was all such seriousness that day in the studio; sun poured in from the skylight and it seemed there were Indians everywhere. William said they were important men, the last great chiefs of their tribes. Of course I know now ten years later—because William told me—the way it turned out. The wilderness land of the Black Hills was taken away from the tribes.

I remember when the old Indian looked at me it was as though with his eyes he brought himself to stand before me. As though his eyes carried him over to me and he was standing so close he could reach out and touch me. And then the next minute he was not standing in front of me at all, but was still in his place against the backdrop.

William said there is no longer a wilderness.

This garden is the wilderness, he said; here, touch, feel. He put my hand on one of the dogwoods and then he walked me very fast from tree to tree and pressed my hand into the tree's bark; or here, he said, or here, or here, even these, the statues, here, feel, and he pressed my hands against stone; horns, fangs, wings of beasts and brutes; the representations of living things with inborn wildness in stone that have always been here in this garden.

I was aware more of William's hands than the creatures in stone. His hand on my hand. On the small of my back. On my shoulder. On my hand. He closed his eyes and touched my face so that he could see the way I see.

I wanted to ask him what he saw when he looked at me with his hands. Of course I didn't ask him. I kept the question to myself.

It has been ten years since that day in the darkroom. I have learned to keep track. Angeline's father, the doctor, over these ten years has provided me with opportunities at The Wills Eye Hospital, and I have learned to read in Braille, and I have my own calendar each year supplied in Braille.

When the Black Hills were taken away from the Tribes, William said, Oh, that was inevitable. That's what William said. Oh, that was inevitable.

William said your darkness is the wilderness.

I feel like stone, like rock, as much like rock as the stone statues in the garden. Except for my hands—the one that moves the pen across the page and the other that guides it.

When I first became blind I thought my parents were not my parents. That's the reason I came to live with Mrs. Martin, Sr. and William's Aunt Lavinia. After time passed I again believed my parents were mine. The initial hysteria that had caused the disbelief had subsided. They were my parents, I belonged to them, but I continued to keep my residence with William's mother and his aunt, and with William nearby, and his wife Angeline, and the doctor visiting, and with my own room and the many advantages they could provide for a blind girl.

Was it from a stone, or a bird? Where did I come from?

Aunt Lavinia had a friend who examined the lines on my palms and the individual fingers of my hands. She took my smallest finger in her hand. She said this is your unfortunate finger. She said it was the finger that contained my misfortune.

Shall I cut it off then, the finger?—the finger that contains my misfortune. Two hands touched me—one belonged to William, one to the old Indian. How else could I know that the Indian's hands felt like the bark of a tree?—like the bark of the tree that William pressed my hand against in the garden. William's hands on top of my hands—and then his hands on my face while he kept his eyes closed so that he could see me the way I saw him. Tracing the features of my face, starting at the brow.

That day William was everywhere in the studio, seeing to everything at once; he was the master. He is still the master, though he says he has gone past his prime. He says he will carry a cane soon, but I have told him he will never carry a cane. He will continue to cut glass plates with a grand gesture the way he has always done, and with great display he will continue to pour the collodion.

Is the moon full yet? I used to ask Aunt Lavinia. I have refused to think about the spirits since she's been gone. And there has never been a word from her from the spirit world. I thought she, if anyone...

Is the moon full yet? I will ask Mrs. Martin tonight at supper. Every night the aunt used to ask, Do you think William will come tonight?

Sometimes I dare to ask the same question. Do you think Mr. Martin will visit tonight? I ask his mother. Or perhaps in the morning?

We have both been robbed, the old Indian and me. Standing upright in his lavish costume he had a kind of beauty. And the look he gave me was full of meaning. I think it said the land will be taken, bad luck, but there was no pity.

When I asked, when I insisted, William explained what the silver nitrate did to my eyes. It does to the skin or the eyes what it does when you develop a photograph. The same wash of blackness that rushes onto the glass plate when the silver nitrate reacts to the salt in the collodion, rushes onto the skin when it meets the saline in the body. Or in the case of the eyes—as was the case with mine—it reacts to the saline and blackens the membrane over the eye. My eyes were blackened, William said—both the whites and the cornea, the same way my hands and fingers used to get blackened. It can wear off the skin, but it can never clear up again or wear off from the eyes. Though he did not say it, I understood—one sees only two black balls in the place of my eyes.

When the accident happened I reached for William with my blackened hands

253

and he took hold of them. It was a sight to see, everything so blackly discolored, though of course I was not able to see it. They tell me that my hands are no longer discolored, and that the discoloration on my face has also faded with the passing of time.

With the passing of time I got on well again with my parents and I continue to get on well with them now; the period of time is over when I thought they were imposters. The word imposter, the way it sits there in the mind. My parents agreed it was just as well I remain with Mrs. Martin and William's aunt. I would have everything there, whereas I wouldn't have much at home with the three other girls, and this one, the blind one.

I remember my skin moist one night from summer heat, how damp, how hot my skin was. I had gone into the garden at night in my dressing gown. I thought I would like to remain there until the night was over.

I thought I heard William coming, saying what are you doing here? The mosquitoes will soon be at you.

I thought he might touch me to guide me back into the house. There's nothing we can do with you, he might have said, wanting to stay out there by yourself in the darkness.

William told me again about the horses that had been taken along for the W___ Survey in the canyons. The horses were with him in his desert, and in and out of the deep ravines between the cliffs. He told me some of them suffered a condition of the eyes, their eyes inflamed, it was called moonblindness.

I inquired about it from Mr. Sachs who owns the stables on Front Street. He was an acquaintance of William's aunt. I asked him if he had ever seen a horse suffering from moonblindness.

He said it was an ancient disease, all the way back to Egypt and the pyramids at Giza, carried by the phases of the moon. When I asked how he knew, he said it was his business to know being a horse man. He said the horses' eyes would become cloudy and pale, whitish-blue like the color of the moon. He said the horses would often go blind.

Our horses did not go blind, William said. We covered their eyes with a cloth soaked in water and vinegar.

Perhaps if my eyes had been covered with the same.

Not marriageable. The blind girl.

You're not to be an invalid, William said. You're not to have an invalid life.

254

And all the time the night getting darker.

There are degrees of darkness to the night,

What difference does it make to me, the garden in the daytime or at night? Except for the mosquitoes which I must constantly brush away, it makes not the slightest difference to me. My flesh is sweet, that's why the mosquitoes go after it. Leaving me scratching until I'm covered with blood.

Covered with blood so that I won't forget they've been on me..

I thought he might touch me, press against me, kiss me, press himself into me, I thought, I seem to remember it...

24, September 1885—written by Lucie Fell

Lucie Fell's writing stops there, I stop reading there—

I've come to the house on South Eighth Street to look in on it.

I fold the pages into squares, attentive to the folding, the corners are even, the pages are creased and I place them back inside the drawer where I've just found them.

it was something she dreamed I might say...I might say I'm dreaming too...

I might say I'm dreaming too and it's night and Lucie Fell is in the house. she's my daughter, she tells me. I'm to give her to her waiting bridegroom. I see the face of her bridegroom, impatient to have her, watching and impatient, waiting for the bridal ceremony to end. you've come home at last, I say. she answers, remember it's only a dream. the girl is wearing her dark glasses with their round lenses black against her colorless face.

what has seeped into the house? absence.

inside the house, the organette. the mechanical musical instrument. it sits on a table-top and has a spool at each end which makes the rolls easier to play. the girl used to play it. she was able to load the rolls into the spools by herself and to play and then re-roll them. she selected from her own rolls of sacred hymns. she played each hymn repeatedly, turning the hand-crank to bring her own tempo to the music. she often started slowly so that the music was solemn and ponderous, and the hymns sounded unnaturally grave. and then she would increase the speed so that they sounded more as we are accustomed to hearing them. but then after a few minutes she would make the instrument play faster again, and then faster still, until it sounded garish and crude and the music had become unrecognizable.

what can I tell? there's nothing to tell. the story existed in its ordinary moments. and Lucie Fell, after the accident, had become sensitive to each of those moments, to everything contained within them, to every sound and every ripple of air. Eventually, she came to call me William. it had always been Mr. Martin, but then one day she called me William. she called my mother, Mrs. Martin, and Angeline was sometimes also Mrs. Martin, but more often she was Angeline. my aunt was always Aunt Lavinia. it had been singular, the girl's relationship with my aunt.

she hadn't wanted her eyes to be seen, and they were not seen. she said she was worried that they would be wandering, or else they might be looking in the wrong direction. she wanted to know if they were badly scarred. I told her they were not. she often asked me if they wandered. I told her they did not.

there are small birds in the garden, *wings of twig* flying up in a mass. they fly up and then they descend again into the trees. the light has changed, the sky is clouded over, the heat is oppressive, the air is heavy with moisture. it will be only a matter of time before it rains. I raise my hand to my neck and wipe away the perspiration. I'll go inside soon and close the windows and return home to where Angeline is waiting. it will rain hard when it begins, and with heavy winds, but now the air is still. I make no move to leave. I feel as though I've become part of the general stillness.

I once took a photograph of Lucie Fell in the garden; in the photograph she appears to be staring directly into the lens of the camera from behind her dark eyeglasses. her hair is worn loose; her face is already angular, having lost its fullness. she's wearing a summer jacket over her blouse and a scarf that drapes the neckline of the jacket. there's the sense she can see, though of course she can't see. her eyes will always remain stained black behind the dark glasses. still, there's that sense she can see and it can't be denied she appears all life in the photograph. she has a sensuality as well. Angeline stared at the likeness a long while the first time she saw it. there had been discussions in the beginning, when it was decided the girl would live with our family, whether she should live with my mother and my aunt in the house on South Eighth Street, or with Angeline, her father and me. it had been decided that she would live in the house on South Eighth Street. time would move forward; the summer would end; the winter would come; the years would go by. but now it's raining and the first drops of rain are large and falling at irregular intervals...

last night I dreamed the wilderness. that's what I told Angeline when I awoke this morning. this morning in our bedroom that has always been too small, and with our continued practice of sleeping together with her arms wrapped around me; and the realization that the flesh carries on in its ability to attract, to arouse, to comfort and to please. her face came near to mine, she looked helpless or bewildered. was it a good dream, she asked? I knew she was worried I'd want to leave and return to the wilderness. you needn't be concerned, I said. but she continued to look worried. it would be hard to be alone now, she said. I could hear the apprehension in her voice. what awful things, I teased, what awful things you want to say about the wilderness. she protested, that's not true. and then she added, you're forgetting that we met in the wilderness—St. Louis was the wilds when we met there, and that hotel was a kind of wasteland. I said, you needn't worry, I've grown too old to return to the wilderness.

the rain is falling hard now, but I remain in the garden. it's a driving rain as I thought it would be. I'm completely soaked within minutes and my feet sink into the wet earth. my good sense urges me to go back inside the house. the basin of the old white birdbath has filled with water, but of course there are no birds. the stone has lost some of its whiteness. I'm standing alone. I touch its rim. I think you prefer to be alone, Angeline, once said. I think you have always preferred it.

there will be a rainstorm, thunder and lightening, possibly hail. several times already this summer we have had hail in the sweltering heat. there's a flash of lightening on cue with my thoughts, followed swiftly by thunder. the powerful resonance of the thunder. it seems no wonder the Indians treat it as they do with respect. it's not 'thunder' for them, but 'thunders.' or 'thunder spirits.' the thunders can choke off the lives of those who are careless, and all the reverence that might be shown them is nonetheless never enough; a man for no reason might still be struck down by the thunders. they can bring the dead back. I'm not the only civilized man to have wished to bring the dead back. graves have been exhumed for one last look. there will be no hail, I am certain. only rain to soak me...

it was around the time I took the photograph. we were alone in the garden. Lucie Fell, using her fingers for sight, was looking at one of the garden statues—it was a figure of a woman. the girl first touched the statue's hands and then felt along its arms, pressing into the metal folds of the sleeves. she had removed her dark eyeglasses and the black balls of her eyes seemed to be staring directly at the face of the statue. her fingers moved up to the face; the statue's head was tilted slightly downward; the eyes were also turned downward, sculpted to appear as if they were almost closed. when she touched them she stopped. the eyes are closed, she said flatly. and then she reached for my face. she examined my eyebrows, my cheekbones, my jaw line, my lips. when I touch your face I can see you, she said. and then she lowered her hands and for a minute was quiet and then started speaking again. I have the image of a white blackbird in my mind, she said. I have been wanting to ask you, are there really white blackbirds? your aunt says there are—have you ever seen one? I have not, I said. I can feel the sun, she said. it's almost as though I can see it, she said. did you know I can see things in my blindness?—I sometimes see a face that frightens me; it has a stern gaze, that gaze is frozen in my eyes; and the statue of the woman I just touched, I could feel by the way it's sculpted it's not smiling, and yet when I saw it in my blindness it wore a smile and that smile frightened me. I can even see myself sometimes. it's not like looking in a mirror; it's in some interior place that I see myself. everything is inhuman there and I'm inhuman too. everything is terror there. I feel terror. and I have the feeling something will touch me, that at any moment something is going to reach out and touch me, and I pull my arms into my sides so as not to be touched.

I think of the accident. the tray of chemicals with the silver nitrate which I had noticed was filled too near to the top. the sense of urgency that had pulled me back into the other room. I had left the girl standing in the dark-room. the unusual way she looked at me—though that might have been my imagination at the time, or my false memory now. there might have been nothing out of the usual in the way that she looked at me. I had gone back into the other room where the others waited. a few minutes later, the accident.

your father will take you today, I said. I think he said to Fairmount Park, or maybe only to Washington Square, to the arboretum. and your mother, too, and younger sisters, maybe to your house, do you miss being there? would you prefer to go back to live there? this is my house now was her reply. she wore a summer jacket over her blouse, the same one she had worn in the photograph. but she was not wearing the scarf around the neckline and I could see that the neckline was shaped in a V. she had tilted her head slightly up towards the sound of my voice; I was looking at her eyes, the entirety of her eyes covered with a permanent blackness. if this is your house, I said, we must have another likeness. perhaps out here in the garden again. will you let me do that? will you let me take another likeness? what do they look like? she asked—my eyes? they are as they always were, I said. where is my stick? she asked—I would like to go inside.

it appears even the soul has been photographed. there has been its literal representation, or rather a likeness of the spirit captured, rising up and pouring itself onto the negative. it's a Mr. Baraduc in France who is said to have accomplished this. on the albumen print the spirit rises as a white mist.

I've come back inside the house, soaked, out of the question now to leave, not with the wind and the heavy rain...

what to make of them? the sounds that come with the wind and the rain. the sounds are outside while I'm sheltered in the house. there are voices present in them. they sound hardly human. they have brought back the memory of the girl telling me that day in the garden that she had seen herself in an interior darkness. in an interior darkness... she said it as though she'd been looking where she was not supposed to be looking... as though I'm now listening to what's not intended to be heard.

the time was still soon last year after my mother had died, and after Lucie Fell had left the house to go live at the Wills Residence. my aunt had had her invalid winter many years prior and then died in the late spring. I had come to check on the house that day, as I am doing now. Angeline was with me; she has been tending to the garden since my mother died. that day she was regretting that she couldn't tend it better. she said the garden seemed to prevent it. I said the honeysuckle was doing well. she said, yes, but it seemed to be going against the will of the garden. I told her I had had a dream the night before, and it had come back to me in the morning. at first I couldn't remember its detail and then its detail returned. it was a dream I'd had before—a kind of recurring dream. in it I am listening through a door to two people talking in the other room, but they are talking low and I can't make out their words, there is only the barely audible sound of their voices, a conversation from which I have been excluded, all the same their voices, which I know in the dream are not for me, become a magnet pulling me to them, and with an overwhelming curiosity until I can't bear it anymore and open the door. it is my father. he is alone. I feel pity when I see him in the dream; he stares at me. the dream stops there. now I stand here soaked inside this silent house.

I feel the coolness of the wood floor beneath my feet, my wet clothes clinging to me. I'll leave when the rain lets up. I find a dry shirt and trousers left years before in a bureau drawer in the room I used to sleep in. I look out the front window down to the street and see that water has collected in the gutter, it will soon reach to the ankles, I run my finger along the sill and I can feel that where the pane meets the wood there are beads of moisture. the clothing from the drawer fits a little large; I've grown thinner over the years. all the rooms are now empty. the house remains empty. the room that had been Lucie Fell's room, which she chose for herself when she came to live here, is at the end of the hallway on the second floor of the ell. I go into her room, the light is dim, there's only the sound of the rain; the sound of the rain and the awareness that time is passing. the room is located just past the turn in the hallway; the girl had wanted it the minute she stepped into it, said my aunt at the time with a suggestion of a deeper significance. I have the sense that time has been suspended. though I consider it impossible for time to be really suspended. it's only perceived to pass differently under different circumstances. now it seems that time has stopped. and the room gives the impression of being naked—stripped down and its occupant elsewhere. I feel as though I'm an intruder and that my presence unsettles the room, or that worse I'm violating its space. or something else altogether: that I'm violating *her* space. or more disturbing still: that I'm violating *her*.

ash is in my mind. now, at this moment. and in my mouth in that way I can taste it. the ashy residue. I had pushed too hard; I had pushed her too hard. afterward I had not pushed at all, never again. one day when I went to the house she was sitting wearing a dress that was very white with many buttons down the front; my mother helped her with her clothes; the girl often wore white. the language of the house had changed. what had been called the small parlor was now the north parlor. we were in the north parlor. the false drawers of the secretary-bookcase in the room had been let down on a quadrant to form a desk. her reflection, which she could not see, came back from the long rectangular mirror that hung on the wall opposite where she was sitting. before I spoke she knew I had entered the room. I touched her hand by way of greeting. there was the impulse to touch her as a substitution for the inability of communication by means of the eyes. it had been a year, a little more than a year, after the accident. she would soon turn sixteen. she had become more womanly and there was some awkwardness between us. her hand remained inert; it seemed to accept being covered by mine, but gave no response of its own. I remember thinking at the time there had been little talk, next to none, about the circumstances of the accident. all talk had been of diagnoses, prognoses, the practical matter of her education so that she could be active to life in her new condition. or about her family coming to see her, when they were coming and where they might take her. or about the cultivation of her second sight— she has *gifts*, my aunt said; my aunt said, mediums are often blind. but on that day when I visited, the girl spoke her feelings about the accident. she said both her father and I had been inattentive—occupied as we were by the excitement in the studio. she accused that I had noticed the tray filled too full, saw the chemicals swimming, but I had taken it as small thing, harmless enough to have been ignored and that the overfull tray caused the accident. and then after she was done with blaming me, she blamed herself: she had been excited, she said, excited and a little frightened too by the Indians. she stopped talking abruptly. her expression did not change. she stared straight ahead; it seemed to me, solemnly.

spit the blood from your mouth. the god is mumbling down its throat. it throws rocks at the heads of the unbelievers.

this is our wilderness, Angeline said yesterday when we were together at Fairmount Park. I know it's not all the marvel you have seen, but there's the famous rustic bridge. and the large rocks oddly placed. and the tall trees rising up, birds landing on their swaying branches. she pulled her shawl around her; the gesture was graceful. she seemed to wait for my reply. but I said nothing. she didn't push for my response. she simply turned her face up towards the sun with her eyes closed and stood there like an animal. it was the way I'd seen a wild animal once being bathed by the sun. her hair was pulled back. it was now rare she wore it down. she pulled closer to me and opened her eyes. we had hired a carriage and I thought of the driver sitting, most likely sleeping while he waited, and the horses standing restless while we walked. we had taken St. George's Hill and the carriage had stopped on its summit. we were walking in the direction of the pines.

it is anyway my wilderness, Angeline said. and then she said she was frightened that something might happen.

what might happen? I asked.

oh, you know, anything might happen.

nothing will happen, I said, at least nothing bad.

anything might happen, she said again. she said it as though it were the last word. and then she said she felt suddenly like going back. I want to go home, she said. I feel tired now; this is perhaps too much wilderness. she laughed when she said it, but her face had gone colorless.

we started walking back to the carriage.

are you disappointed? she asked. do you feel regret, or remorse? are you disappointed you have no heir?

heir. that's a strange word, I said, as if this were a kingdom and we a royal house. I went to her question then. no, I said, I prefer it this way.

she said nothing, but stared ahead. I couldn't give you progeny, she said.

I did not marry you for progeny, I replied. I married you for you. and for me. yes, I married you for me.

this morning I awakened after a restless night.

I heard a voice reproach me for my self-interest.
it was spoken by someone who misread or misinterpreted. it had never been self-interest. it had been interest in the life of the self.

before ash, earth. now it's fire-ash. fire. and a cloud hung over the earth as I was walking here this morning. the cloud was backed by a pale red fire. a

263

bird messaged the sky. the sky had darkened for rain.

I don't die, the voice said. time has passed with its hours. the story existed in its unalterable moments.

again the sound of rain.

and the language of the faces in the photographs, the faces are frozen as though it were stone that had been photographed. or marble with its hardness. I stare at the faces which give every indication of staring back.

I woke up this morning after a restless night, in my restlessness I saw them, everyone was again alive.

take out your spell for me. it's part of a song from the Indians. before I lose my voice. *take out your spell for me. take away your spell from me.*

no sign of anyone.

the bowl is too pretty for harm, the voice said. why not just leeches to lap the blood? there are all those I don't see. I won't be back among the suffering bodies.

do you want to know what I think? Angeline had asked. she has never lost her beauty. and now past youth, but not yet old, she is her most beautiful. and always with that calm to sustain me. I answered her, yes, I want to know what you think, what do you think?—

the house continues to stand as it always has. over the years there were those who made themselves known in these rooms.

when my late wife, Lucie, was alive and in bed sleeping next to me, I would often suspect by the sounds she was making that she was dreaming. and I remember that I would think to myself: she is dreaming; I thought it was my own dream when I woke up that night and saw her on her knees on the floor. It's always the dreamer's story. The dreamer's story when I woke and saw her.

And the dreamer's story too when I woke and saw my father.

I was still a child and had just returned from Arkansas with my mother. my mother could not flee fast enough back to Philadelphia after my father was murdered. I had been saved, but my father had not been saved; he had been attacked and mutilated by savage men who were not Indians. later everyone came to know that. and everyone came to know about the men who hired them to disguise themselves as Red Indians and to maraud and kill and blame it on the red men. and everyone was surprised to learn that they were not Indians. for years after my father died when I had returned with my mother to Philadelphia, and when I was in my childhood bed in the house on South Eighth Street, I would wake in the night's deep darkness to find my father standing over me. his wounds were no longer visible, nor was I afraid when he appeared; it was the opposite, I felt consoled; or if not consoled, at least safe, waking to find my father standing over me to keep me safe. other memories have crowded him out now, there have been other painful memories in between. but despite the violent way my father died, there in that darkness whenever he appeared to me his face was tranquil; his face seemed to have settled from that which had transgressed him; he was composed and quiet when he appeared to me, he would rarely speak, there was only his ghost-face hovering. he appeared to me many times back then in my childhood; at certain periods he appeared almost every night. and then it was the same when Lucie died—for a period of time her apparition was always in front of me. but now neither of them appear to me except as memory; unlike that earlier time when it was not memory, when it was something more tangible than memory; yes unlike in that earlier time when it was each of their ghosts suspended in front of me.

sometimes in the morning when I wake I see a flock of mourning doves from our bedroom window; the birds fly back and forth over the trees, first they fly to the left and then they make an abrupt turn to the right; they fly to the right furiously and then they turn back to the left. this repetition continues until finally the birds fly off. I've seen this pattern of flight many times before and I've pointed it out to my wife, Angeline; I've seen it in the garden in the house on South Eighth Street, and in Fairmount Park, and I've seen it in the canyons too; I've seen the black birds that inhabit the canyons flying back and forth between two columns of rock, the canyon walls reaching up, and the birds darting back and forth, looking as though they could not make up their minds, going in one direction and then the other, while I watched from below at the lower edge of one of the rock walls.

it always pleased Angeline's father when I talked about the wolves in the canyons. he said he didn't know there were wolves there. yes, we could hear them at night, I told him, always in the distance; we rarely saw them, but the sound was unmistakable. it filled the canyon. we recognized it the minute we heard it. there was no need to have heard it before to know what it was. the Indians said they were black wolves. Angeline's father's eyes seemed to flicker as he listened. he would listen to as much as I had the energy to tell; it seemed with a yearning; I can't know for certain; he never said he was yearning to see the canyons or hear the sound of wolves. in fact once he said his one trip to St. Louis had been enough for a lifetime and as close as he needed to come to the West. all the same, he listened to my descriptions with his eyes flickering with excitement: the gullies and the valleys; the dry beds of streams that would appear late at night, shallow with water, but enough to sustain us, and the water disappearing with the sun; and the canyon walls rising in a reach toward the sky, all rock and aridness, and the Indians. and like the rest of the family Angeline's father had been unreserved about revealing his high spirits the day the Indians came to the studio to be photographed; he had been as eager as the women to see them first hand.

and then the accident—

the girl wrote on long sheets of paper in her own little room. the room was on the second floor; the day she chose it, she had gone inside and touched all its objects, along with the window and the bed. she touched the bed last, then she sat at the desk and asked for paper and fresh ink. when they were brought, she placed the paper straight in front of her and dipped the pen into the inkwell. she held the pen in her right hand. she used her left hand to steady the paper and keep track of the line; she would write to the end of the line, then move her finger down a space on the page and dip the pen again, and then she would move the pen to the waiting next line. she wrote that way everyday, producing a diary or journal. my mother would read it aloud to her when the girl asked. paper and ink were always kept there for her. but what does she write everyday? I asked my mother. descriptions of things, my mother answered. she has described the desk as it is, an accurate description filled with detail, and the view of the garden from her window as she imagines it, or else the dress she is wearing. but sometimes she does not describe; sometimes she only puts her thoughts down on the paper.

we had been in the garden when she first called me William. where is my stick? she had asked. and then she had said, I would like to go inside now, William.

I had been struck by how tall she had grown. she was now almost as tall as I was, and she had become much thinner. and then I imagined, or that is to say, the image came into my mind of blood between her legs. there was no good reason for this appalling image to come into my mind. but the thing that had put it there caused it to stay no matter how I tried to erase it. there was a moment she had become hysterical that day, and then her hysteria stopped and was replaced with an unyielding calm. her expression was pitiless and yet standing in front of me was a young woman with reason to pity. she had reached for my face and there was nothing reticent in that reaching. she touched everywhere on my face, her fingers lingered everywhere in order to see. she will perhaps add a description of my face, I thought at the time, to the descriptions in her papers. I don't know if she ever did write a description of my face. I read some of her papers—she sometimes asked me to read them aloud to her when I would visit. she would have the bundle in her hand and hand it toward me. she sometimes asked Angeline to read her papers to her as well. my mother reported that the girl had different places to store her papers; in the desk there was a drawer for those that could be read by anyone; and another for those that could be read only by my mother; and a third drawer for those that could be read by no one. as I read, Lucie Fell listened with full attention to her words: *yes, the blanket chest in Mrs. Martin's bedroom. it has three drawers and a lift top. it is grain painted so that it will look expensive—I can feel the ridges of the paint which are intended to suggest the grain. inside, in the summer as it is now, are the winter blankets that are stored. there are six such blankets in Mrs. Martin's chest...*

allow that the blood will not disappear, I cannot erase the image,

she is sometimes in me, the girl said.

who is in you? I asked.

you know, she said, that person you are always thinking about—your wife, Lucie Martin. it is as Aunt Lavinia says it is, she comes and goes in me.

my aunt says that?

yes.

perhaps I was wrong to bring you to live here, I said.

no.

that person is dead you know.

yes, I know.

she lies beneath a stone, I said. shall I bring you to the cemetery so that you can touch the stone?

no, she said. and then she asked, where are we now? I've lost track. are we anywhere near that old dogwood?

no, I said. we're near the new garden sculpture, the bronze of a woman.

then she had asked again about her eyes. were they as they always had been? she insisted that I tell her about her eyes.

they are as they always have been, I lied.

I examined her face, with its new angularity, and her eyes which did not see. she leaned forward and the shift in movement brought her forehead to my chin; then she quickly moved back as though to step away from me. it struck me again she'd grown taller over the months, and in becoming taller, also thinner. for a moment the image of blood returned, and then disappeared from my immediate thoughts. the girl stepped back from me farther, appearing undisturbed; where is my stick? she asked—I would like to go inside. I handed her the stick and we went into the house. once inside, I thought about the house with its history, and the way the girl had now entered that history. and then I went home where I reexamined the events of the day. the images of the day returned and it crossed my mind that if I wrote them down I must lock them away; they must be locked away just as the girl's papers were kept locked away; in some undisclosed place; in a drawer, to be read by no one.

now the figure is me, standing at the south window in the parlor with the curtain pushed aside; I look out to the garden where it's still raining, my hand is still holding on to the soft fabric of the curtain that I've pushed aside. a fragment of a certain night returns. I had dreamed that I was standing at this window looking down to the garden. I was looking down at the flowers on their thin stems; it took nothing much to move them, only the slightest breeze. there were two women in the garden. Angeline and one who was younger; it was Lucie Fell. Angeline's hair was unbound and she was leaning protectively towards the girl. their faces were turned full towards me. I was present and watching them. I remember thinking, 'I'm watching them and it is to me that their faces are turned.' I remember thinking too that there was delicacy in the way that Angeline regarded the girl; I had the impression

269

she was about to draw her close, perhaps to comfort her. and then I had another feeling—it comes back to me now as I stand here remembering—that something was approaching in what I would describe to be a threatening way. I wanted to warn Angeline and the girl because they seemed not to be aware of it. I wanted to warn them and I kept trying to get their attention, but I was not able to reach them.

and then Angeline turned to me. it is only that it is unfamiliar to you, she said—there is no cause to be alarmed. come sit with me a while, though I think it's too nice for sitting in. perhaps we could sit for a while and then walk to the wharves.

both women were looking at me and Lucie Fell's eyes shifted their direction. she turned her head to face me and I had no doubt I was the object of her attention. her eyes were wandering the way she was always afraid they would wander. and I had the thought that it was strange because her eyes had never wandered before, or I had never seen them wander. I continued to think that and then I said out loud: I don't know if she's aware that they are wandering. my wife kissed Lucie Fell's forehead. we have become like sisters, she said. I didn't know if she was talking to Lucie Fell or to me. my wife repeated it again: we have become like sisters. and all the time this was occurring I was aware I was in a kind of trance, but knowing that didn't give me the ability to wake from it.

I think of the time that has passed; I bring it out to examine once again. like on a summer night when the weather was good. after supper in the garden and Angeline near the flowers as she had been that first night in the garden. and Lucie Fell with one hand on Angeline's arm and in her other hand a jar to capture fireflies.

after the periods of my absence Angeline returned to me much the same as I returned to her—her word was: *hated*—she would say, I *hated* the time you were away from me. and I would reply, but it is the time you were away from me as well. or at night in our bed when she would let herself go in a kind of abandon—so much so it would surprise me, and excite me too, to hear her voice husky, and to feel her body against mine, her strength becoming suddenly the strength that directed our bodies towards each other's flesh, and the sound of her voice when she asked with the words: have you really returned? have you come back to me? come closer, William, you have returned and now I must feel you against me. now I must feel you... and my surprise at the touch of her soft flesh, as though I had never taken hold of it before, or had never taken her, nor taken pleasure in her before. it made me think of the abandon of whores, which is always a false abandon. but this was my wife. there was nothing false. there was only frantic striving and then the silence. there were the simple things too, like buying honey from the market. going from one stall to another and winding up at the honey stall; the range of color of the honey in the row of glass jars, from light to gold to dark,

moonblindness, Angeline said. tell me again, just as you told Lucie Fell, tell me about the horses you saw in your desert. or was it on your mountain?— the horses that were suffering from moonblindness. you said that their eyes had become inflamed, but they weren't really blind. or else tell me about the old monstrosity that you found in the ruins. you said when you found it, it seemed to be staring out from the centuries that had passed. you said, it is still there staring; it is waiting for someone to come who will understand what it's trying to say. do you think it's very important, what it has to say? and then she said, listen, the Age-to-Come Adventists, over near the food stalls on Market Street the Age-to-Come Adventists are bawling. they're bawling about the end of the world again. they've taken to walking up and down Market Street. they shout out their awful predictions and take aside anyone who will listen. but I wanted to tell you I went by the cemetery today and placed flowers on the graves of all our dead. all the graves that belong to us, the ones holding our family. my father, and your mother and your aunt, and your first wife, Lucie. yes, I put flowers on your Lucie's grave too. it seemed a small thing to do and I felt I must. the leaves were gathered all around the stones and the headstones were pointing upward, all the different shapes and sizes, all of them gray, and some of the oldest ones shorter now, starting to sink into the ground. I was thinking how even gravestones grow old and sink into the ground.

moonblindness, Lucie Fell said. the horses sometimes go blind, but not always. I was told that by Mr. Sachs who owns the stables on Front Street. he was a friend of your aunt's; he came sometimes to call the spirits when there was a gathering at the house. but he kept it a secret from his wife. he told me about moonblindness. he said it was an ancient disease, all the way back to Egypt and the pyramids at Giza. the disease is caused by the phases of the moon. when I asked how he knew, he said it was his business to know, after all being a horse man. the word is pretty don't you think? moonblindness. he said the horse's eyes would become cloudy and pale, whitish-blue like the color of the moon.

our horses did not go blind, I said. we covered their eyes with a cloth soaked in a mixture of water and vinegar.

a feeling of distance. of white blankness. of having been searching for something that I thought was lost only to find I already had it. the certainty I did not have it all along. that it was lost. that it had been lost. the memory of displacement.

or of finally reaching towards some kind of conclusion. surprised by memory. as though I am not entitled to retain it: this sudden memory. as though it has been placed in my hand but I'm not entitled to retain it. I had been staring at the overdeveloped print, where there was too much black, so much so that it seemed to be pointing in a direction that had overstepped the place of its origin. the image was now buried inside itself. it was an image of an Indian with a bird, the corpse of a hawk affixed to the Indian's back, the top half of the bird extending above the head of the Indian. there is little that shows through clearly from the blackness of the overdevelopment, but what does show through appears to have deepened. there has been a deepening of the lines on the face of the Indian, who is staring in profile, and the thin strips of leather that are visible hanging down along his shoulder and down his arm. and the bird is like something seen in the imagination, or like a visitation, or an apparition, or a ghoul— both the Indian and bird gaze directly ahead. the bird's wings are so close to its body that the animal appears to be wingless. perhaps the bird *is* wingless, perhaps the wings have been removed. the image, in actuality, is a consequence of reflected light, but now that light has been diminished and the print darkened, the image has become more clearly identified with its essential significance... it is an image of coming forth from or re-turning to...

we had arrived at the food sheds on Market Street where there was all con-gestion and the assault of the hectic environment: baskets of produce wait-ing to be sold; the produce spilling out into the street; cabbages and potatoes and green beans. Angeline lead me to George Stockburger's butcher stall. he wore a white apron, a black sweater underneath, a white shirt beneath the sweater, and on his head a black round-brimmed hat. behind him was the wooden enclosure that held his equipment, rows of hooks all across and ice cabinets below. there were large pieces of meat hanging on hooks and on uncovered counters; he brought the meat each day in a wagon from the slaughterhouses in the North East part of the city. that's where all the slaughterhouses are located, and my aunt called it the blood and flesh dis-trict. Mr. Stockburger lifted a slab of meat down from a hook; he placed it on the table and further butchered it down. it will make a good roast, Ange-line was saying.

or returning to...

do you think it was torches that lit the ancient ruins? the rooms of the cliff dwellings. there were 60 rooms or more. at night the ladders were taken up. a handful of men, even women and children, could defend themselves once the ladders had been taken up. or on nights when there was nothing below to threaten them, perhaps they sat at the cliff's edge with their legs hanging down. towards the canyon floor below. the *little death*. the Indians talked about *the little death*. the death that comes by way of initiation. and then the rebirth that follows. speak the truth. speak the truth before language. speak the pre-linguistic truth.

I went with my camera. perhaps I was the first, or perhaps one of the first to record it. to record what can be seen only with the camera in the remains of the ruins.

Angeline's face became solemn as she got older; and even more beautiful. people often stared at her beauty. and when Lucie Fell was with us, which she was often, they stared at Angeline's beauty and then they stared at the girl in her dark glasses. there had been an afternoon at Sea Breeze, and Angeline was standing facing me. Angeline and Lucie Fell were wearing wide-brimmed hats to keep the sun off their faces. we had taken a steamer, the John Warner; it cost us sixty cents each for the day and it left from the Chestnut Street wharf at 8:15 in the morning. at Sea Breeze we sat on the shore watching the fishing boats and the fishermen who had laid out their nets. when they pulled the nets in they were always full; fish were abundant there even in the relative shallows. we might do that, Angeline said. we might fish; they have boats for visitors to fish. but Lucie Fell wanted to remain on the shore. we had eaten fried oysters and cold chicken, and ice cream and fruit. when we walked, Lucie Fell took Angeline's arm, or mine. we searched up and down the beach for shells. Angeline had a pouch for collecting, and Lucie Fell had one too. the girl would crouch and run her hand along the sand until she touched a shell and then she would examine it with her long fingers. she didn't want our help. she wanted only to crouch, again and again, and to reach out with her fingers until she touched a shell. I was aware of myself standing there with them; the sun was brilliant and very hot. after a while I took my shoes off and walked down to the shoreline where I put my feet in the water. Angeline remained a way up the beach with Lucie Fell. they have bathing suits for twenty-five cents, Angeline called to me. no, I don't want one today, I called back. perhaps some other time we'll all take one. would you like to go into the water? I asked Lucie Fell. she didn't answer me, but stayed fixed on her shells. Angeline looked at her and then back to me. Angeline was dressed in white, standing; and Lucie Fell was also dressed in white. I remember thinking at the time that in their white dresses in the bright light, they seemed to embody some feminine ideal. or they looked like two phantoms together, with the light on them that way. I turned back to the water and rolled my trousers, and then I waded a little way out. the waves rolled in one after another and I kept stepping back to keep my trousers from getting wet.

I was afraid you wouldn't be here.

wouldn't be here...

I'm standing in the silence of the house... silent because it is empty... de-spiritualized, my aunt would have described it. the house has become de-spiritualized. I've kept it empty since my mother died, and since Lucie Fell moved out, unable to remain alone here after my mother died. Angeline and I come here often to care for it. the memories given back. the house waiting for the return of the those who used to live here.

imposters, Lucie Fell had called them. she said it *out of the blue*, out of the blue were her father's words to me; Edmund Fell had shaken his head in an expression of disbelief and helplessness. she thinks my wife and I are not her parents. his daughter had asked him to come near so that she might touch his face and then she made the same request of her mother. you are not my real parents, she said when she finished. the girl later accepted, because we told her so often, that they were her parents, her real parents. but in the beginning she insisted that it was simply not true.

through the mists of the photograph the head appears, all but forgotten, and the impression that the teeth are clenched, the breath labored; a wall stands behind, and what looks like a door that leads to another room, or to a series of rooms, but I know the door is painted on, it is only part of the backdrop.

the girl wanted it described, she wanted everything described that she could not get at with her sense of touch. when I came into the room she was sitting side-by-side with my aunt in the small parlor. my aunt was reading to her from The Spiritualist Register and describing the photographs that appeared on the various pages.

      this one is a clever photograph, my aunt was saying, it is a photograph of a photograph in a frame sitting on a side table next to a vase of flowers.

      what about the spirit? the girl asked.

      of course there's a spirit. there must be a spirit or they wouldn't publish it in the Register. and oh such a poetic spirit! I cannot decide, Dear, if it is a male or a female. it's slender and leaning gracefully with its hand on the frame of the photograph. it wears a white robe and a wreath of flowers on its head in the style of the Greeks.

      what is that style? the girl asked.

      the Greeks wore narrow wreaths on their heads, my aunt answered, the wreath went all around the head, it was made up of flowers. I've decided that the spirit is a man, Dear; the face is too masculine for it to be a woman. but it is delicate. that is just what makes it so poetic.

luminous visitations

apparitions

when my aunt died, we provided her with a grave bell in accordance with her wishes. the coffin was fixed with a bell that sat above ground and had an air hole for my aunt. its inventor had been a man named Franz Vestor of New Jersey. if my aunt had awakened, she would have been able to alert the sexton by pulling the cord and ringing the bell.

a feeder put there many years ago, filled with water and sugar for humming-birds, but there were never any hummingbirds that came to the garden. nonetheless, my mother hoped she might attract them. there are certain moments, and the inconsequential actions we are in the midst of at those moments, that act as a gateway, like the false doors of the Egyptians, rec-tangular and gray, *a niche through which the dead can enter and communicate again with the living.* I've come back out to the garden. the feeder for hum-mingbirds. I stop to examine it; it's still wet from the rain. the past is there again, immediate and in evidence: a day when my mother and I went out to examine the feeder. we were excited, eager; it was an innocent moment after our return from Arkansas. and we were able, for that moment, to become distracted from the fact of my father's death. it had been only a short time since we moved into the house on South Eighth. my father's body had been left behind in its grave in Arkansas. come with me, William, my mother had said, wouldn't it be wonderful to see a hummingbird at the feeder? with her critical eye she examined it. none have come yet, William. look, you can see it's full. let's sit on the bench as still as statues so that when they come they won't be frightened. would you like to sit here and wait? we'll be able to see them very well from here.

the death of Smith and Windmill islands. it was as though a stage had been erected for viewing the removal of Smith and Windmill islands; a prosce-nium which was visible from the wharves where one could stand watching on the edge of the dock. the sky was an indeterminable color; haze, gray, at moments a luminosity that could be seen behind the gray; sometimes an af-terglow, orange, disquieting, as though a herald of death, and it's true the removal of the islands was a kind of death. it was a long and drawn out af-fair. I watched them working that day, just as I watched on many days. the work went on for several years, little-by-little, with infinite patience. there was first the removal of the ten buildings on Smith Island: the hotel, the three dwelling houses, the ice house, the gas house, the bowling alley, the blacksmith shop, the two pavilions. and then on Windmill Island: the log-wood factory, the three dwelling houses, the two coal offices, the shed, the removal of all the trees, all the structures, all the machinery, all material, everything artificial and everything natural. removed to where? the question was weighed up until the destinations had been determined. and then the trees went down, flat against the earth, the islands which had stood up out of the water. the boats are called scows, I said to Angeline, referring to the large flat-bottomed boats with their square ends, some of them pulled by tugs. the scows carried the debris away. the islands were dredged down to eight feet below and the scows carried the dredging. until the earth sank down lower and lower into the water. the explosions and demolitions and the death of the islands. I realized that islands can also die, can be put to death so to speak; can become inconvenient to the measure of progress. so for both the islands they dredged eight feet below the surface of the river. there had been warnings that the stuff of life could otherwise reconstitute itself, so they had to be dredged down to eight feet below, where the ghosts of the islands would remain out of view below the water.

I must return home, Angeline will be waiting. I told her this morning that I'd only stay here a short while, that I only wanted to make certain all was well in the house. but we were there only yesterday, she said. I answered, yes, but I want to look in all the same. now I see the silent clock in the entranceway, in its case of fretted gold and bronze. the clock is one of the heirlooms. I've come back inside the house.

the mirror takes me by surprise, as it's done in the past, coming upon it at the top of the stairs, it doesn't matter that I know it's there, I'm still taken by surprise and my reflection is caught as though it's another. I stare fixedly at it: that other person. until it seems to be absorbing me into itself.

beneath my feet the touch of the carpet and then the wood of the floor.

Lucie Fell had the idea she might still take photographs, become a photographer, despite being blind. the smoldering darkness, she said—that too should have its representation. will you help me, she asked? then she turned her face in the direction of the sound of the approaching footsteps. Angeline was coming. Lucie Fell lowered her voice: will you help me?

she is your creation, a voice says, referring to Lucie Fell. she is something you have created for yourself. not only since she's been blind, but always, from the beginning, you brought her forth, you summoned her, the way your aunt's mediums used to summon the spirits. in your eyes she has her place always with you. and in her eyes—in her poor eyes which have been sentenced to be in this world forever as two black balls, with even their whites made black, and with all of the membrane blackened—she imagines light.

there had been the utter stillness of the canyons. the light hitting the rocks like ghost light. the stone image of an animal. small and meant to be held in the hands, meant to be rubbed and worshipped.

here's the center window on the second floor landing in that stretch of the hallway that faces out to the garden and gives a clear view of the Dogwood trees. there had been talk all those years ago that the trees were too close to the house and might set the house ablaze if they were struck by lightening. of course it never happened. nonetheless there was a flurry about it. I was too young at the time to be consulted, but my mother and aunt had deliberated about having the trees removed. finally my mother said the trees were too short to be struck by lightening and my aunt agreed to the sense of that. that is the reason the trees remained.

do you think you can leave off with me? you can't leave off with me.

you. the way it was written. as though the girl had addressed it directly to me in the bundle of her papers I had been earlier reading—I believe she meant them for me to read. that was the reason they had been left behind only half-hidden in the drawer. something in me said I must go to the drawer. *something said.* that old expression. they were by intention in the drawer: these old letters written many years before she left the house. left in the drawer in the room that had been her room. her room was the smallest room in the house because she insisted it must be hers.

you can't leave off with me. do you think you will go to your wastes and leave the rest of us behind? I won't be left behind, but you can tell me, are my sentences straight and proper on the page? I do my best, but I can never be certain. I can't see them, you know. and remember, they were in the drawer marked: to be read by no one.

I'm no longer certain if it's day or night. when I arrived it had been dark with the rain, but the rain has long stopped. it seemed for a while there had been light filling the house, coming in through the windows. now it's dim, the sky had darkened, perhaps for more rain, or else it is simply night...

the girl said, I wanted to wear one of those ghost shirts, you know. you are a bad father not to have gone back out to the West again and brought one back to me as a present. you went out there so often, you could have gone out there one more time. I know it is childish of me and I am no longer a child. but the way you described it, it made me want one. you said they called it a ghost shirt. that name would be reason enough to want to wear it. you are a bad father not to have gotten one for me. but then of course you are not my father.

...or else it is simply night and I'm sitting motionless. in her small room where there is only one window. it looks out to the street. I hear voices from the people down below. or sometimes I hear footsteps. and the wheels of the carriages and the hooves of the horses. and I remember a horse had appeared without a saddle or a bridle. I was sleeping and I was aware I was sleeping. there was some observation I was making. about that strange and wild expression there seems always to be in the eyes of horses. now I'm holding Lucie Fell's pages in my hand. all those I've found that have been addressed to me.

...nor did I think of you as my father, the girl said, except perhaps at moments like this moment. and I think there was something in you that I wanted that a father might provide. and I was certainly not a child then, already thirty, getting on in years, but I wanted that ghost shirt.

a piece of paper in my hand. a stack of these pieces, all with her peculiar scrawl. it takes an effort to read them, the words wander on the page, at times they're impossible to read, one word is too high on the page and covers another already there, but at times she's precise, passages that are precise in the way they appear, one letter following on another, neatly and precisely, I'm holding the papers in my hand. the words that were written. the blind impulse of the blind girl. I've stared into her eyes as though they were sighted. and she's reaching out for me again. as if to take hold of me. but the time has gone past.

I've stared into her eyes as though they were sighted. coaxed her to remove her eyeglasses with their dark lenses. take them off, won't you. there's no reason you should hide your eyes from me. and then gently with the utmost care my fingers came to rest at the sides of her face. I could feel her start when I touched her. she held her body rigid. she was still very young. not yet sixteen. there is a way, I said, and I am certain of it, that you can take things into yourself, the things of the world that you no longer see. I believe you can take these things into yourself with all the same strong impressions as though you have seen them. I could feel her stiffen and the muscles of her face grew tense against my hands.

my mother often made the comment that the girl didn't eat. she has no appetite, my mother said. she eats less than a bird. she lives off the air. she doesn't eat. William, why don't you see if you can encourage her to eat.

I moved my hands a little higher along the outside of her face until my thumbs reached the top of her cheekbones and then I began to remove the dark glasses. she raised her arm as though to stop me with her hand. but then she let it fall back to her side.

the dogs were barking. it was the dead of night I heard them. it seemed they had been barking the whole night long. they were howling into the air and I remember wondering why my father didn't get up from his bed to go outside to quiet them, or at least to see to them, to investigate what it was that had disturbed them. it might be an intruder and the dogs had cornered him, holding him as prey. our dogs were black and very large, all of them ugly, they would tear their prey apart with their teeth. I remember wondering why I didn't hear the screams of a human, or of a wild animal, or both. but there were no screams, there was only the night which was black the way my father described the nights as being in his native Wales. he said there were hounds there many times the size of ours. he said we would go to see them one day. we would go back to his native Wales, he said. he still had family there, he said, and I must meet them—they had all remained there except my father.

black as coal, as all that is black. the black of darkness and unseeing. impossible now to remove the thought of it from my mind, it is fixed in my mind, everything that comes from darkness. it is against the will of the Lord, it is said, to remain behind in that darkness; time is squandered irreversibly there.

black as coal

do not look into that darkness. but where else will Lucie Fell look? where else will the blind girl look? but there is also darkness that is comprised of light, a light too brilliant to set the eyes on. the girl's head turns to follow a sound as though she is staring directly at it, but she is only staring into the black film that covers her eyes. her eyes have disappeared. she doesn't know it, but she senses it. she fears she is a grotesque, complains to me of her fear of it—I must be shocking to see, she says. there are other fears too. it is sometimes unbearable, she says—to have someone touch me. it is as though that sense too has become distorted, as though my flesh is now too responsive, too acutely aware of its experience, as though I am thin-skinned now and easily bruised. sometimes I feel a tiredness, she says, as though I am dead. the sense of my breath rising to leave my body. and then: give me my glasses, she demands—I don't want you to look at my eyes. if they are to be looked at it should be in a circus. what do you think of that? in a circus where I might be gaped at.

the repetition of a scene playing itself back to me again. repeated, though lost in the past, and I am only dogged by it. had she ever been inside a circus tent? I had failed to ask her. I would never ask her now. the fact would remain unknown until it dissolved with all the rest that would dissolve.

of course there was sometimes talk that could be heard of the tent shows when they came, though they were mostly put up in the smaller towns outside of Philadelphia. the city itself was for the larger circuses.

and everything comes back on itself of its own accord, now or at one time or another. it had been all those years later in a tent show outside of Philadelphia where I stumbled upon Laurent again. it was a chance encounter. and Laurent revealed himself to me for a second time in a kind of innocence. innocence on his part and mine. he was raw in the manner of youth, but he was no longer young. and of course he still possessed that abnormal union of the sexes. in its own way, I thought, it is perfection too. and I confess that Laurent is a secret I carry as a haunting, another haunting. it had been in one of the small rural towns in Pennsylvania that I saw him again, barely a town, in no way a city. and it was no longer Mabies' traveling show when I stumbled on him again. Mabies was dead, he told me. Laurent said he had worked his way north. he was years older now and much of the beauty had gone out of him. but some remained. enough of his beauty remained—his beauty and hers. and the same word was printed on the sign which hung over the tent flap: HERMAPHRODITE. and the implication contained within that word. her expression was still as striking to the eye as it had been when I had first encountered her, way back, those years ago; when I had come to her broken from the death of Lucie. it comes back to me now, it never left. and I trace that second encounter back through the years not knowing what to make of it now. it had been late in the morning. Angeline had been waiting for me at the Inn. we had been on an overnight trip to the Moravians. I had noticed the advertisement for the tent show in the Philadelphia Inquirer, and I told Angeline there was something of a business nature that I must do. she didn't question me, but let me go. there was a millinery shop close by the Inn; she said that she would take the time to look at hats. we two would meet later. it had been late morning. just as it had been the first time. I found Laurent waiting on the other side of the tent flap, again wearing his white shirt like a Spanish dancer's shirt. he was standing the way years earlier I had posed him when he asked: *do you want me male? do you want me female?*

the tent show hadn't yet opened, but it was only a few minutes away from opening. over the tent flap, the sign said: HERMAPHRODITE. I sensed it was Laurent waiting inside, waiting to receive, but not to converse. he was waiting to offer himself up to the sight of the men and women who paid to see him. there would soon be a long line and excitement to see him.

and there is no need any longer to deny the truth of it. the truth that haunts.

the secret of Laurent.

was there a moment that day those years ago when I desired her?

the air smelled like rain and they had thrown down sawdust.

I want to see him, I said. I know him. he was a friend of mine. and whatever else I said to them convinced—

the clouds were dark that day and I stared at them. I entered the tent and thought about what the girl had said about belonging in a circus. it had been soon after her accident; darkness was her permanent condition. we can expect, Doctor Stille had said at the time, that her state of mind, too, will now be at its most vulnerable. I think because of that fact we had never taken her to a circus or tent show.

when I entered Laurent's tent my vision was obscured for a few seconds by the darkness within and I strained to see him, realizing he was straining to see me too. there was a chair on which he sat. he stood up. what, is it open? he asked. open? I repeated. no, it's not open. I've come in early. and then I asked him if he remembered me. do I remember you? who are you? draw closer. oh, I remember you.

there is time, the voice says, the time that is stretching before you.

all the time in the world, my aunt used to say.

but now I will sit here in the house for a while until my breath returns. any movement seems to exhaust me as though I am unwell, and all things considered it might be true that I'm unwell. my hair and my skin are still damp. the rain had soaked me.

it will end because it must. there is the silence of the empty house. I am brought to attention by something that goes by me in a quick, strange movement. I don't know what it is. a shadow perhaps, or a flying insect that got into the house. the rain has long stopped. all day there had been the unusually high temperatures of the hot summer, now it's cooled down and day is giving way to night.

I go in one room and then another. sitting in each room as the hours go by. has it been hours? or in actuality has it been much less time than hours?

in one room then another. sitting for a while in each of the rooms, getting up and walking from one end of a room to the other, and then sitting again. sitting on one of the mahogany chairs in the dining room, with its cabriole legs and claw-and-ball feet. or on the caned side-chair in the front parlor. I am that… it is said. I am what I have thought myself to be. sitting now. I am tired. it is tiresome. it wears me down. sitting on the cane side-chair. the way I sit perched here. the chair uncomfortable to sit on.

there, now you can see it, you can see exactly the way that it works. one falls into a dream. one begins to dream. the dreamer is no longer separated by the world from the thing he is dreaming.

and it is said living our lives is about living our selves.

although I've been accused of being occupied only with my self.

or the memory of my aunt struggling with a piece of hard bread after her teeth became bad. she couldn't bite into it properly with her new poorly-constructed teeth; she had to use her hand to break off small enough pieces so that she could eat it. but she loved hard bread and would not give it up, nor would she dip it first into her tea, or into any other liquid to soften it before biting into it. I'd rather not eat it at all than to eat it soggy, she said. though she was self-conscious she looked a mess. she was afraid that she looked like the old women hanging around the food stalls on Market Street. she pointed the old women out to us on every trip that we made to the market.

I am in the quiet of the house, in its emptiness. but it's more than its emptiness—it's that state of being that pushes emptiness to its extreme degree of desolation. the objects in the room sit quietly all around, retaining for a time the traces of those who once lived here.

intangibility. pity.

traces.

I sit here.

feeling the sensation of knowing that I'm alone.

the painting of my aunt sits across from me in the gilded oval of its frame. a string of pearls is worn high. her dress is cut low (though she's not young in the painting). I don't remember her wearing a dress cut so low. the dress is green. a rose-colored shawl slides off one of her shoulders. but it's her face that draws the attention. her hair is pulled severely back so that her face is only a pinch of features sitting just below her exaggeratedly elevated forehead. her eyebrows are thin and arched, there's the indentation of a slight frown between the eyebrows. her eyes are narrowed and her lips are pursed as though she were going to start talking in a kind of consternation. large clusters of earrings are on her earlobes and the small shaft of her nose is slanted a little upward.

it was my mother's voice that answered when I knocked on her closed bedroom door. is it you, William? open the door and come in; I've been waiting
for you to come and help me down to the garden. Is Angeline with you? she
does so much to make things easier for me. and of course our Lucie Fell, I
don't know how the girl manages it, but there seems to be nothing she can't
do—despite her eyes. I feel something has changed, William. I feel an enthusiasm in my blood to flow a little more strongly through my veins.

and Lucie Fell came up behind me while I stood looking at my mother. Lucie
Fell said to her are you certain you feel well enough for the garden, Mrs.
Martin?

the decisive moment between life and the last breath drawn. those I have
been present with at their moment of dying.

now I see them again.

the claw and ball feet of the dining room table.

when I was a child, I thought that the claws would reach out and grab me.

of course they didn't reach out and grab me. and when I was older...
pathetic imagining.

the distance between one room and another. the rear stairs lead to the apartment of rooms which I used to occupy with my wife, Lucie. we had only a

short time in those rooms. and on the floor below, tucked away in a corner, at the back of the house is the tiny, sparsely furnished room that used to be occupied by Lucie Fell. the house is not a mansion, my mother said, it is generously sized. there are those who say it's too complicated in its structure.

I'm met at the top of the stairs by the mirror. the mirror dates back to Colonial times—it was originally purchased in John Elliot's famous mirror shop on Walnut Street. it's placed to confound the mind, coming upon it at the top of the stairs so that the reflection takes one by surprise, and when I catch my reflection in it, it's as though the reflection belongs to another person, someone other than myself. no matter how close to the mirror I stand, the person reflected back seems to be someone other than myself.

Angeline will be waiting. she has so often waited. I've not been a good husband, I recently told her, being mostly absent and keeping you waiting. she said that was the way she accepted it; and that though it was unspoken those were the terms of the marriage. it could not have been otherwise, she said; we have had a perfect union.

I wanted to say—but I held back—I wanted to say I don't know any man who wouldn't have wished to possess your beauty.

but Angeline did not hold back. she said, I know she's never stopped calling out to you over the years. I was afraid of it because I thought she would take you. she must have been so angry she had to die so young, and so angry at the way she had to die. just as you were angry too. I could feel your rage. I believe you loved my barrenness because of it.

I don't remember what time it was when I left to come here. early I think. perhaps the sun had just come up. or earlier. it seemed when I came in I turned the gaslights on.

289

there have been thoughts to sell the house. to move back into it or to sell it. but one must think. one must consider.

it seemed I turned the gaslights on when I came in. and then I sat for a while in the dining room at the table with its claw and ball feet. I was still young enough, when I came to live here, for my imagination to be stirred by the claws. it seemed the table had a bestial life to it.

it seemed I turned the gaslights on when I came in. and there was a chill in the house despite the excessive heat of the day that would be soon coming. I might have thought to light a fire in the fireplace, but the season is summer and the chute has not been cleaned. there was an old log sitting in the firebox covered with ash. the log looked skeletal, brittle, as though any disturbance would cause it to crumble.

a while later it started to rain; it had been a hard rain, unpleasantly cool, I was getting soaked but I didn't want to leave the garden. the smell of earth, the thickening of vegetation at the back of the garden, everything stark in the rain, the ornamental bushes in the far rear, and still in a corner by itself the white stone of the birdbath, the stone was turning gray but it still caught the attention, as it had that day when I first saw it from my bedroom window and had the impression it was something else.

when Angeline comes here to the house she does her best with the garden, but she has no gift for it.

I've been soaked through, so much so I'm shivering. if my mother was still here she would say, you must take the dampness out.

the boxes are in my old bedroom—I have moved them many times—the boxes containing Lucie's photographs and notes. *this is where I used to live.* her words accompany a poorly lit wetplate of the house. it shows a partial view of first floor hall through the open front door. dark, but still visible, is the stairway dado. as I pulled the boxes away from the wall, each of them struck me as a kind of a coffin. the coffins that contain her work: the faces, the gazes from the eyes of her subjects. and I read her words: *the face of any living being, even the face of an animal, seems to me to impart to a photograph the greatest opportunity for authenticity.*

we are ordinary flesh. the words are written on a piece of paper that has been clumsily attached to an albumen print made from a wetplate. the portrait to which she's attached the words seems to say nothing of flesh. it's a young boy who has been posed for the camera, perhaps eleven or twelve years old. he is in semi-profile. the lens has come close. it is a bust of the young boy, his chin rests on his fist, his eyes are looking down so that they appear to be almost closed. his nose is straight, his hair sits almost sparsely on his head. she has intentionally made the likeness slightly out of focus so that the boy's outline is softened. light plays on his forehead and hair, his hair a veil of light. *I prefer to work in this form now, the wetplate,* she wrote. *I find it is more in attendance than the daguerreotype.*

I have no body now, I hear the voice say. her voice is like air. *I must wear some- one else's body as my own.*

the air touches me, touches my lips, like a finger that runs itself lightly from one corner of my mouth to the other and then back again. the spirit touches me gently. and I am wild and still covered with sweat from the violence with which I pulled the boxes away from the wall and then ripped the photo- graphs from inside them, along with the leather bound diaries and scraps of loose papers covered with her handwriting. her handwriting is narrow, the letters and words placed so closely together they are difficult to read.

there's nothing she can tell me. there's nothing I can ask her now. nothing can be conveyed. only her work remains, the thing she regarded as her work. I concede it was her work. it was her work and now it is buried in the coffin-like boxes.

Lucie Fell, even in her blindness, wanted to see my late wife's photographs again. perhaps you will describe them to me, she said. or if you don't want to, then perhaps Mrs. Martin Senior will. the girl pleaded with me, her coal black eyes staring as though they could see.

let them remain, I said and stopped with it there.

let them remain buried, all those faces that my late wife fixed on her albumen prints, giving to them that kind of quasi-permanency that is given by a photograph. busy at her work waiting for what she knew would be the right moment. waiting. waiting for the light. that's the way I remember her, working in tandem with the light.

where are the ghosts now? the house feels empty, a concluding emptiness, which means that it is utterly empty, or finally empty, on each of the floors, in each of the rooms. there is no possibility of return, there has never been that, there is not that now. not even through its ghosts which prefer to stay silent.

again the mirror takes me by surprise. the reflection looking back is not my own. it's related to me, but it's not me. it strikes me as intentional the way it has tricked me into believing that it's myself. the gaze is willful and deliberate; there is no question it has come from some other part of me. I stare at it until I'm taken over by it. there, it seems to say, you are the one I have set my sights on.

through its apparitions. or its ghosts.

my aunt objected to the word ghost; she preferred the word spirit or soul. or yes, the word spirit.

earlier, damp from the rain, I went into the kitchen to make a cup of tea. I managed it, although it was a little bitter.

to be the first. to see for the first time. and then to record what I had seen on my photographs. as though I had to account for my life. and it might be argued by some that the sights had not really been unseen. all those places on my photographs that people later gazed at in a kind of astonishment. there had been others, the others who had been there first, who also had lived, who had seen them.

succumbing to heat and exhaustion. or to cold and exhaustion.

injuries. loss of equipment. the gloom of the canyon.

Camp Beauty.

and then later the Dream Dance.

but before that the interior posts and the mountains.

and I think of death as it might come—in the mountains in the snow; it always seemed to me that there would be no fear there. only the white beauty that had poured itself upon the earth for an entire day. and by nightfall the drifts so high that I would sink down into one of them. completely covered by the snow. the cold turning to warmth.

I imagine that was the way the young Indian girl died. she was Mohave. her determination was to die. it was thought of as a dark act for her to go into the storm, into the cold and the snow to escape a man. she had no way of knowing that her fear of him had become groundless. that he could no longer touch her, that there would be no wedding night, no coarseness and desire. coarseness and desire had been taken from him along with his mind. he was occupied with his death now just as she would soon be occupied with hers. in the howling wind nothing would touch her. she would sink into the snow and the deep snow would warm her.

anything can break a spell or bring a spell.

I think of the old woman at the fort hanging on to a piece of wood that had been carved to look like a wolf; rubbing it all the time, eyes half-closed, rubbing it day and night.

her worn leathery skin.

better weather for dancing.

addressed to Mr. William Wright Martin
December 21, 1891
Washington
I send first my good wishes for your health, which I am sorry to learn has been weak.
I have enclosed several copies of prints taken for Mr. James Arthur as part of his work in connection with the Indian Messiah religion. they were taken for him by W.J. Lenny, using the dry plate process. the copies I have sent depict the ecstatic dancing of the Ghost Dance (or as it is also called, the Dream Dance). the photographs are attentive to the trance condition and to the hypnotic and mystical effect of the dance. you have most likely already heard about it. it is reported that they [the photographs] were taken in the early months of this year, January and February; you will see that snow is still upon the ground. the photographs have come to me along with a report by way of the Commission on Indian Affairs from Mr. Arthur. he reported that when he arrived the ground was covered with snow and it was necessary to wait for better weather for dancing.
here in Washington it is believed that the now famous outbreak at Pine Ridge associated with this religion and its consequences have brought an end to the Indian wars.
based on our friendship over many years and your own excellent work in some of these same regions and among the peoples inhabiting them, I thought the likenesses and news of more recent developments would interest you.
very truly yours,
George H_____

there is that moment when one must let go
you agree, don't you?
there can be no progress if you don't let go?

when I got out of bed this morning the sky was just beginning to lighten. no color of the sunrise was visible, only a dark glow. and from the window I could see the other houses set off dimly against the coming light.

the Indians reach with their arms to the sky in W.J. Lenny's photograph, or else they have flung themselves forward so they are looking down to the ground.

a light wind must have been blowing. it is unmistakable because the grass is swaying to one side. I can also see evidence of wind in the way their hair is caught in the midst of movement; or else in the movement of the fabric of the blankets draped long like capes across the shoulders of some of the Indians.

I brought the photographs of the Dream Dance to the house on South Eighth Street to describe them to Lucie Fell. she asked me to take her hand and guide it so that she might trace the figures. I told her that the shirts the Indians were wearing were called ghost shirts and the Indians believed that bullets would not go through them. I told her the Indians believed that the shirts were unassailable.

Lucie Fell had repeated the word: unassailable.

and W.J. Lenny's photographs reminded me, excited me. the Indians had gathered to call upon their god in a place that was hostile and severe. but it had beauty too. I was squinting at the photograph to discern the image. a vastness of land and sky, flat and far stretching, so much so that at its outer edge it began to look like something else, it began to look like water, like the shoreline of an ocean, and the dry grass looked like waves. it was here that the Indian people had gathered to dance.

now from the window it's no longer possible to see all the way to the far end of the garden. the rain has left fog which obscures it and only a layer of mist can be seen; a grayish haze that conceals what is there. and I have the sense of returning, of coming back to myself, as though my soul has decided at last to return to its body. and it will tell me about the places it has inhabited during its absence, or it will tell me about some particular place it has inhabited. perhaps inside a stone, or in the roots of a tree.

and I have a certainty at times that something intended for me to know is reaching me from far away; that something that has happened, although many miles away, is reaching me. there are no limits on the distance; it can be as far away as across the country. for example there had been a small, out-of-the-way article in yesterday's Inquirer about a fire that had broken out at a travelling circus in the West. several of the exhibition tents were said to have collapsed and been engulfed by the flame. it occurred to me that Laurent would be old now, almost as old as I am. and then it struck me with certainty he had perished in that fire.

I imagined the fire and the way Laurent died. that last moment and the terrible certainty that his death was moving towards him, that nothing would stave it off, not with the flames lapping at the canvas fabric of the tent.

and his soul sent out to wander.

there is the sense I should be finishing up.

I ask myself what else is there?

and I think of those who are gone with their souls wandering.

if my mother were here now she would say that we should go outside and walk in the garden. she would like it that there's mist, that we can't see all the way to the wall at the end; we must walk carefully she would say. we must walk in the fog, she would say, so that we can feel the moisture in its composition on our skin. and everything that was in front of us that we couldn't see would be revealed once we arrived at the place where it was no longer hidden by the fog.

the feeling that my soul resides inside of me and at the same time elsewhere. in some secret place that I must find; some secret 'other' place that has taken its fancy. and it's all so secretive this business. the way this other place is kept secret from me.

Lucie Fell stood stricken when my mother was dying. like the statuary in the garden she stood in a corner of my mother's bedroom; she would not leave, or she left only for brief and necessary intervals. but most of the day and night she could be seen standing in my mother's room. she stood in her dark glasses and there were times when I looked at her that I thought she was the angel of death; the angel we've been promised to have present when we die. it seemed she was waiting, insisting on waiting, to take my mother with her. at times she would sit on a chair near to my mother's bed, but most often she stood out of the way in a corner. she remained even when the doctor was there. the doctor said she could stay; he said it didn't matter she was there. it was because she was blind it didn't matter; her lack of sight gave her only a half-presence in the room. but she can hear, Angeline said, perhaps there is something private your mother wants to say. my mother can no longer talk, I said. Angeline continued to object: but there may be something you want to say to your mother. it's all right, I replied, Lucie Fell will leave the room if I ask her.

I always had the thought that I would find a place so distant on this earth, so unfamiliar and strange, with so much to teach it would wholly consume me.

thoughts come back. it's strange the way that thoughts come back. when I was in the mountains wintering over one of the Indian wives was giving birth. it was a difficult birth and she was screaming. and in that corner of the room at the wintering post where the birth was taking place all the other Indian women had gathered around her and were screaming too.

the thing that makes an impression.

the thing that's remembered is the thing that make an impression.

when the Ghost dance surfaced I was no longer able to go there to see it. the god that descended, the Messiah, the Indian Christ in the paradise of the West. I was only able to see someone else's photographs and to hear the rumors and read the official reports. so I am left now with what can only be my imagined idea of the dance. the prevailing tone was an expression of grief. to dance toward trance. to dance toward unconsciousness.

and I seek silence now, a kind of graceful solitude.

I listen for Angeline's footsteps on the hardwood floors at the side entrance to the house with its old cooking fireplace. the fireplace remains intact but is no longer used. when I first came to live here it was already long out-of-date and the large stove had already replaced it. now the fireplace sits cold and all the rooms in the house are quiet. hours must have passed. the clock in the front hallway is no longer working. I miss the ticking sound that used to be made by the clock's escapement as it counted off the seconds. though it never chimed to sound the hour. what hour is it? it's no longer raining. only fog. Angeline's certain to come looking for me, to investigate what's keeping me. what is keeping her? why hasn't she come looking for me? when the doctor died, she grew thin in her grieving for her father. when I touched her in the night, I touched the bone of her frame. for weeks we went every evening to the house on South Eighth where my mother encouraged her to eat. Lucie Fell sat at the table, at most times silent, always wearing her dark glasses; there was nothing in her blindness that she was not able to tend to with dexterity at the table: her plate, her knife and fork, the serving platters filled with food. the loss of my sight, Lucie Fell said one evening, is a kind of death too. she had said it to Angeline.

but Angeline's footsteps do not come. there are only my feet, still bare, walking on the floor, silent because they are naked.

an evocative power.

or to be awakened out of sleep in one's bedroom, in the half-light, in the mythological room with birds. it was dark and cold, the room in late November. I saw my wife kneeling on the floor in her nightdress. everything was red, beneath her, red as the walls of the room were red, and the small winged figures carved into the headboard, the figures suspended and facing in opposite directions.

the thoughts that one keeps secret, the thoughts that I have kept secret over the years. they are thoughts that have crystallized into mental images. there were two sides to my life, that is my thought now as I stand with my bare feet on the floor, in the small room just inside the rear entrance to the house; in the old days of the house it used to be the kitchen, and the enormous fireplace immediately to the left as one enters through the rear entrance had been used for cooking and not just for warmth. that had been before the rear wing was built, where Lucie and I had our apartment of rooms on the third floor. but now the rear entrance room is not used as a kitchen anymore, but only as an entrance room just as it had been through all my years of growing up. and it leads to the back staircase which in turn leads to the apartment of rooms I used to live in with Lucie; and also to the austere little room on the second floor that had been occupied by Lucie Fell. I continue to stand in the entrance room looking at the old fireplace. I hear a crackling sound that can only be the sound of fire. but it is not fire because there is no fire and I become aware of how damp it is in the house and how damp I still am from the rain. the windows on the wall opposite the entrance look out to the garden, just as the windows in the small parlor, which is adjacent to the entrance room, look out to the garden. the dampness seeps in through the windows and the house holds it. without life.

I am being led, but I don't know where

and I don't know who is leading me

and I forget for a moment where I am, which room I'm in, which house it is, if it even is a house.

there is the sensation of losing consciousness but I know I am not losing consciousness. I am only light-headed for a minute. the sensation of nausea rising. yesterday, or was it the day before, at the Athenaeum there was talk of indigestion and the pain that it can cause. but I am not losing conscious-ness; I am only light-headed. and perhaps it is the sensation not so much of losing consciousness as of returning to it.

strange the way the spirit enters; I call it a spirit, but I might call it some-thing else, something less apart from me and more like impulse or inclina-tion; a voice inside my head that can only be mine.

when I watched my late wife die, when I watched the life go out from her body, staring as I was at the moment that defines death.

the rooms in this house have witnessed death even before I was born and lived here to witness it. there's that moment of knowing that life is irretrievably lost and no further struggle against death is possible.

there is no use trying to turn away from it.

when I was a child I slept in the other part of the house, in the old part and not in this wing that somewhere along the way, long before I came to live here, had been added, and that can only be accessed by climbing the rear staircase. my room was near my mother's when I was a child so she could hear me if I called out in the night. I don't remember calling out. I was a brave boy, my mother said. I heard her say that to my aunt.

in the places of the mind where we hope to be certain of privacy.

my mother and my aunt were in the small parlor and I had been standing almost exactly where I'm standing now. I had just come down the stairs, there was that silent way I had of moving that made my mother sometimes complain. you are so silent you seem to appear out of nowhere, she would say. or else she would tease and say: oh, it's my spook, oh, it's the spooks again. Just before I had come down the stairs I had been playing in the back wing, perhaps it had been in one of the rooms that had later become the apartment of rooms I lived in with Lucie. I had stopped when I heard my mother's voice, not because I intended to eavesdrop on her conversation with my aunt, but because I thought I was not supposed to play in those rooms and I didn't want her to see me, the rooms were unoccupied then as they are now; only the housekeeper entered them to clean. in fact the first time in many years that the back wing had ever been occupied was during those six months that I lived there with Lucie; and then the wing was occupied once again during the years that Lucie Fell lived in the small room on the second floor.

the voice lingers, as though in the air.

the odor in the house of old fire. fire not burned in the fireplaces for a long time. a piece of wood that had not completely burned before the fire was put out.

be reasonable, my mother would say. I sometimes used to have fits of temper when I was a child. be reasonable, darling, my mother would say. it was intended to soothe me. and the words did soothe me. the words and the tone. yes, why not be reasonable. and the fit of temper would continue a while longer, but in the end I would be reasonable.

but that day as a child when I heard my mother and my aunt talking I had just come down from those rooms where I thought I was not allowed, whereas now I am going up to them.

the Indians are already a defeated people when W. J. Lenny photographs them for his studio portraits. look at the slope of their shoulders. one of the five braves has his eyes closed. the faces are taciturn; the expressions distant. everything about them is quiet and reticent. there is no resistance. there is something written across the bottom of the photograph by way of a title— the words say: *as they appear in everyday life.*

it is perhaps the doomed part of the house. everything that falls to the rear, up the rear staircase. from the side entrance. ice was brought into the house by way of the side entrance. with its heavy wooden door at least five inches thick. and then into the side entrance room where there's a bank of windows that look out to the garden. it's stopped raining, but the sky is still dark. everything is gray. the house is built in an L-shape around the garden.

Lucie Fell's room was on the second floor, the apartment of rooms was on the third.

who reports?

everything is here that needs to be here.

a small tired weakness.

it has stopped raining, but the sky is still dark. the house is built in an L-shape around the garden. and from the window in the entrance room I look out from the side view to the rear wall of the garden. two Dogwood trees stand there. a stray cat appears. I watch the start and stop of the cat's walk; its manner is aggressive, but all the same it retreats when I tap on the window. it's getting darker. as though it will rain again. or is it just night? I'll soon need to turn on the gas light to light my way up the stairs; or else make my way in the dark with my hand upon the banister. the stairs. the banister. the places that will make a noise when I step down. on my way to the rooms. the house with its quiet. when I was a child I avoided the parts of the stairs that made a noise when you stepped down.

like the closing song of the Ghost Dance.

     go around five times more—

the words are written in a careless script at the bottom of one W.J. Lenny's photographs.

the dampness of the earth after rain.
it was not ordinary.

oh, but you must—

single phrases that rise up

from down below

I'm on the stairs

about to climb up

I'm on the stairs about to climb up because I didn't stay long enough when I climbed up earlier. I didn't see everything I wanted to see. that was hours ago or longer, although I'm certain a twenty-four hour cycle has not yet passed.

Angeline will be waiting, she'll begin to worry.

Strange that she hasn't come looking for me.

...this is the thought that enters my mind as I climb the stairs. and I remind myself I'm climbing them again because I didn't stay long enough when I climbed them before; I didn't see everything I wanted to see, and yet I can't say what it is I wanted to see. I have only an inner urging that I need to see it again. this is my thought, I'll take all of it in. I start to climb towards the third-floor landing. the third floor landing that will take me directly into the room that had once been my late wife Lucie's study; and then through the small passageway that leads from that room into the bedroom; the myth of the bedroom; and then to the dressing room; and then finally off and apart from the other rooms I'll find what was my own narrow study with its sky-light window. the stairs are dark in the dusky light, though I'm not yet in total blackness; even before I turn the gas lamp on, I'm able to see as I climb the stairs; I'm on the lower stairs and the day's last light is coming in through the entrance room windows. the entrance room is just below, but the higher I climb, the dimmer it gets; and there are not windows on all of the stairway landings. I have the thought I'm climbing away from the light. climbing away in the quiet and shadow. the sense of the forbidden returns to me from when I was a child; it's that same excited feeling that used to rise alongside the fear; when I was a child it was the fear of being discovered here, despite the fact it was the truth that neither my mother nor my aunt minded if I came here; they were co-conspirators in a game with me only pretending that they minded; and that lent excitement engendered by the idea it was forbidden. but there is no one to forbid it now, no one to forbid me anything and the sensation of excitement takes me by surprise. until this moment there had only been dread when I would think of coming up here. dread during all the years since Lucie died. and dread even after Lucie Fell came to live here. Lucie Fell chose the smallest room to be hers in this wing on the second floor. but I have not climbed the full flight to the second floor yet; there are still stairs ahead. I continue up and when I do the lightness I felt only a moment before turns heavy and at the second floor landing I find that I'm winded. I stand for a moment to catch my breath. the door to the room that was Lucie Fell's is visible just off to the right on the landing. the door is still open as I had left it when I was in there earlier. but it's not my intention to go into her room again, or at least not just now; only to stand for a moment to catch my breath, and to shake off the tiredness that has taken hold of me. there is almost no light now and it feels that the house has become even more silent in the darkening light. at least it strikes me that way though it might be my imagination. nothing but silence, and the stillness more pronounced. the hallway appears to be smaller with nothing moving. the staircase, the landings, the rooms themselves—all large when I was a child—appear smaller as I stand here. in fact they look really quite small. of course it's true that in this wing of the house the scale was smaller than in the others. but that alone does not explain it. no, everything is smaller now than it had been when I was up here earlier, as though it has shrunk, is shrinking still, and will keep on shrinking until it becomes like one of those toy houses.

...or as though the silence is taking on a deeper meaning, and there is the sense of departure in the silence, it is an absolute silence and contains all that has vanished or is vanishing; all that is fading, like the fading of a life at the bedside of the dying. departure, everything that was, but is no longer; everything that is gone and will not come back; the struggle towards remaining; the desire to remain; or to return; but that's impossible; there can only be hollowness now; only emptiness.

on the second floor landing I have the irrational thought that Lucie Fell will appear in the open doorway to her room, as though she has been in there all along and heard me coming up the stairs. she will be pale and thin when she appears. she has become increasingly thinner with the years. no longer young now, but not terribly old. and when she appears she will act as though it's natural she's here, as though she still lives here and has just been sitting at her desk writing on her sheets of paper, she fills them with words but can't read the words for herself. she arranges the sheets into stacks and carefully marks each stack with the name of the person intended to read it, or else she marks it to be read by no one. I have the sense she's returned to the house, that she came back sometime between now and the hours earlier when the day first began and I read what she wrote on the sheets of paper she had left behind marked: *to be read by no one.* she may be angry that earlier I read her writings despite the impression she left the sheets behind precisely so I would read them. did she know when she returned to the house that I was here? she will have a frown on her face; William, she will say; William, you cannot take it back. and now there's the scent in the air of the perfume she liked to wear, violets, the scent of violets. I can smell it in the air where she is standing, in the hallway now, just outside the door to her room. she wears a pale colored dress that seems to give light to the interior darkness; the light has faded more now since I started up the stairs. and

Lucie Fell is standing before me. she is standing without her dark glasses. her eyes robbed of sight. the blind girl. I never thought of you that way, I say into the darkness. and then I move closer to her. I pass close to her. when did you return, I ask? I thought I would stay here, she answers. but you wanted to go, I remind her. you wanted to go to live and work at the Wills Institute, where you said you could do the most good. yes, because there was no one left in the house here who needed me, she responds.

I see her standing oddly just outside the door, where she has taken a step to the side so that her back is flat against the wall. I was brought around in a horsecar, she says—you know I like to ride in them. she stands like a sentry or a guard, she's no longer standing in the shadows. I didn't hear you come in, I say. but I knew you were here, she says. the entire journey by horsecar? I ask. yes, the entire journey by horsecar, she answers. alone? I ask. yes, alone, she says. but how? I ask. with schooling, she says—there have been advances for the unsighted, you know; more is possible for us now. which door did you come in? I ask. through the side door, she says. and then she tells me that she came directly up the stairs.

conceal yourself, a voice says. hide.

of course I know full well that she's not really here. the woman, Lucie Fell, is in an ordinary moment of her life—at home at the Wills Institute where she resides. it was her expressed wish after my mother died to go to the Wills Institute. she had said it seemed her purpose in this house was finished. and besides there would be a life for her there, a contribution to be made, and though no longer new to her blindness there were still skills she might learn, new steps to take her forward, and now it occurs to me that the spirits of the living can inhabit like the spirits of the dead. she inhabits still standing just outside the door to her old room with her back flat against the wall, as if lingering, this spirit of someone who is still alive.

    it is impossible, she says.

    what is impossible? I ask.

I thought I saw light coming into my eyes, she says, as though my vision is restored. do you think that it's possible that my vision is being restored? that the persistence of light has begun to penetrate the black film over my eyes?

but before I can answer she has moved away from the wall, taken a step towards me, brought herself closer to me.

her eyes with that absolute blackness, without whites, so that they seem to be empty, but filled with darkness and perhaps with a strange ability to see.

she remains quiet. tense.

I am old now, I say.

I am old now, I repeat.

she says nothing.

and I have repeated it the way in the songs of the Sioux every phrase is always repeated. every phrase sung twice.

this one says—Ye' ye!

this one says—Ye' ye!

that day in the studio I remember you were afraid of the Indians, I say. there was so much going on. your father and I were preoccupied with so much activity.

oh, it's old now, it's the past, she says.

yes, it's the past, I agree.

one can't bring the past back, she says.

no, one can't bring the past back, I agree.

it's gotten darker in the hallway, the remaining light, the light, to the extent that there is light. and directly in front of me are the stairs that lead up to the third floor.

there is no flow of words, no flow of words, no flow of words, no return to the physical.

still, there is the sense that she is being intentionally cruel. yes, I have the feeling her intention is to be cruel.

as though she

or maybe it's only an imagined cruelty, just as all of it taking place now, at this moment, is imagined; it's a deception that I know is deception; I might even call it a self-deception; entered into willingly; even willfully; in which case it is not deception, but a kind of truth presented in a way that makes it acceptable to my mind because it has this aspect about it that enables me to say it's not real.

and I have entered my willed deception the way I have entered this house—

I can imagine many things when I'm in this house because there is nothing that inhabits it which is not imagined or remembered; memory being close to what is imagined; and again the suggestion presents itself of that which is inhabited. I think about the spirits of this house existing in a languorous habitation; they retain a tenderness of mood, or I imagine them that way, or perhaps the truth is that they are really in a rage. or perhaps they are only silently angry the way Lucie Fell is silently angry; but ready to pounce all the same, in the enchantment of the house; and the enchantment is that anything can be imagined here, a life can be relived after all, or at least some of its moments.

      one day I touched your face, I say. I wanted to see you the way you see me. I imagined your face as I might see it if I had no sight and I could only see it by touching it. I thought at first it would be impossible to imagine what you looked like only by touching your face. and I thought it was unfair because I had the advantage of being able to see you with my eyes. I played a game of touching your face, I could see it before me even with my eyes closed. and then I reminded myself that you weren't always blind.

      I asked you to do it, she says. I wanted to feel your hands on my face.

there is reluctance to leave it alone, or to leave it behind. there is something too satisfying about the imagined content—that sense of a willed reality. and it's real enough, the hallway for instance, my feet on the carpet, and Lucie Fell's old room. there are sounds in the house that are also real, the sounds of the house settling.

      I know who you belong to, she says.
      what do you mean? I ask.
      she lifts her head and raises her eyes towards the floor above. always strange to see it, the way she uses her eyes as if sighted.
interesting the way empty dwellings become historical objects. and what is present in them, or the meaning of what is present in them—the residue if you will—becomes again apparent, or can at least be sensed upon investigation.

      oh, but you should go up now, she says.
      go up? I ask. or rather I repeat it flatly. the sound that I make in saying the words is a dry sound as if to purposely obscure her meaning and mine. but when I examine it more closely I decide that is not my intention to obscure.

because all empty dwellings are filled with the presences of those who used to dwell in them.

like the cliff dwellings in the canyons... from all those years ago.

there had been the night, the mule, the Indian, the canyon floor, the dwellings in the cliff alcoves above. I seem to remember something like a mantel, still intact, situated over one of the interior archways.

it was never the smallness of man against the vastness of nature; it was something else; it was an opening for the soul and for consciousness.

you should go up, she says again.

the way a moment can be traced, or the way we might think we are tracing it; and I have the idea that Lucie Fell's accident traces directly from the canyon and the cliff dwellings, from the heat and the blinding light, from success which led to greater success, from demand which led to greater demand.

greater demand for prints of the canyons to be used for the Survey albums, to be delivered faster, and in larger numbers, and then the day we took the photographs in the studio of the Indians who were on their way to Washington to present their side and the side of their tribes in the conflict that had been roiling concerning their claim to the Black Hills. the Indians were Red Cloud and Spotted Tail. there were other Indians too. it was Red Cloud I think she referred to when she talked about the Indian who 'saw' her. she had said it unnerved her to see him staring at her. those were her words, that it 'unnerved' her. and the accident happened in the moment of her becoming unnerved.

don't think about it now, she says.

she has a look in her eyes, if it can be said that her eyes can look, but now there's a look in her eyes, or an expression on her face, an expression that sometimes comes in intimacy. and I've seen such looks before, moments when there was without question something in her eyes that constituted a look of intimacy; a look of intimacy, I might almost describe it as a devilment.

she reaches out to touch me, places her hand on my face. are you able to see that I'm old? I ask. it's nothing, she says. is that lace at her throat? the cutout pattern through which her skin shows. and because it's a dream anything can suddenly appear, the way the image of a woman might appear, on the wall of one's bedroom in the middle of the night, and the woman on the wall might be doing something ordinary, she might be wearing a rag wrapped around her head, and she might have a knife in her hand, but it's only a kitchen knife and a kitchen task she's performing, again some ordinary task, though unexpected, but the way the image appears it can't help but be startling. Lucie Fell uses her fingers to trace the features of my face, she moves her fingers along my jaw line, with her fingers she parts my lips, the gesture is a small one, she begins to whisper and there is something unapproachable in the way she is whispering, but then she stops and it is silent.

the inside of the house has the feeling of dampness from the heavy rain.

the light, to the extent that there is light, comes from the open doors of the rooms: there are only two rooms on the second floor, the one that was Lucie Fell's and one other at the end of the hallway.

because of the odd way the house is built, the third floor contains only the apartment of rooms.

and the luxury of the house is that rooms remain empty.

313

what silence speaks of. there is that apt gesture of silence, the hand closed in a gentle fist, the index finger raised and placed over the lips. there is a moment while I'm still on the stairs when I try to see the third floor rooms in my mind, to remember them clearly as they had been when I lived in them... to remember them as clearly as if I were in them now... but the images will not come. all that comes is the red of the bedroom walls. yes, the walls of the bedroom and the winged figures carved into the headboard—

...suspended in the air and facing in opposite directions. in the bedroom, in the mythological room with birds.

...it was early dawn, perhaps not even dawn. I remember that everything stopped during those minutes, the minutes of waking, the room, my wife on the floor, then coming into awareness of what had happened, there were the hours that followed, more than a day's worth of hours, but the fate of everything was known in those minutes.

...the desire to continue up the stairs, to go into the apartment of rooms, to lie down on the bed I used to sleep in with Lucie. the coolness of the air as I enter. with all the doors open I can see the red of the walls of the bedroom. the bed facing the door. the dark wood of the floors, the small area carpet on the side of the bed. the wood floor is cool beneath my feet. I become aware I've stopped moving and that my body is rigid, I'm standing with my head raised and with my eyes closed. *it's silly to stand there, the voice says, when you can lie down and rest.* yes, rest, I repeat, rest in this bed with my wife Lucie. *enough time has passed, the voice says—too many days. how many has it been? do you remember? you look worn. you look tired. it's time. you agree that it's time, don't you?*

do I agree that it's time? I imagine I do if the condition of the body is any indication—I think about the way my body has grown old and the feeling I have of disembodiment, or the feeling of weariness. *you look worn, the voice says again.* I make no protest to the voice. I recognize the truth of what is said. everything is slowing down now. I stare at the wood frame of the bed with its hand-carved headboard. the wood is mahogany—it's a dark, heavy heartwood. I'm aware that I'm staring, that I've moved closer to the bed, that I'm reexamining it—is this the bed? and I look at the bed the way I sometimes looked at things when I was a child; it was a game I played, to look at an object hard enough to retain it, as though I could imprint it on the forefront of my brain. that's the way I'm now looking at the bed, in an attempt to imprint it; it's necessary to do that because in the past it had never been imprinted. *so that you will see it all the time, the voice says.* there's no need to protest to the voice, there's only uncertainty as to its origin, and the sound of the rain...

...it has started to rain again. I turn my head to the window, but it's dark now and impossible to see out from where I'm standing. there's only the sound of rain beating against the window and a dampness in the room. *if you were to die now, the voice says...* I move closer to the bed; and to the figures carved into the headboard; birds or angels? right now I take them to be angels. I find a reassurance in that, though a reassurance of what I cannot say. *if you were to die now, the voice says again...*and I recall the image of a horse, a wild horse that had been captured and was lying on its side with its feet bound. the horse's body was rigid, but the animal was breathing rapidly. and it comes into my mind that the winged figures on the headboard are neither birds nor angels, but beasts that engage in battles. engage in battles in the mythological room, in the bedroom. and it comes to me again, to be awakened out of sleep in one's bedroom in the dim light of an early dawn. *if you were to die now, the voice says again. but don't think about that now, the voice says. you are tired, you look worn, it's time, you agree that it's time don't you? come and pull the covers down, it will be so good for you to rest; lie down beside me, you're not frightened are you? you've never been frightened, I think you look distinguished with your hair turned silver. but do you see I haven't changed at all? do you see how one thing can become another? rest for a while and then we'll go sit on the rocks on the other side of the creek. I was reading A Life Struggle by Miss Pardoe while I waited for you to come here; reading slowly through the chapters: Brother and Sister; The Letter; The Ball; Guardian and Ward; Storm Warnings...*

315

too much time has passed. don't you think too many days have passed? do you re-
member how many? there's no doubt that the rain is beating hard again, I
have no need to go to the window. and I realize I'm tired now with the tiredness rain brings. it comes to me again: to be wakened out of sleep in the dim
light of the bedroom, and to have the sensation that something had happened, or is happening still, and to see my wife kneeling on the floor, and to
see her face when she looks up at me. but I can feel how warm it is in the
bed now, despite the dampness of the room, and I'm in the bed where the
voice has urged me, invited me, and the cool dampness has disappeared, and
there's only the voice urging me to come close, come close again in the bed,
where there is only the warmth and the tendency towards sleep.

I'm in the bed

where it seems that I'm waiting

and Angeline has not found me

the sensation of something terrible happening, a loss of breath, the breath
being taken from me, BREATH, and a buzzing sound like that of an insect
on the intake of the breath.

the tendency towards sleep brought about by the warmth and the rain. to
be wakened out of sleep in the dim light of an early dawn with the awareness of something terrible happening. my wife is kneeling on the floor a
little distance from the bed. she is stifling her screams. fear and pain on her
face. a piece of sculpture has appeared in the garden, the sculpture of a
young woman, a high forehead and the exaggerated oval of her face, her
hair is pulled away from her stone face, and she holds her arms out in front
of her. my wife is looking at me, the room is cold, there's perspiration on
her forehead, I lift her up from the blood, and the flowers are in bloom, all

316

the clusters of flowers. at first I can't say what they are, but then I see they're honeysuckle despite the season. the oldest headstones have started sinking into the ground, there's no way to prevent it, the leaves have gathered around the graves, the eyes of the white sculpture. and now it's warm in the bed even with the dampness of the room, the movement of the seasons, the late summer, the seasons repeating, the voice is urging me towards sleep.

urging me to enter the darkness

the sun has gone completely down, the room is dark. there is still the sound of birds coming up from the garden

whether you are dead a day, a week, a year, it's all the same, the voice says.

in the medicine garden tansy is for fever…there's a sculpture of a woman, the voice says…

it's the sculpted figure of a woman suffering from a debilitating disease. she is emaciated, her frame is bony,

her breasts, though, young, are ill-shapen and sagging, her belly is bulging.

the sensation that I have that something terrible is happening, a loss of breath, breath being taken from me, BREATH, and a buzzing sound like that of an insect on the intake of the breath.

now there is only that which can still be written and I'm no longer certain of what can be written. the piece of sculpture in the medicine garden of the woman with her belly bulging, she's only a young woman, but emaciated by disease so that her breasts, though small, are sagging. and the mind with its tendency to trick me into a state of abandon. as though I've returned again to the last time I was in this bed; the last time I was in this bed I was with my wife; the way time becomes fluid and the moments of my life enter into the fluidity; the last time I was in this bed my wife was next to me; it was late fall; it was already cold; colder than she liked; she said it was already cold and getting colder; and then she moved close to me in the bed; we can share the warmth of our bodies, she said; the room was dark; the lamps were turned off; and I turned on my side to face her. there is only that which can still be written and I'm no longer certain of what can be written. but there's no stopping it, the memory comes back in that odd way of memories. *you can never be certain, the voice says.* but I am certain, I want to say. I want to say it out loud, but I don't want to hear the sound of my voice break into the silence. memory merges with the present. her breasts were small, did I detect a change in them that night? I believe I did, I remember a greater roundness, fullness, something approaching a state of ripeness, the thing that happens to wives, to women. and it was one of the moments approaching the concluding moment, the concluding moment, irrevocable, the irrevocable moment which cannot be recalled, cannot be recalled although there's nothing else to do but to try to recall it, to call it back into the present.

we can share the warmth of our bodies, the voice says. I turn on my side to face her, to bring her close, to bring her to me,

her eyes are fixed on me, as in a photograph, where her eyes are in the shadows because of the uneven light.

her eyes darkly shadowed

in the night

to have a wife in the bed

to be wakened out of sleep

wakened out of sleep, my wife was kneeling on the floor, now it's warm despite the dampness, the season is moving, and the voice is talking to me from the bed. from the bed where it is warm, the voice is coaxing me down into the warmth, the image of the bed, the half-open door, or less than half-open. the door is only slightly cracked and the bed is the only visible object in the room, the thickness of the mattress, the white sheets, and the white spread, my wife's body next to mine, we are silent, we remain silent, what words can there be between us, the tongue that enables us to speak. and now the tongue which is the instrument of all human speech floats up between us breaking the surface of the night. I feel the heat of her body next to mine, on top of us white sheets, a shaft of light from the window, from the gas lamp on the street, our bodies in the bed, where I feel the heat of our bodies. I reach for her, aware only of her heat and mine, aware only of hunger, aware of the desire to swallow and to devour, remembering the way it was to possess then, where one was gentle until one became wild, and aware only of the alternating gentleness and wildness, and alternating gentleness and violence. if I open my eyes I will see her open eyes, lit from the light that is coming in the through window. a surprise to see her eyes again, dark. I stop and then they close. and I continue, aware only of the need to continue. the need to continue until it is finished.

...unaware of the self that might have been born, that for several months she had been carrying inside her.

...or the self that is my self which will soon be unborn.

the indwelling power

and the rocky cairns

and I feel myself emptying.

emptying.

and I hear the sound of footsteps.

I hear something now
what do you hear?
I hear an animal
what kind of animal?

Angeline's footsteps on the stairs. but Angeline is not coming. no, no one is coming. but then no, or is it yes, the sound of her footsteps.

and she will say

come, love

the innate wakefulness of love

come, lamb

the innate wakefulness of human beings

the sensation of something terrible happening, a loss of breath as though the breath is being taken from me, BREATH, and a rasping sound like that of an insect on the intake of my breath.

splintering,

come, love... come lamb

Angeline

I hear her voice
she's kneeling beside me
come, she is saying

the desert wind
all kinds of life, she is saying
all kinds of life living

let me uncoil you
a certain composure for uncoiling

the sensation of something terrible happening, a loss of breath as though the breath is being taken from me, BREATH, and a rasping sound like that of an insect on the intake of my breath.

and when they're ready to receive me I will tell them I have decided to remain and run with the order of the—
that strange and solitary animal which runs with the—

Angeline

unafraid

I hear her voice
she's kneeling down beside me
come, she is saying

spit the blood from your mouth

I will take it from you

memory settles it

...and I have the sensation of something terrible happening, a loss of breath
as though the breath is being taken from me, BREATH, and a rasping sound
like that of an insect on the intake of my breath.

Notes

Page 24: *when you want to go into the Mysterious...* Re-rendered from Ella Deloria, *Miscellaneous Papers,* as recorded in BEFORE THE GREAT SPIRIT, Julian Rice

Page 36: *Aura means wind, breeze, and breath.* From INVENTION OF HYSTERIA: Charcot and the Photographic Iconography of the Salpêtrière, Georges Didi-Huberman.

Page 44: "in ancient times the earth and trees of the burial place..." The I CHING, Wilhelm/Baynes, Hexagram 28, Preponderance of the Great

Page 63: ...head snapping... inspired by and re-rendered from STUDIES IN SPIRITISM, Amy Tanner

Page 73: "There are the little ewes crying with cold feet." Diary of Mrs. Amelia Stewart Knight, pioneer of 1853, entry Thursday, April 14, 1853

My choice of the name Laurent for the hermaphrodite (starting on page 77) is a homage to Julia Ward Howe and her 1840's unfinished novel, THE HERMAPHRODITE.

Page 125: "Dusk. The Angelus." Title of a drawing by Georges Seurat: Dusk (The Angelus) 1883

Page 149: "I shall never forget our experiments with a so-called light when you took a bottle of red liquid." STUDIES IN SPIRITISM, Amy Tanner

Page 149: "Above the door there was a key." ibid

Page 209: *the birds have gathered to decide who should raise the human infant...* Re-rendered from THE SIXTH GRANDFATHER, Black Elk, as cited in BEFORE THE GREAT SPIRIT, Julian Rice

Acknowledgements

Gratitude for early reading to:
Luna Tarlo especially and at all times, my first and always perspicacious reader, and this time also for our out-loud reading of the entire manuscript; Alisa Field for giving me Philadelphia and for her encouragement and generous support throughout; Karen Luper for embracing and believing in it, for support through-out, and for watching over the manuscript on her long solo drive from Santa Fe to Portland, Oregon; Lloyd Lynford for his kind and generous support all along the way and for the key that unlocked it; Anne Palermo and Marina Levertova for their valuable insights and their kind and generous support. Gratitude also to Frances Schorr for always being there.

Grateful appreciation to:
Editors Rob Cook and Roland Goity for publishing excerpts of the manuscript in their stellar literary journals: *Skidrow Penthouse* and *WIPs* (Works [of fiction] In Progress) respectively.

Grateful thanks to the following:

In Philadelphia:
The Mütter Museum
The Mummers Museum
The Morris House
Independence Seaport Museum
Philadelphia Historical Society
The Athenaeum of Philadelphia

In New York City:
National Museum of the American Indian
New York Historical Society
Metropolitan Museum of Art
International Center for Photography

In Santa Fe:
San Miguel Mission – oldest church in the US

In Sedona:
The Red Rocks, and to the guide who safely directed my climb and brought me into the ceremony of the 4 directions.

Grateful thanks also to:
The Navajo Guide at Canyon de Chelly who gave me time, information, understanding, words of anger, words of wisdom, words of caution, and what I took to be a blessing.

Long-time alternative photographer Quinn Jacobson, widely known for his work in the Wet Collodion Photography Process, who so generously instructed me in the effect of silver nitrate on the eyes.

Those dear friends who read various sections of the *The Absent* in its early iterations at the Summer Writers Institute at Skidmore College and provided much encouragement: Mamta Chaudhry-Fryer, Jody Hauber, Rochelle Low, Lisa Sardinas, Kathryn Ugoritz, Amy Wallen, and Lola Willoughby. And of course my very special thanks and gratitude to Mary Gordon. And also to Robert and Peg Boyers.

Sarah McElwain who applied her outstanding creativity and talent to the book's beautiful design and also for her never-ending patience.

And finally, but foremost, my deepest appreciation to Stephanie Dickinson, the brilliant, visionary, and indefatigable publisher of Rain Mountain Press, whose own writing lives at the core and shines with great beauty.